LET IT BE ME

HEALING IN CINCY
BOOK 3

ELLEESE BLACK

LET IT BE ME

Healing in Cincy Book 3
A fake dating, age gap, and sports romance

AUTHOR'S NOTE

While this is book 3 and it's more of a standalone from the first two, there are references from events that take place in those first two books. It's not 100% necessary to read those, but if you'd like to avoid spoilers and confusion I would recommend you read The Night We Met and Make It Without You (in that order) before reading Let It Be Me.

This book contains on page spice, explicit language, mentions of infertility and adoption, car accident, cheating, and parental loss.

CONTENT WARNINGS

Cheating (not between the main characters)
Explicit language
On page spice
Car accident (off page)
Adoption (briefly talked about)
Infertility (not the main characters)
Parental loss

PLAYLIST

Delicate by Taylor Swift
My Church by Maren Morris
Simply The Best by Billianne
Slow Dancing by Aly & AJ
Shadows by Sabrina Carpenter
Sign of the Times by Harry Styles
Sad Forever by Lauren Spencer Smith
Uncrazy - Acoustic by AFSHEEN, Rebecca Ferguson
The Way You Love Me by Faith Hill
This Kiss by Faith Hill
Grow as We Go by Ben Platt
Hide and Seek by Imogen Heap
Cosmic Love by Florence & The Machine
Let It Be Me by Ray LaMontagne
Liability by Lorde
Chasing Cars by Snow Patrol
Colorblind by Counting Crows
Since U Been Gone by Kelly Clarkson
Thinking out Loud by Ed Sheeran

Flux by Ellie Goulding
Look After You by The Fray
sun to me by mgk
Fallingwater by Maggie Rogers
Unsteady by X Ambassadors

Let it
BE ME
HEALING IN CINCY
ELLEESE BLACK

*To those who've been made to feel hard to love.
Go find someone who makes loving you the easiest thing in the
world and then yell about it from the rooftop.
This one's for you.*

1

SARAH

"Sarah!" *A voice called out to me as soon as I pushed out of the air conditioned basketball arena to meet my parents and into the sweltering South Carolina heat. It's nothing I'm not used to, but after having my body chilled to the bone, this heat and humidity is a slap to the face.*

"Liam. What's up?" I asked and changed direction as I walked towards him. I noticed Kamryn, my college roommate and bestie, isn't with him, so he either purposefully dodged her on their way out or he made up an excuse to talk to one of his former teammates.

"I want you to help me get drafted," he pleaded, as graduates walked by us in their black gowns and colored hoods.

My eyes widened. "Me?"

"Yes, you. I have faith."

Is his faith misplaced? I barely know anything about the business and this summer was supposed to help me learn the ropes before diving into the actual work. But, still. Is his faith in me misplaced?

"Okay," I said slowly. "I can't attempt to do anything until Monday."

"No problem. Just call me when you can."

Liam quickly hugs me and I mutter out, "Sure." And then he's off to find his and Kamryn's family's. My feet held me in place as I watched him walk away. Sweat formed on my neck and trickled down my back. Not just from the heat, but from Liam wanting me to get his name out to scouts. Excitement courses through my body and I use the diploma holder to fan myself before I go in search of my parents. The entire time as I wove my way through graduates I thought how perfect that this is the way my life could head. A sports agent.

I found my parents by the fountain and accepted their congrats while thinking about the next steps in my future. Can I do this? I mean, this is a male-dominated field. Am I good enough? I did my best to stay present while we were at dinner at some fancy steakhouse. My parents were talking excitedly about me moving back home. But as I was pushing the mashed potatoes around on my plate, I couldn't stop thinking about Liam and his asking me to help him succeed, and how utterly sick to my stomach I feel at the mention of moving back home.

I STUMBLE over my feet as the memory hits me out of nowhere. I pick up my pace trying to outrun that part of my life. Sweat forms on my forehead and trickles down my face while also sliding down my back.

Breathe in.

Breathe out.

Breathe in.

Breathe out.

One foot in front of the other.

An uptempo EDM track flows from one ear to the other through my headphones as I pump my arms and feel the stretch in my burning legs when I see my driveway come into view from the end of the street.

My watch vibrates and I look down seeing I've done ten miles in under two hours. It beats my last personal record, but maybe that's because the memories of the past made themselves known today of all days.

Run.

Run.

Run.

The truth is that I have been running. Not only in the physical sense, but in the metaphorical sense as well. It's been two years of growth. Pain, too, if I'm being honest. Because you can't grow without pain and if it's one thing I've learned, is that growth is painful. And that eventually the painful memories run up to catch you.

I'm in the break room at the office, pouring a cup of coffee, when my cell phone rings with a call from Chance, one of Liam's best friends in college.

"Hey, what's up?" I ask into the phone that's wedged between my shoulder and ear. Nothing greets me from the other end and I pull my phone from my ear to see that I'm still connected. "Chance?"

He lets out a breath. "There's been an accident."

"What? What are you talking about?"

"Liam. He uh...Sarah he died last night."

The coffee mug I'm holding falls out of my hand and shatters on the floor. My boss flies into the break room and stops short when he must see the distraught look on my face.

My thoughts turn selfish for mere moments. What does that

mean for me? How do I move forward? What happens next for me?

"I—um, what?"

What happened next was a blur. Chance tells me what little he knows, which as frustrating as his lack of information is, is better than nothing. I took off from work, packed some clothes, and drove straight to Pennsylvania. I remember Kamryn doing her best to shut me out. But I put aside my grief and focused on her. That may have been where I went wrong in neglecting myself to help her. But if I refused to focus on myself, then I could focus on her. And that seemed like a better choice at the time.

I STUMBLE AGAIN as that time plays like a movie in my mind. The realization that I failed my friend when he put his faith in me is something I rarely talk about. Not only that, but it's been hard for me to talk to Kamryn, my best friend and roommate from college, without thinking about Liam. While she lost her best friend, I lost someone I grew close to while helping him reach his dream. And since then, I've continuously doubted my career choice path. What did that say about my ability to wanting to become an agent?

I remember the day I met Liam. His good looks tripped me up and for a brief moment my mind went to some not so friendly thoughts. But then I saw the way he looked at Kamryn and knew that they had the potential to have something incredible. So I nixed those dirty thoughts and placed him firmly in the brother-friend category. But who knew that the something incredible between the two of them would lead to tragedy?

When the news broke on the accident, a lot of lives were

changed that day. The invisible thread that tied us together snapped in the middle.

A lot of Liam's friends placed the blame on Kamryn which sent her into a deeper hole. A deeper spiral. I lost two friends that day. The Kamryn I grew to love was a shell of herself. The shadows that I never imagined would weave around my best friend, proved they were there to stay. Kam wasn't the only one to lose something. Her childhood best friend, Emily, lost her fiancée that day. Those two suffered a loss that no one their age should have had to. But eventually things turned around. Both of them are slowly finding happiness in their own way and on their own terms.

While I'm...not. Happy, that is. I'm not sad, but I'm not overflowing with happiness. I figure that's normal. We can't be happy all the time.

When I was reevaluating what I wanted to do with my life, I found love. I've been with my boyfriend, Paul, for three years. We went to the same high school but rarely crossed paths. We bumped into each other when I came home after college and things clicked with him. Our friendship was new and easy and watching each other succeed made our friendship blur to more. Happiness finally became more attainable with him because he gave me a sense of worth.

And when I got the job offer in Cincinnati over a year ago, it was too good for me to turn down. It was everything I wanted. But since then, we've been doing long-distance and it is not for the faint of heart. And because of that, our relationship has been strained. And I miss him. So much that my heart aches.

Missing him is what's at the forefront of my mind when I see a car parked at the end of my driveway and a figure pacing the length. My stride falters before I realize I'd recognize that form anywhere and sprint the last twenty yards home. His head flips up at the sound of my feet smacking the pavement.

"Baby!" I exclaim as I run into his arms and he hooks his arms under my legs to keep me from falling. My legs are high around his waist and I bring our lips together. The physical connection is what we've been missing. That was the easiest part for us to grasp while the rest clicked into place like the final puzzle piece. Where my drive was high, his was higher. It made for more than one sleepless night and zombie-like mornings. But it was worth it. He was worth it.

Paul breaks away from the kiss and I look into the sparkling brown eyes that stopped me in my tracks that Monday at the coffee shop. His chocolate brown skin is still holding onto the summer glow, which is easier for him to keep since he lives at the beach and spends most of his weekends playing beach volleyball. He keeps his hair trim with a fade and his beard has not one hair out of place.

My face drops when I don't see that familiar light when he looks at me. No smile to greet me and no teasing quip about how I'm sweaty and probably ruining his clothes. He slowly releases my legs and steps back when I'm on two feet.

"Oh." My voice drops, not only in volume but in strength too. "You're not here for that kind of visit." It's not a question as much as it is a statement. His lips are pulled taut as he shakes his head.

I've never felt dread around him. Elation? Yes. But never dread. I guess that's what happens when someone puts you on the highest pedestal. Their disappointment never touches you.

Paul and I talk on the phone as much as we can. But with our busy jobs, those calls and texts have become less and less to where we're lucky if we talk to each other once a week.

Motion from the side is a reminder that we're in my driveway. And I don't want anyone to bear witness to what might happen.

"Come inside," I say without any of the excitement I was feeling when I saw him in my driveway.

I turn, not waiting to see if he's following me. And each step I take to the door feels like a death march. My vision blackens on the edges until all I can see is the step that's in front of me. My mouth pools with saliva and I feel like I'm going to be sick. This can't be happening. How is this happening? I've always made sure the people in my life knew how much they meant to me. That's my cursed people pleaser tendency that's been my driving force since high school.

I unlock the door and push through, holding it open for Paul and flicking the lock when he's in my foyer. Resting my back against the door, I watch him survey my space. He's been to the city once and I wasn't even living in this house. I suspect he asked my mother for my address instead of asking me. But now that I feel the end is right on the other side of the door, what does that say if I couldn't even read the signs that were big and neon right in my face? Were my rose colored glasses that thick?

He finally turns to me and I take in his appearance. His shirt is crumpled and I'm not sure if it's from the hug or his flight here. But he looks less put together than usual. He looks less like that man I've been loving for the last three years. Has our distance been a factor in this distraught look?

"I love you," he starts, although he might as well have just shoved a dagger in my chest because no good conversation ever starts with a declaration of love. "But this is too hard."

"What is?" I ask, almost desperate.

"The distance. Dealing with your freak outs is not what I signed up for. And if I'm honest, just being with you is hard, Sarah." Paul says and tucks his hands in his pockets. "I can tell you I love you as many times as I want to. But the truth is that you're hard to love. And I realized that loving you is not the solution."

I don't touch on my "freak outs" that Paul calls them because he's always made it clear where he stands on mental health. You're either fine or you're not. And if you're not fine, damaged, or broken, in Paul's eyes you're not worth the work for him. So I did my best to hide my manic episodes from him. Apparently my best wasn't good enough and he uses this chance to bring it up.

"How am I hard to love? Is it because I didn't fold the first time you said it? Was it something I did? Tell me, please." I hate myself for begging and I almost feel like I'm clinging to him, my life raft, to keep me afloat and tell me what he needs.

"If you were easy to love and I loved you as much as I thought I did, I would have come with you when you asked me. But you are too hard to love and I need an easy love."

Ouch. I rear back like he slapped me. The realization that I'm really not good enough hits harder than it should. But Paul pointing it out in not so simple words is him shoving that dagger in further. "Am I really hard to love or is there someone else?"

His gaze drops to the floor and my stomach falls out of my butt. "She just got out of the first trimester."

My keys fall out of my hand and clatter to the floor making him jump. "So while I've been missing you and blaming myself for our lack of communication, you've been with someone else." I'm angry. Angry that I stayed with someone through this move. Angry that I tied my happiness to him. I'm angry that I let him put me on that stupid pedestal. Angry that I told him I loved him. And I do. Well— did. I did love him. At least I think I did. Now I'm questioning if what I felt for him was actually love or was it contentment? Was my love for him tied to how dependent I became on him? Because in my grief of losing Liam, I clung to Paul to keep me afloat. I let him keep me afloat. I let him mold me to who he wanted me to be. Is that love? "How long?"

"Don't make me answer that," Paul says, and I know, despite my resistance to wanting the truth, that I need it. Because despite my need to not want the details, for my sake, I need them. I need to sleep peacefully at night and know that none of it was on me. I need to be able to move on knowing that none of it was my fault. But despite my need-to-know, I'll always blame myself for us falling apart. But I'll also blame him for letting us fall apart.

"How long have you been with her?"

"Nine months."

I cross my arms over my chest and bring a hand up to my lips. Squeezing them together with an attempt to keep them from trembling. I think back through the last year and try to catalog when we went sideways. In my haze I can picture that moment. When his text responses came back hours later instead of minutes later like they used to. When he would always tell me to hold on as he went into another room and I'd hear the door close. I chalked it up to him wanting to talk to me in private. It was always him though and I walked around life blissfully unaware of what was happening back home.

"Come on, Sarah. You knew things were going to change between us the second you decided to move up here." He says as if that excuses his stepping out on me.

"That is no excuse for cheating on me, Paul. I asked you to come with me. You could have come with me!" I shout. The tears of anger clog up my throat. Making it hard for me to speak. I feel weak. Weak that I'm letting him see a side of me that he's responsible for. Weak that I'm crying over a man when I watched my best friend cry over two until she finally pulled herself out of the dumps.

He shakes his head like that suggestion is idiotic. "No. I was–we were building something there."

"We could have re-built anywhere," I say, as all the fight finally leaves my body the longer he stays here presenting his horrible case.

"No." He says and ends that topic. Something I admired about Paul was his ability to switch topics at the drop of a hat. Because of it our relationship was never stale. But I never thought I'd come to hate his ability to end a conversation until it pertained to me. "I flew up here because you deserved some sort of closure from us. Because let's be honest, our relationship was on the downslope the second you accepted the job up here. I'm just putting a name to it: a break-up. And I also want you to know that I'm proposing to her as soon as I land back in Charleston. I just wanted you to hear it from me first."

I bite my tongue as the tears fill my eyes and I know that I can't look at him anymore. Three years down the drain. A friendship so solid, ruined in his selfish moment. "Get out." I spit as the first tear falls.

He walks a step forward and pauses as if he wants to say something more. But I move to the side, not wanting to hear whatever he wants to say and pull the door open as I do.

When he crosses over the threshold I slam the door shut and lock it.

I cover my mouth with my palm as a sob lets loose. I cry over my stupid heart for opening up and letting someone in. I cry because I wasted three years on someone who gave me everything without my having to ask. I cry for being so stupid. I cry for being a stupid, hopeless romantic and naive enough to let someone in.

Hard to love, my ass.

Swiping off my tears, I head up the carpeted stairs, taking them two at a time and going straight to my bathroom to shower.

I bring my phone and speaker into my bathroom and find the most "female scream, I hate boys" playlist to yell in the shower. When the water is to my liking, I hop in and exfoliate my body from head to toe. The only way to make myself feel my best is to start from square one. And that involves an everything shower. As Kelly Clarkson sings about breathing for the first time, some of that post-breakup tension melts away from my body.

They say the best way to get over someone, is to get under someone else.

Well I vow to not only change the game, but to never fall in love again.

2

SARAH
SIX MONTHS LATER

It's a chilly December evening and the club is packed, making it the perfect place for an inconspicuous hookup. The lowlights of the club and the bass from the music vibrates through my body. I drove up to Columbus for the weekend under the guise of a 'spa weekend' and my friends were none the wiser. My hotel that I chose for my stay is a block away from the club that I'm at. Honestly it was more for convenience than anything.

I finish my second drink of the night and weave my way back through the crowd and onto the dance floor. The music drowns out attempts at conversation with mid-level guys and thankfully stops any logical thought attempting to run through my mind. This night is about shutting off my mind and having an orgasm or two.

I'm in the middle of the dance floor and my body sways and rolls to the music as sweat begins to form on the back of my neck while my hair tumbles in thick auburn waves around me. What I thought would be a smart choice, the black backless mini dress I'm wearing, unfortunately does little to cool my body off. Sweat sits on the surface of my skin when the song fades and bleeds into another when I feel a presence at my back. My body reactively flinches and then relaxes as I feel the weight of sure hands land on my waist and wrap around to my lower stomach.

The strangers scent of cedar wood and leather cocoons us to where the other scents of Chanel No. 5 and Dior, in the club don't invade us. His body is firm and dwarfs mine from what I can tell. No inch of space is spared as he tentatively pulls my body flush to his. My body grinds into his groin and I hear the hitch in his breath. Good god what is he hiding in his pants? He takes my hand and pulls it up, wrapping it around his neck and my fingers slide up to weave into the hair that's at the nape and I give the silky strands a tug. His hands roam my body and down to my thighs, trailing up to the hem of my dress and I can't stop the moan that lets free. I'm thankful for the music being so loud as he and I are the only two who know the effects of what's taking place.

I feel the heat from his mouth on my neck and my head falls back on his shoulder, rolling to the side to give him better access. His tongue laps out and licks a drop of sweat off my neck. The noise that escapes me spurs him into action and he latches on. Trailing kisses and alternating sucks as our bodies continue to move to the beat of the music. His hands lock me in place to his as our bodies move in a way that's reserved for the bedroom and his lips trail up before he pulls on my earlobe. My libido goes haywire when he dips his tongue in my ear.

The foreplay has gone on long enough. I turn around and wrap my arm around his neck again, pulling him down for a kiss. No hesitation, no resistance. Just pure lust fuels this kiss. Even in my heels he still towers over me and I feel him lower to my height as our lips connect. A zing that goes far past attraction moves through my body. I choose to blame it on the alcohol and music because I've never felt anything like this. Is what pumps through the air vents at Target pumping through the air vents in the club? His hand presses into my lower back and he rises to his full height. I slip my hand into the back pocket of his jeans as my head tips back while he devours me.

We're no longer dancing.

We're lost in each other as the magic in the club takes over our senses.

This is what I wanted. This is what I need.

To be devoured and treated like the goal is to make me feel like a first choice.

We dance like this for another song. Front to front. My arms around his neck. His arms around my waist. When he slides his leg between mine, my body stutters. I use the music pumping out of the speakers as a reason for my gyrating on his thigh. Each rub of his jeans against my core has my body reaching higher and higher to the peak. Before I know what's happening, we're moving off the dance floor and to a secluded corner of the club. We're still in view of the other patrons but we have enough privacy to continue what we're doing. As soon as we're hidden away, he presses me up against the scratchy felt wall and places his thigh between my legs again. A whimper escapes as he presses firmly against my aching core.

"Is this what you want?" He huskily whispers as his lips find my neck again and he trails his hand back down my thigh to the hem of my dress. A gentle back and forth sweeping of his fingers on my upper leg has my mind short circuiting. *Seriously, get it together Sarah!*

"Yes." I pant and shove my fingers through his hair. I pull

him back so I can get as good of a look in the dark club as possible. "But not here."

His hands come up and gently wrap around my wrists that are still locked around the back of his neck. "Do you have a place around here?"

I nod my head and pull my hands from his grasp, leaving our hands linked together. "Mm-hmm. I'm at a hotel a block away."

"Okay," he says and pulls me with him as we move out of the hideaway.

I follow close as we wind our way through the gyrating bodies and stop at the coat check before heading outside. He helps me into my coat, making sure to button it up, before slugging his on and together we fall in stride towards the doors, hand-in-hand, and out into the Ohio tundra.

I had thought his appeal would disappear when we left the club. But as I tell him which hotel I'm staying at, his allure amps up when he wraps his arm around my shoulder, shielding me as much as he can from the cold and the spectators loitering on the sidewalk. The walk to the hotel is charged with an undeniable chemistry. One I've never felt with any of the guys I attempted to date in college. Or even with Paul. But I force my mind to forget about anyone else as we take a slight turn to where the hotel is located and stroll into the lobby, right towards the elevator. Luckily, we have no wait and the doors open instantly. Hot stranger and I filter into the car and I press the number 8 to take us up to my room.

We both plaster ourselves to opposite sides of the car. And in this light I feel metaphorically knocked on my ass. He's beautiful. His dark blond hair is tamed, but slightly trussed up from my fingers running through it in the club. And will probably look messier if the way we danced is any sign. I see a peek of ink trailing up his neck and it makes me wonder if he has any more tattoos or if he just decided to tattoo his neck. His dark blue eyes survey me and when our eyes clash a breathtaking smile is almost enough to make me screw the one night stand and ask if he's looking for a relationship. Which goes against my new rule, but for his smile I would throw out every last rule I had about falling in love.

"What's your name?" He asks as the elevator car gets closer to my floor.

"Why?" I ask because this isn't normally what I do when I just need a release.

"Because I need to know whose name I'm going to groan out and you need to know whose name to scream when I make you come over and over."

Well, shit.

"Are you always this cocky?" I ask and don't deny that his words did something to me.

His answering smirk is answer enough. Usually, it's a turnoff. But tonight, when I feel like all he needs to do is brush against my leg, his smirk does the trick.

I cross my legs in a nonchalant way but I can't deny the way his early statement hits me right in the core. I also don't miss the way his eyes twinkle at the movement. "Sarah," I say after a beat. "Yours?"

"Theo," he tells me.

God, even his name is hot. I open my mouth to say something when the elevator stops on my floor. He steps forward and takes my hand in his to drag me out of the car.

"Left or right?"

"Right. Three doors down." I say and he drags me in that direction. I manage to fish my room key out of my small purse as we're walking hurriedly and hand it to him.

Theo swipes the key against the door and when the light turns green we file into my room. As soon as the door closes, we're flooded in darkness as I didn't think to turn on the bedside light before I left. But my eyes slowly begin to adjust with the sliver of light filtering through the crack under the door and I see him still leaning against the door. I set my purse on the small table and that sound must wake him up. But I decided I need to be in charge. I move to turn on the small light that's on the table and when he steps into my space, I hold my hands out and press against his firm chest.

In this dim light he almost looks devilish. Like he's not so gentlemanly after all and my pussy quivers at the thought. He quirks an eyebrow at me and a smirk lifts on one side revealing a dimple.

"I'm in charge tonight." I declare and slide my hands down his torso. The clench of his abs as I reach the hem of his shirt and trace the line where his shirt meets his jeans, has me rejoicing that I can make him feel this.

"Oh, really? And what are you going to do to me?" His question comes out in pants as I continue to lightly trace my fingers over his skin.

"I think the question is, what am I not going to do to you?"

His eyebrows raise in surprise at that. One thing I decided to change was my approach with men and hookups in general.

"Hmm." He starts and shucks his jacket off. "What are you not going to do to me?"

"Well first, let's get unsexy. Are you clean?"

He nods in quick succession and it's the most serious I've seen him. "Yes. I just got tested last month. I even have the results on my phone if you want to see them."

I shake my head with a slight smile that he'd go that far

to reassure me. He's been nothing but honest as far as I can tell. "Good. Me too. And I have an IUD. Next, I want you to take off all your clothes and climb on the bed."

His movements are slow and it's almost as if he thinks I'm not serious. But when I back away from him and lean against the wall he moves slow, but with each inch of skin revealed he becomes more determined. I watch with my legs crossed tightly over each other as each piece of clothing is removed. My earlier observation that he's an athlete is confirmed when his pants are shimmied down his legs, revealing muscular thighs, encased in black boxer briefs, that one can only get from the gym and playing competitively. My curiosity over his ink is satisfied when I see intricate designs of tattoos on his legs that move up to his thick thighs and I can only assume that they do in fact cover the majority of his body.

My eyes eventually make it up his body and I see him watching me. Waiting for me to make my first move. I pacify him and slip off my heels. Height-wise, they put me at 5'10" and without them I'm hovering around 5'7". When Theo stands to his full height, I have to crane my neck further to look at him. Judging by the look in his eyes he likes that.

"Shirt too." I order and do my best to hold in a moan when he pulls his shirt off from behind him like all of the guys do. My mouth fills with saliva and I swallow it all down as his torso stretches and abs flex with the movement while I count each delicious abdominal muscle. I was right about the tattoos. His body is a full canvas and I doubt he has any room for more ink.

The sound of his shirt hitting the floor with a light thud, sends a thrill through me and I erase the space between us. I don't know if I can wait anymore. The ache in my core has me ready to combust with each step I took closer to him. My hands land on his heaving chest and I get a closer look at his tattoos. His ink gives nothing away about who he is. Just scripts and quotes mixed with shapes and florals. Not being able to help myself, I lean forward and flick a nipple. The action earns a groan from him. My lips trail across his chest and I rise up on my tiptoes to kiss along his neck. He angles his head and allows me more room to claim his body. I dip my tongue in the spot where his neck meets his chest and kiss over to his Adam's apple.

I slide a hand down his body, into the waistband of his briefs and my hand lands on his growing cock. My fingers encircle his thick length and I give him a firm tug. I run my thumb over the slick head, coating him in pre-cum as I run my fist up and down his length.

"How quickly can you come just like this?" I ask as I pump him with more precision.

"Pretty quickly," he groans out through clenched teeth.

He flinches when I lighten to a feather-like touch on his cock. I look down and see his fists clenched and then look up to see his jaw fluttering from the force of keeping himself together.

I lower myself down to my knees, his briefs coming down with me, and take him in my mouth. I skip the buildup, the teasing, and the light touches.

"Jesus Christ." Theo says and lays his hand on my head. He doesn't force himself on me and I like that.

I take him to the back of my throat and my nose meets trim pubic hair. I moan around him and move my hand between his thighs to tug on his balls, fondling them while he swears above me. He curls his fingers through my hair and that's one of the only signs he gives that he's affected. My hand holds onto his thigh as I bob up and down on his length. I pull off his cock and leave the tip in my mouth, fluttering my tongue over his slit and alternate sucking.

"I'm two seconds from coming. Tell me I can come down your throat," he begs.

I look up at him, mouth still full with the tip of his cock, and moan around him. His grip in my hair gets tighter and I feel him swell before he goes still and comes down my throat roaring my name. I work him through the rest of his release, not letting his cum seep from between my lips, and only when he's stopped coming do I slip him out of my mouth with a pop. I kiss my way up his chest and dip my tongue back into the divot at his neck. Licking up the drops of sweat, I reach behind me and pull down the tiny zipper at the bottom of my dress. The straps fall down my arms and I let the material puddle on the floor leaving me bare except for a tiny scrap of lace covering my pussy.

Theo backs up and swears under his breath. My curves are in all the right places; to my ample breasts and hourglass shape. I'm not overly toned in the mid-section as most of my exercise is running and my go-to comfort food is french fries. But I don't think he cares as evident by his growing-again erection. My fingertips press into my thighs the longer his gaze roams over my body. My deep breathing is almost embarrassing.

He stalks towards me and lifts me up by the back of my legs. Theo lifts me so high that my legs go over his shoulders. He presses me up against the nearest wall putting my laced covered pussy in his face. The heat from his breath has me tightening my thighs around his head and my hands fall into his hair.

Theo looks up at me with an almost too innocent look before hooking his thumb through the useless scrap of material covering me and taking a swipe through my entrance.

"Fuck," I rasp out. His tongue flicks my clit in fast swipes and my toes curl against his back and my hands tug hard on his hair when he inserts two fingers in my opening. Theo pumps and curls his fingers inside of me while never letting up on flicking my clit with his tongue. "Theo..." My orgasm can't be coming that fast. He can't be that skilled.

"Come all over my face, Sarah."

The bass in his voice vibrates through me and I shoot off like a rocket, moaning his name as he continues to eat me like a man starved. I'm floating. Scratch that, I'm moving. Still on Theo's shoulders and braced securely with his arms bracketed around me as he walks us to the bed. His hands come up and cradle my back as I'm laid in the center of the bed.

Theo places another open-mouthed kiss on my pussy, pulling down and flinging off the scrap of fabric over his shoulder and sliding his tongue inside my opening, before he kisses up my body. He pays close attention to my aching breasts. Pulling a taut nipple into his mouth with his teeth, then soothing the sting with his tongue and then sucks, sending the signal to where I'm aching for him. I can't close my legs as he's cradled between them, so I rub against his lower stomach hoping for any type of friction.

"Your cock. I wanna come on your cock," I demand, close to hysterical tears from my arousal and the need to come again. How is he this good? It must be a fluke.

"Then put it in," he tells me while still lapping at my breasts.

I push at his chest and roll him onto his back, following until I'm straddling his hips. My mouth falls to his and our tongues tangle. I moan into his mouth as I pull his bottom lip between my teeth and suck. His answering groan at the sensation is heady. Running my hands up and down his chest, I break the kiss and follow them down. Taking my time to cherish the work of art that is his body until I come face-to-face with his cock.

"You have the prettiest cock." I tell him and pump his length in my fist again. I hold eye contact with him as I lean down and let a drop of spit fall onto his cock. His legs tense under me as I work my fist over him and watch his eyes go from a deep sea ocean blue to a midnight black.

"You have the prettiest pussy I've ever seen. I bet it would look prettier with my cock inside."

I rise up on my knees and move back up his body, rubbing the head of his cock through my opening. "Let's test that theory."

Theo places his hands on my hips to steady me as I slowly sink down on him. I lift up to coat him in my juices before sliding back down on his length and bottoming out.

His head flies back and the grip on my hips intensifies. "Christ, you fit around me perfectly." Theo swears when he looks down to see where we're joined.

"You were right," I say and finally relax my body to accommodate him, as my hips start to move up and down his length. "My pussy does feel prettier with your cock buried inside of me."

My hands fall to the headboard and I use that to help me ride Theo like he's a mechanical bull. With my chest in his face Theo flicks each nipple with the tip of his tongue as it moves past him.

"Your pussy feels even better wrapped around my cock than on my face. But I think it's time for you to come on my cock. What do you say, Sarah?"

"Yes," I pant out. "Play with my clit." I order as I feel the telltale sign of another orgasm.

"As you wish." Theo starts rutting up into me as he plays with my clit and my climax flies forward. "God damn, baby," he grits out. "I feel you fluttering around me."

"Come inside me." I demand.

He pauses and looks up at me to make sure I'm sure.

"Do it, Theo. Mark me," I wail as my orgasm doesn't seem to end.

Theo flips us without separating and pounds into me. The headboard smacks against the wall and he holds my hips in place as he chases his release. I feel when he does. His cock swells and his strokes get more messy, more wild, as my third orgasm hits with his and he yells out my name. The sound of our cum mixing echoes throughout the room and it lengthens my orgasm. I play with my clit as another orgasm hits me and I throw my head back on a silent scream.

"Fuck, baby." Theo's hands fall to the sides of my head while his strokes slow.

I run my hands through his hair. The silky strands are wet with sweat and I can't ignore that this position is more intimate than it should be for a one night stand. I get the sudden urge to kiss him and start another round while still coming down from this one. But I resist and I think he's on the same page as I am.

With a kiss to the tip of my nose, Theo pulls out and I wince as I feel the loss of him. He rolls off the bed and I watch his very firm athletic backside move towards the bathroom. I hear the water running in the sink and two seconds later he waltzes back out with a wet washcloth.

I hold my hand out and he shoos it away to clean me up. I've never had anyone clean me up after sex and I can't deny that it does something to me. The intimacy of aftercare should be studied. I watch his face while he cleans me. His mouth is set in a firm line and with his face angled down, I can see the slight tilt to his nose which tells me it's been broken a time or two and poorly reset.

Theo tosses the towel to the side and moves to pick up his discarded jeans. The notion that he's leaving shouldn't have me feeling lost. It's the orgasm, Sarah. It'll wear off.

"I assume you didn't want to cuddle?" Theo asks as he slips his shirt on.

I lift my hips and pull the covers out and sliding under them to give me some sort of barrier. "Nope."

He smirks and walks over to the bed. Resting a knee next to me, he leans over and lifts my chin with his pointer finger and thumb. "I didn't think so. Thank you for tonight." He tells me and presses his lips to mine. His tongue traces the seam of my lips before leaving me breathless and pulling away. With a final kiss to my forehead he backs away from the bed and walks to the door. I'm still left dumbfounded by his parting kiss when I hear the door clank shut.

I fall back on the lone pillow, as the other ones were shoved off the bed, and stare up at the wall. Stumped that, in my quest for a weekend release, I had someone rock my world, if only for one night. Maybe coming to Columbus wasn't such a bad idea. And if I play my cards right Theo and I will run into each other again.

3

SARAH

SIX MONTHS LATER

I look up from my phone as the elevator stops and opens to the fourth floor of the office, with our logo 'It's a Match PR' lit up and greeting me from behind the receptionist's desk. I step out and wave to Tessa as I walk past her towards my office. With my phone forgotten in my hand, I take in the empty office as the sound of my clicking three-inch black Louboutins on the hardwood floors breaks up the quiet. As I make the final steps to my office, my phone vibrates with a notification that has me scowling at the device.

I open up the drawer at the bottom of my desk and drop my purse and work tote into it and close the drawer with my foot. Standing up straight, I push my thick auburn hair over my shoulder and go back to my phone. I re-read the score from last night, showing me that Cincinnati's baseball team lost again so now Mason is going to gloat because he's an Atlanta fan. Speak of the gloating devil.

Mason: Pay up Callahan.

Me: No way. The series isn't even over.

Mason: You think they can come back for the next three games?

Me: Yes.

Of the small client list I have, Mason is my favorite. After the blind side of his trade, he fired his team and took me on as his publicist when he found out what I did for work. It was easy working with someone who not only is in love with my best friend, but who I have a childhood history with. Eventually I took on a baseball player that was traded last season after five years playing in Washington and a soccer player in Cincinnati. Both were looking for a new public relations agent who could revamp their image. Since I love small projects, they were perfect. I even have them in a group chat on my phone named: Problem Children.

The agency I'm with is small but takes on all of the teams in the city and surrounding areas. When my schedule allows me to, I travel to where my clients have games. Not only is it work, but it helps feed the travel bug in me.

It's been a year since the breakup. And while I have moved on, the pain is still this living thing that's simmering just beneath the surface. It somehow reminds me that I'm not enough. That I wasn't enough for him to stay. That I wasn't good enough for him to choose. And learning that your ex not only cheated on you months after you moved states for work, but got someone pregnant, stings more than anyone can know. It brings the not enough feeling to the forefront of my mind anytime I think about what I could have done differently.

I still haven't told Kamryn the real reason Paul and I broke up. She had other things going on in her life. But even if she had asked, saying it out loud makes the situation more humiliating than it should be, so I just haven't.

I've moved on to thinking about bigger and better things. Yet, the only bigger and better thing I can't stop thinking about is the hot one night stand from six months ago. I swear he cast some sort of spell over me to where no other hook-up seems appealing anymore.

Alas, I've been advised that burying myself in work is merely a weak band-aid to the stitching that's required. But, so far, I'm happy. At least, that's what I feed my therapist in our bi-weekly sessions.

On top of working harder than ever, I've filled my time with my girls and their boos. I'm glad my friends have found their happiness. And I'm more than happy to seventh wheel it when need be.

I'M LOOKING over the contract for an upcoming photoshoot for Nate, my baseball player in his fourth year, when my boss knocks on my door.

My head pops up at the noise. "Hey, Jeff. What's up?" I ask and take my glasses off.

He shuts the door and comes to sit in front of my desk. "Have you checked the headlines?"

"No," I say skeptically. My eyes flash to my computer that's gone on screensaver mode having not been used in the last thirty minutes. I really should change that setting as my inbox is usually flooded with a dozen emails after thirty minutes.

"Hockey," he says with zero context clues.

"..is a sport," I say as I finish his sentence for him.

He gives me a look that's earned me more smacks to the back of the head from my parents than allowed.

"I know you were looking to expand your client list in the next year. But we're going to have to rush that."

Behind the scenes I've reached out to other agents to see if their clients needed new reps in terms of publicity. I have a few who are looking for partial representation, which works for me. But if I fear this conversation is going to go the way I think it is, then I'll have to nix the other contracts.

"Why?"

"Riley Jones. Have you heard of him?" Jeff asks.

My mind flips through the hockey players that I have heard of and his name pops up in my mental rolodex. It's sort of my job to know the athletes in Ohio because at any moment, any one of them could need new representation. "Sure. Hometown golden boy. Drafted his first year in college as a right winger, but he committed to playing all four years at Columbus State before starting his first game with the Blue Jays. And that's about all I know. Why?" I feel like that word has left my mouth one too many times since Jeff set foot in my office.

He gives me the look I've seen him give his daughter on more than one occasion. The one that says more than words. The look that makes her do what he asked of her despite the moaning and groaning it took to get to that point.

I shake my head as realization settles in. "No. Absolutely not. Jeff, I was joking last week when I said it wouldn't be a bad idea if he had a babysitter. Plus, I don't have the time to reform, babysit, whatever you want to call it, a twenty-three year old hotshot who thinks he's God's gift to the sport and women." I sit back in my chair with a huff.

"Sure you do. Mason's schedule is light, Nate's on an

away stretch right now, Jordan is doing fantastic in Cleveland, and Miles is crushing it with FC. You have time."

Not only do I cover ground with my athletes in Cincinnati, but I'm also in Cleveland, which is my furthest trek for work, as well with three clients there. Columbus would be my first and while I have been looking to expand my client list to the minor league teams in Akron and Dayton, I wanted to do so in the next few years. Not right now as Jeff is proposing.

"Why can't someone else do it? Like Travis?" I feel bad for throwing him under the bus. But really? Why me?

"That's the thing. Riley was with his agent, who's a guy, when–"

I groan and drop my head to my desk before sitting right back up. "What's in it for me?" I ask, because if I know Jeff, it's that he won't stop until I say yes. And when an athlete is in hot water with his agent, that means the team is doing PR damage control and needs to "rehabilitate" the athlete before they decide he's no longer worth the hassle and choose to trade him or drop him altogether.

"A raise, more vacation days, and really anything else," he says as he lists off each item. Jeff loves this company. He started with a few athletes before he brought me and eventually a few other agents on. Again, we're a small agency but we have some big name and rising star athletes on our roster.

"First class seating on every flight I need to take plus a guest, whether it's for business or pleasure. The rest of my student loans paid off, paid lunches, and anything else I will bring straight to you." I throw at him.

Jeff chews on his cheek in thought. I know he'll agree. Just like he agrees to everything else I bargain with. My boss is like the older brother I never had. Being an only child, I made friends quickly and made sure to hold onto them with all my might. Really, Jeff got lucky. I'm a catch. Which I reiterate to him weekly. "Deal."

My shoulders release from my ears and I stop swinging my foot when Jeff makes no move to vacate the seat he's taken. "What else?" I ask because I know there's something else. Jeff always sugarcoats things with me, despite me telling him I don't want or need that.

"He's here."

I slam my head against my headrest this time and clench my fists. My manicured nails dig into my palms as I clench my fists. "Jeff…" I groan out.

"Did I mention you're the best employee ever?"

"Unless you want to pay off my mortgage too, you should stop buttering me up." I tell him as I sit up and unclench my fists.

Jeff holds his hands up in surrender. "Fine. You're right. But I think with you as his rep, he'll shape up."

One of the reasons I became so good at my job is that I had zero distractions. Everything had a place and nothing shook me. Because, really, what else did I have to do? I have no love life to speak of so all of that saved time went into work. My clients fell in line. I worked press releases to their advantage, got them photoshoots that no other publicist could, I made their reputations squeaky clean, and in the end, the community and fans love them. I became a shark in a male-dominated field.

"Will you send him in here?" I ask.

"Sure," Jeff says and gets up. "Again, I know this is sooner than you hoped. But you're saving his ass from never playing hockey again. I'll send you an email of what he's been up to so far."

I give Jeff a smile that doesn't reach my eyes. As soon as he leaves, my phone dings with a text.

Emmy-Lou: Cookout this weekend.

Me: Do I finally get to meet this elusive man you've been spending all of your time with?

Emmy-Lou: Yes.

Emmy-Lou: But Kam doesn't know you know more than her. So please keep that under lock and key.

Me: What's in it for me?

Emmy-Lou: The strongest and largest margarita poolside?

Me: You drive a hard bargain, little bird.

Emmy-Lou: Love you!

I'm smiling at my phone when a knock sounds from the other side.

"Come in," I announce without looking up and place my phone face down.

I move my gaze to my computer and wiggle my mouse to wake it up when the familiar scent of cedar wood and leather invades my senses along with a hulking figure that darkens my doorway. My head swivels to the doorway and my eyes slowly take in the man standing at my door. From his crisp Air Maxes with worn black jeans that encase his muscular legs to the long sleeve henley that's pushed up to his elbows revealing the tattooed forearms I remember holding onto as an orgasm ripped through me. A silent fuck leaves his mouth as the surprise at seeing each other is more than we ever thought.

Words seem to fail me. If he were anyone else they'd be so easy to pull out of thin air. But, this. Seeing him after replaying that night while laying in bed. What do you say to that?

"Take a seat, Theo," I say and open up my email. I do what I can to avoid his gaze for as long as possible. I have no other reason than trying to avoid looking at the man who made me come harder than anyone ever had. Shaking myself out of those NSFW thoughts, I see the one promised from Jeff and quickly scroll the contents. "Or is it Riley?"

I can't believe my one night stand is Riley Jones. What are the actual odds? Considering I went to Columbus when we hooked up, the possibility was more likely that I thought.

He finally steps into my office and closes the door, resting his back against it. "It's Riley. But my middle name is Theodore and I usually go by Theo when I'm out on the town. I didn't know if you just wanted one night because you knew me as 'Riley Jones the hockey player' so I went with my middle name. Well, the shortened version of my middle name anyway." He tells me this while still resting against my office door. His body is tense and I'm not sure if he's afraid to say or do anything that'll cause me to fly off the handle.

My forehead scrunches. "Back up. How would I have even known it was you? And you approached me in case you've forgotten."

Riley pushes off the door and strides over to the chair that Jeff was occupying and slumps down, crossing his ankle over his knee. His cologne wafts towards me and he exudes masculinity, power, but also cockiness that I fear has been his go-to for so long he doesn't know how to stop. "I did and I don't regret that."

We stare at each other. Separated by a desk. In the light

of day we're nothing but strangers. But our night together might as well be playing out between us like a hologram the longer we sit in silence.

I shake out of my memories of our night and get back to business. I do my best to ignore what happened between us and turn my professional hat on. "Were you happy with your last team? Your agent, publicist...that team."

He stares at me as if he can't believe my switch up, but then he too, shakes off the daze. "They were okay. Some of them turned out to be in it for fame rather than helping my career move forward. I didn't really catch on until it was too late."

Figures. "Right. Well I'm going to do my best to get your information from all of them. If that doesn't work, I'll see if Jeff can pull some strings. If you are looking for a new agent, which I highly suggest you get a new agent as soon as possible, I can ask around and see if any are looking to take on a hockey player. In the meantime, I can assume the role of your agent and publicist temporarily." I say all the while drafting up an email to his former team. My talent for multitasking should be studied. I then draft up another email for Columbus's front office regarding his agent status. It's unnecessary but if they make any moves without him knowing, it won't go over well.

"You're not gonna have me do tutoring or anything, right?"

My fingers halt on the keyboard and I turn to face him and raise an eyebrow at his blasé question. "All of my clients are involved in the community. Whether it's camps for kids or community clean-up. No exceptions. It's part of having a sparkling clean reputation, which you now need. And this is where your last team and I differ." I push my keyboard and mouse to the side and lean forward so he knows I'm serious.

"As your publicist I need to be on the same page as your agent, your coach, your manager, your personal trainer, and so many other people that it would make your head spin. Since I'm now your temporary agent, that job now falls to me. If you want your team to respect you and the fans to make your jersey the top seller in the store, then you'll do what I have lined up for you. That includes reshaping your social media and real life presence."

Riley's gaze challenges mine, waiting for me to waver in my demands. If he thinks our night together will soften my approach to him, he'll be waiting until hell freezes over. Our time together was a pebble thrown into a still lake. Enough to shake us both, but not enough for me to bend on how I do my job. And when he realizes I won't bend on the way of my working to make him more successful, he finally gives in. "Fine. When do I start."

"I knew you'd see things my way. In a couple of weeks there will be a Fourth of July event downtown. A bunch of locally owned businesses will be there along with some athletes for the teams who aren't in season. Fans flock to this event every year because they look forward to it every year. It's a great way for you to market yourself and get to know the area."

"You know I don't live in this city," he says like I don't already know.

"You have a car, right?"

"And a motorcycle. If you ever wanna ride again," he replies cockily as a smirk teases his lips. His innuendo is not lost on me and the memory of me doing just that hits me full-force.

I won't lie when I say that Riley is handsome. A fact that was not lost on me that night. But he's a young athlete, making money he never dreamed of, with his tousled dirty blond hair, tattoos climbing up his neck that I know covers the majority of his body, and his dark blue eyes that sparkle with mischief when he looks at me. But I won't fall for it. At least not again. Not even as the cedar wood scent from his cologne fills my office and takes me back to that night.

Because as a woman in a mostly male-dominated field, I'm already at a disadvantage as this career has presented some not-so-friendly men in this field. Some athletes felt they had a say in what I can do because they were men. But with my icy persona when it comes to this job, I've fended off their quips, jabs, and come-ons in the most effective way that I could.

By becoming the second highest paid public relations agent in the United States.

Riley is no longer the exception to every other athlete in this country. So it's now my job to look at me as a sort of sister to him and not a friend. I have to remind myself that because the thoughts that were just running through my head weren't very sibling-like.

I copy and paste his email from Jeff and pull up another email. The sound of outgoing mail breaks up the silence.

"I just emailed you events to attend for the rest of the year," I say, ignoring his quip about the motorcycle. "I'll get in touch with your coach to work in a mandatory skate with kids either here or near home base. Either way I'll be there."

I look up and see him looking around my office and I follow his wandering eyes. Since I'm here a lot, I realize I've made it my second home. Pictures of my family and friends fill the walls and shelves. Along with my degrees showcased by pictures with my team here and my clients. I have an area rug that is woven with blues and oranges to break up the cold interior that this office originally presented. A candle warmer gives my space a cozy feel to it and Riley getting a glimpse into my life has me wanting to take the pictures down and unplug the candle warmer so he has to earn the right to know me.

Riley's gaze comes back to me and I have to look away before I look back up at him. "You got it boss lady."

"My number is also included in that email I sent you. Do not, under any circumstances, send me unsolicited pictures. Got it?"

He leans forward and the Tom Ford scent I know like the back of my hand, invades my senses. "What kind of pictures should I send you then?"

"Goodbye, Riley." I dismiss him.

"Goodbye, Sarah." He leaves with an arrogant chuckle.

4

RILEY

Unbelievable. I think to myself as I walk out of Sarah's office and towards the elevator. My hot hookup six months ago is my new publicist.

And basically my babysitter.

I have a babysitter at twenty-three years old. I mash the elevator button more forcefully than I should and stomp in before pressing the G button. It's not enough that my last agent and publicist were a box of rocks, but now this one seems like a real ball-buster.

It's going to take a lot of effort on my part to not bring our time together in the hotel up. I could see it in her eyes as we sat in her office and I won't deny that I looked for Sarah after that night. My internet stalking gave me nothing as I only had her first name to go off of. At least she gave me her real name. Whereas I used a shortened version of my middle name to protect my identity.

The elevator opens and I hurry out of the building towards my Range Rover. I didn't lie when I said I have a motorcycle. But since I was needed here at the last minute

and my bike is at my parents place as it needs work done…
well my Range Rover was the logical choice. When I get in, I
start up and pull my phone out of my pocket. Checking my
email, I see the one from Sarah. I scan it and am baffled
with the amount of events she wants me to attend. Todd, my
fuck face agent, always said he was "working on something"
and then asked me what clubs we were going to that night.
But almost a year into the league and I still had no endorse-
ments to my name, hadn't been to a single charity event, and
saw maybe five people at our games last year wearing my
jersey. So, in hindsight, maybe it's a good thing I'm getting a
whole new team.

I find my playlist of choice before I pull out of the
parking lot and make the hour and a half drive back home.
Does it suck that my agent is now based out of Cincinnati?
Yes. But it doesn't hurt that the city is beautiful. Maybe if
Cincy revives their pro team, I'll see about a trade. For now,
I'm content playing at home in Columbus. In fact, I love
playing in my hometown. It works as my parents still live
there. Although they've made their opinions crystal clear on
how I've fallen off track. I hate being a disappointment to
them. They took me in when my birth parents were taken
too early from this world.

Momma and Pops were college best friends with my
parents. They were in each other's weddings and got jobs in
the same city. And when my parents had me, Momma and
Pops became my godparents. But they never could have
predicted that they would have to raise me as their own.
And so soon. I owe them more than I ever could imagine. So
how do I repay them? By fucking up on and off the ice. I
think my fuck-ups off the ice are more disappointing to
them than anything.

No. I know it's more disappointing to them. Getting

photographed at a party with drugs spread out across the table like a feast was finally the wakeup call I needed. Actually, getting benched until I fired my team was the wakeup call I needed. Not being able to play hockey because of the choices those close to me made, put everything into perspective.

I've loved hockey since the day I got my first pair of skates. It's my first love. Originally, it was something Dad and I bonded over. But when my skills far surpassed his basic ones, that's when my parents decided to sign me up for a league. Oi, I remember those first days of tryouts like they were yesterday. The first day going home I almost told my parents I wasn't cut out for hockey. I played for fun. So to have to abide by rules...well, that was an adjustment.

But I had a lot of good days once I learned how to accurately play hockey. But some days–some days I wanted to quit. Especially after the night of the accident. I don't remember much. But I do remember that we were on the way home from one of my games, singing along to a song on the radio when out of nowhere a truck struck us. Like I said, I don't remember much from that night. Matter of fact, I don't really remember anything from that night. What I do know is that I woke up to Momma and Pops flanking me, with twin haunted looks on their faces, while I lay in the hospital bed. My leg was broken, I had a concussion, and no one would tell me where my parents were.

At ten years old, I just wanted my mom. Her comforting rose and fresh laundry scent that soothed me anytime I needed a hug. I needed my dad and the accompanying scent of sweet mint from the gum he was always chewing to stop his smoking habit. But what I got at ten wasn't just a broken leg.

Now at twenty-three, memories of my parents are dulled

by my own mind. Regression is what the doctors called it at the hospital and that it would be a possibility that as I got older I'd remember the night of the accident in its entirety. I'm not hopeful for that, because who wants to remember something like that? How can my mind pull out memories about two people who've been gone for more than half my life? Momma and Pops do their best to keep their memories alive when I do need it, but I think they're terrified of rubbing it in my face that they knew them longer than I did. Speaking of, my phone rings with an incoming call and I answer it.

"Hey, Momma," I greet and put my attention back on the road.

"Hi, Riley. How was your meeting?" Her voice floats through the speakers.

I set my cruise control when I see nothing but open road before me. "Good, I guess? My new publicist, from what I can tell, is tough. She's temporarily taking over as my agent until I can find a new one."

"That's a good thing. I never liked your agent. He seemed more of a taker than a giver."

"Ugh, Momma." I cringe.

I hear the sucking of her teeth. "None of that."

When I moved in with Momma and Pops, we took some adjusting. They had to adjust to having a third person in their house. I had to adjust to living with people who weren't my birth parents. While we would do vacations together before my parents passed, that was different than living together full-time. And as the kinks were eventually ironed out, some things were still tough to talk about. Sex being one. I don't think Momma or Pops thought they'd have to give the birds and the bees talk to me. But it was wholly uncomfortable for all of us. What they left out, due to all of our embarrassment, I learned on my own and from experience as I got older.

With Momma working as a part-time sex therapist, it became easier to talk with her about the act and why my body reacted in a certain way when it saw something that my body liked, especially when I hit puberty. But sometimes, like now, I still revert to childlike ways when it comes to talking about sex.

"What did you call me for?" I ask, getting back on track.

"Oh, right. We're having a barbecue this weekend. If you want to take a break from your hockey life and head over we have a plate for you."

"Is mac & cheese on the menu?" My mouth is already watering just thinking of the flavorful dish.

Momma's laugh is audible. "Of course it is. That's one of the only ways we get you to come home."

"Momma, don't play. I come home once a month."

My parents live just a thirty minute drive away. But with how busy my schedule gets during the season, they act like I have to travel by plane to see them.

"I'm plenty aware, honey," she tells me. "My other line just buzzed. I'll see you Saturday."

"Okay, bye. Love you."

"Love you too, honey."

AN HOUR later I make it back to my condo and pull into one of my assigned spots. I get out and take the elevator up to my seventeenth-floor home and use the key fob to get inside. The clattering of my keys being tossed in the bowl is deafening in the silence of my home, along with the front door closing shut. I'm in the process of taking my shoes off when the sound of feet pitter-pattering towards me brings a smile to my face.

"Hello you two." I greet my cats. That's right. I'm a cat dad. A Certified Cat Daddy, if you will. At least that's what my teammates call me. I've been a cat lover since I was little. When my parents passed away, there was a question about where the family cats would live. I begged and pleaded with Momma and Pops to let them live out the rest of their lives with us. They said yes and it felt like a bit of my parents lived on until they crossed over the rainbow bridge.

When I signed my contract and bought this place, I knew I wanted cats as soon as I got my own place. And that's exactly what I did.

Sasha, my ragdoll, jumps on my shoulder before I head towards the expansive living room to turn the television on for some background noise. She did the jumping one day as a kitten and has been doing it every day for the last two years. While I wait for my streaming apps to pop up, I scratch under her chin and take a look outside at the view of Downtown Columbus as the city comes alive after what I'm guessing was a long work week. After I signed my contract, I took all of the advice Momma and Pops taught me about staying financially responsible and bought a nice place that isn't too extravagant. In fact, I live quite modestly compared to my teammates.

If by modest, I mean my condo is three-thousand square-feet with floor-to-ceiling windows and an unob- structed view of the city. I have a kitchen that serves its purpose as I've been known to cook up quite the feast when I have guests over. A double burner stove top and a flat top in the center for when my cooking calls for that. Along with a dining room that's off to the side where those big feasts take place with a table that seats eight.

When the apps on the TV finally load, I select a show that I've seen hundreds of times and place Sasha on the oversized couch before petting Pixie, my Maine Coon who is more on the reserved side, on the head and wander to the kitchen. On days I don't cook, like today, I have a few meals stockpiled from the meal delivery service I use. Rifling around my fridge, I find a salmon meal that's high in protein, with plenty of veggies and sweet potatoes. My phone vibrates right as I pop my food in the microwave.

Baby Pucklings

> Max: The Ally tonight?
>
> Noah: Can't. Going on a date.
>
> Max: Boo!
>
> Max: Logan? Riley?
>
> Me: I have a workout in the morning and my parents have a barbecue.
>
> Logan: Do Cassie and Dean have room for one more?
>
> Max: Logan, dude!
>
> Logan: Food significantly outweighs a night on the town.

I leave them to bickering in the group chat and take my food out of the microwave after it finishes beeping. Call me snobby, but I hate eating out of plastic containers. So I transfer my food to a plate and slide it over to the bar. I pour myself a glass of water and dig into my food with nothing but the noise from the television.

I think back to my meeting with my new publicist. Before I walked into Sarah's office, I took a moment to look at her uninterrupted while standing silently at the threshold. The smile that crossed her face as she stared at her phone uncovered an animalistic side of me and I wanted to know who it was that got her smiles. But the longer I stared at her like a creep, I couldn't believe my luck that it was her.

What attracted me to her all those nights ago was her hair. Although the club lights did nothing to accurately depict what the color was. I knew when I finally saw her hair in the elevator light that it would become one of my new favorite colors. Regret slammed into me the second the door to her hotel room closed. I had lingered in the hallway for a few minutes, hoping that she would rush and open the door to call out for me, before tucking my tail and heading to the elevator bank. Thinking that if it was meant to be, then it would be. But never did I think she would be my publicist.

Without thinking, I grab my phone and pull up Instagram. Yes, I come from the generation where we love to stalk people on the internet. However, my internet stalking after that night was extremely unsuccessful. I couldn't exactly type "woman with red hair in Ohio" into Google. Who knows what those search results would be. But as I think back to this afternoon, I recall seeing a picture of her with Mason Brooks in her office and decide I'll try my luck to find Sarah that way. It doesn't take me long as she's best friends with his girlfriend. Crossing my toes, I hope her profile is public. Clicking on her username, I feel like I should do my celly when her profile is presented to me like a hat trick.

I scroll through what she's shown of her life as I finish

my food. Her profile is not over-the-top like I'd expect and she doesn't post as much as I assume someone her age would. Sarah posts with reds and blues in her feed and it makes me wonder if those are her favorite colors. Deciding to be bold, I click the follow button and close out of the app seemingly afraid of what might happen if I stay on the app for too long and push my phone away from me. God help me if I accidentally like a picture from four years ago. I may be bold, but that can only take me so far.

I continue to mull over today and take it as a good sign that I have a new publicist. Sure, I was resistant to think a woman could handle my career. And if Momma could hear my thoughts she'd whoop me into next year. I spend more time than usual spacing out and when I look at the time and see it's a little later than I'd prefer. So I close down my kitchen and living room and go through my night time routine to prepare for the long day of tomorrow.

When I bought this place, I wanted to make sure my bedroom was a sanctuary of sorts as I knew this would be the one room where I could completely decompress. My one request was that the dark oak, four-poster California King Bed I had my eye on at the furniture store be the focal point of the room. So my interior designer ran with decorating to where this place feels more lived in than the almost year I've lived here. I have a matching dresser that sits off to the side of my bedroom and matching nightstands, although one is empty. Naturally, I have a massive cat tree that's set in the corner of my room and two dog-size beds for my cats at the foot of my bed and a few more spread throughout my condo. Can't say I don't spoil them.

I head to my bathroom and start the shower from the wall panel next to the light switch. My clothes meet the hamper and I drop my towel into the towel warmer. When I see the steam from the shower, I walk-in and still can't believe that after six months Sarah is back in my life. I don't necessarily believe in fate or destiny, but it can't be that much of a coincidence that she's my new publicist.

Here I make a promise to be as professional as possible. But make myself look as appealing as possible so that one day the client and employee line won't be too much to blur.

5

SARAH

"Hi, Mom." I greet her when I push through the front door of my house after a long workday. The last thing I wanted after onboarding a new client was a call from home. I've always thought of my mom as my best friend and with me being an only child she got her dream of a built-in mini-me. I received solid advice from her, that was more like what I assumed an older sister would give, while she still managed to be stern in her parenting. Yet, my mom eventually always found a way to blur the line between parent and friend. And my dad, while he was more firm than my mom, he let her take the reins when it came to me. I love my parents and how they've provided for me. But I never had the type of relationship with them the way Kamryn has with her parents.

My relationship with my parents was great in college. They gave me the freedom to choose my own path as long as it more or less fit the plan they had for me. I'll admit, I held some resentment towards them because I always loved fashion and wanted that to be my dream. But again, that wasn't in their plan for me, so I pivoted to appease them.

Being a Callahan meant I had to live up to the family name. So that meant veering towards a business degree that most of the women in my family have but no longer use. I must have drank the kool-aid at school as that was never my plan. I never wanted that to be my plan in the first place. My family is old money and that meant I had a lot of things handed to me. Money being one of them. And going against that path was the first splinter in my relationship with my parents. But that splinter turned into a full fracture after Paul and I broke up.

My parents loved him. They loved us together. They loved what we could have been together. He was the son they never had. So they could never grasp how I could lose him. Never mind the fact that it was him who stepped out on me. Never mind the fact that when they saw him around town with his new girl they never said a word to me. My mom suggested I turn a blind eye to his infidelity and that was the final straw. Our relationship is icy at best. But it turned into a full blown blizzard. I think that betrayal hurts the most and why I began pulling away from them. It's been over a year since I've had real conversation with my parents, that wasn't surface level, and I wonder if they're finally noticing.

"Hi, sweetheart. I haven't heard from you in a while–" *by my own doing* "–so I wanted to check in on you. Are you getting enough sleep?"

Leave it to my mom to ask about my sleeping pattern and not make amends. "I get as much sleep as one can hope for." I tell her as I toss my keys on the console table and slip my heels off as fast as possible.

"Good. That's good. And how are the girls?"

"Your daughter, that's me by the way, just got a new client. Thanks for asking. As for the girls? They're busy."

As much as my parents love me, I don't think they supported my dreams to not only become a publicist but also move away from the only home I've ever known. Yes, they pushed me in that direction. And they supported my dreams just like every parent should do when their child has a dream. But I think they placated me for longer than I knew and secretly wished I would marry someone who would take care of me financially and that's not who I am. Which is why they constantly pushed the "You're a Callahan" narrative so much. I think that's part of the reason they loved me and Paul together. His last name and job more than provided enough for him financially and it was hard to ignore my moms jabs about us taking the next step in our relationship. Paul and I never talked about taking that next step as we both were focused on moving up the corporate ladder. Or, so I thought.

I hear the clinking of ice in a glass through the phone. And if I know my mom like I think I do, she's either got a tall glass of iced sweet tea or a glass of whiskey she's sipping on. "Your father and I saw Paul–"

"Mom. I'm gonna stop you right there," I say as firmly as I can, without being too disrespectful while I head out onto my screened-in patio. "If you called to talk to me about the man who cheated on me and started a family with someone else, I will hang up on you." The summer breeze rustles my hair as I take a seat on the couch. I'm finally at a place where talking about him doesn't sting too badly. But the phantom ache does pulse from the reminder.

"You don't speak to me that way Sarah Jane. I am your mother. Besides—," she starts but I cut her off.

"Then act like it. As my mother, you should know when certain people who are not in my life are no longer up for discussion. I am your daughter, not your friend." I let my words hang between us. This is the problem with a mom who got a daughter and a built-in bestie. She wants me to have what she has with my dad no matter the consequences. And because of that, the line between parent and child continuously blurred more times than I can count. "You know what, I have to go. I'm exhausted and this phone call isn't helping. Bye, Mom."

I don't wait for her response. I simply end the call. I try not to let her reasoning for calling soak in. Did she really call to check in on me? Or was it to talk about my ex? Some days I feel I can't win with being who she expects me to be. Does she want me to be successful? Or does she want me to be a housewife?

Do I wish I had a partner? Of course! It's bittersweet and lonely watching all of your friends find their peace, their happily ever after, while you stand off on the sidelines just waiting for your turn. I hate that I'm lonely because I've refused to give someone else my heart. I hate that I know the feeling of loneliness more than the joy of happiness. And I hate that my mind goes to thoughts of Riley and how he made me feel in that one night when he's now off-limits.

But I let myself picture the unthinkable. Him patiently tearing down the brick walls that I've carefully constructed around my heart and making room for himself inside the tight space. Him proving everyday that I'm not hard to love. Him not giving a damn about our working relationship. Him being the man from the club that night and taking what's in front of him.

Yet reality is less exciting than fantasy as we do have a working relationship. And I won't give that up for anyone. No matter how many butterflies take flight when he looks at me.

My phone buzzing knocks me out of that fantasy with a

notification from a hookup app I've been utilizing. It's not perfect. But when your past is finally fading in the rearview and the future is nowhere in sight, you have to focus on what you can.

And that's the now.

~

Kamryn: Are you riding with us?

Me: Yes.

Kamryn: Then get your ass here.

Me: You're mean.

Kamryn: You're late.

I AM RUNNING LATE. And as someone who writes out every event down to the minute, I despise when my time gets thrown off. Blame it on the walk of shame I did at four this morning. I didn't sleep with the guy from the app. I tried to. He had some very sensual music playing in the background, the big lights weren't on, and a mahogany teakwood candle was burning in the background. That should've been prime hookup time. But nothing. We were making out on his couch and I tried to will my libido into action. I moved his hands over the hot points on my body and nothing. I wanted to cry in sexual frustration. And after thirty minutes of over the clothes groping and grinding, my lips bruised from our kissing and beard rash on my neck, I made the excuse of no longer feeling well and high-tailed it out of his place. But when I got home, all it took was one remembrance of my time with Riley and I shot off like a rocket with the help of my trusty vibrator.

With a huff of annoyance, I throw sunscreen and an extra change of clothes into my tote bag. We're finally meeting Emily's new boyfriend who she's still been tight-lipped about. I know she's happy. I saw it that night when she was getting ready for her date. And that's all I want for my little bird. She and I have gotten closer these past few years. It's not the bond that I have with Kamryn. But it's… simple. Where she's soft-spoken, I'm as outspoken as can be.

I've never been great at cultivating friendships. Let alone friendships with women. The backstabbing, endless gossip, and silent competition never appealed to me. And for that I was a loner for most of my childhood. But that changed when I met Kamryn. Yes, I put on a front when we first met. But the longer we went on as roommates, the easier it was to let her in. The first year, she was my only true friend. And as the years went on she became my best friend. Same with Emily and Jax. I liked them instantly. Not because they were an extension of Kam. But because they were gentle with their approach to friendships. Now we cheer each other on and give each other shoulders to lean on when need be. They're my people.

Heading downstairs and into my kitchen, I snatch my car keys off the counter and I lock up my house before skipping down the few steps to my BMW. As soon as I start up, my car connects to Bluetooth and I turn on Maren Morris's latest album on Spotify. I back out of my driveway and make the short drive to Kam's little house. Pulling up, I park behind Jax's car and make my way up to the door. I don't bother with knocking and am surprised when heated arguing from the backyard greets me when I walk inside.

"Kam?" I ask as I walk down the hallway and pop my sunglasses on top of my head.

"In the kitchen," Jax calls out.

Finishing the short distance from the foyer to the kitchen, I see Kam and Mason talking on her patio. Her arms are crossed which is a sign that she's agitated and maybe hurt. Jax is at the kitchen bar tapping and scrolling on her phone with her brows furrowed and more than likely annoyed that they're arguing.

"What's going on with them?" I ask and lean on the counter next to her.

Jax sets her phone down and exhales heavily. "Kam has been going on and on about being in the dark with Emily."

"Huh," I muse and keep my focus on the squabbling two-some outside.

"Do you know something?"

I slide my gaze to Jax. "Do you know something?"

"Are you asking if I've seen a man in a truck with tattoos covering his body make his way to Emily's apartment building the past few months? Then, no. I don't know a thing." Jax says with a smirk.

I snort at the same time Kamryn and Mason come back inside. Mason with a smile on his face and Kam with a scowl still on hers.

"Hi, lovebirds." I greet and try to cut through the thick tension that followed them back in here.

Kam greets me with a kiss on the cheek and Mason with a high-five. Alrighty then.

"Are we ready?" Mason voices as he cuts through the tense silence.

"Yep." I say, looping my arm through Jax's and we head towards the door.

"Is this it?" I ask from the backseat when Mason slows down in front of a large two-story brick house that's set about half of a football field away from the road.

"Yep. That's Em's car." Jax points out.

I see Kam attempt to glance at Jax, but Mason turns the car into the driveway and luckily she doesn't say anything. I'm hoping that whatever her spat was with Mason doesn't bleed into the rest of the day as I've been anticipating meeting the man who stole Emily's heart. When the car is in park, Jax and I swiftly grab our bags and head to the door arm-in-arm.

"Nervous about Kam?" Jax whispers.

I sneak a look behind me and see Kamryn walking towards the door with a scowl firmly back on her face. "Aren't you?"

"Yes. Emily is happy and that's all we want for her."

I give Jax an agreeable look and then knock on the door. I hear a murmur behind me and am about to turn to see what's happening when the door opens.

"Hi, friends!" Emily greets us. "Come in." She motions us in as she steps aside and holds the door open wider.

We step inside and a whistle of impression leaves me as I survey just the foyer and what I can see through to the back-yard oasis. The stairs that lead upstairs is off to the left with Emily's bag dumped on the bottom step and a spacious home office with glass doors is on the right. The foyer, however, gives off the impression that people live here but not in a messy way. "Nice place," I say.

"Thank you," Emily's boyfriend says.

Emily introduces us to her boyfriend, Adam, and points us all out to him.

"I've heard incredible things about you all from Em," he

tells us and I like him instantly. Honestly I trust Emily's judgement when it comes to people.

"Well she's been incredibly tight-lipped about you," Kam snips.

Until now.

Jax freezes next to me and I hear Mason swear under his breath. Emily tries to make eye contact with me but all I can do is shake my head. In all the years I've been friends with Kamryn, she's never disappointed me like she has now.

"Kam!" Jax snaps at her.

"Sorry."

Oh goodness. It's so quiet you could hear a pin drop. Don't even get me started on how awkward this is now. Ground, swallow us whole to spare us from finding our way out of this.

Adam pipes up after the awkwardness is too much for him to stand. Can't blame him. "Does anyone want a drink?"

We all take that as a cue and follow him into the kitchen to let Emily and Kam talk it out.

"Your kitchen is insane," I blurt out.

Light oak cabinets and marble patterned countertops with stainless steel appliances gives off a home-vibe. It's a space where I envision Emily watching Adam cook as I know she can't cook anything edible to save her life.

"Thanks. At first I thought it was too much. But now I like that it shows Dylan that men can do more than yard work. And when he's older he'll be able to fend for himself."

I barely know Adam, but I like that he's teaching his son to be domesticated. If that's even the word you would use.

"Nice," Jax says. "I'm sorry about my sister."

"Don't worry about it," Adams shrugs it off. "Now who wants a drink?"

"I was promised the largest margarita you can make me," I claim.

"Coming right up. You three help yourselves outside," Adam tells us and I like him instantly. We all grab our drinks, margaritas for Jax and I and a beer for Mason.

"It's like paradise," I murmur when we step outside. "Now I'm starting to see why Em keeps you to herself."

Adam, Mason, and Jax snort like they're not thinking the same thing. A pool with a waterfall, cabanas, a fire pit, and a hot tub adorn the space. That's not including the spacious patio we're standing on with the outdoor kitchen enough to make any suburban dad drool.

Adam moves to fire up the grill as Jax and I whip our cover-ups off and walk into the pool. Turns out this is a salt-water pool and the temperature is warm enough to not have me sprouting goosebumps or my leg hairs on the fast track to growing. Movement from behind the boys drags my attention there as Emily and Kamryn come out of the house brighter than they were twenty minutes ago. And that's good. They've been friends for over a decade and for something like Emily dating someone in private to come between them would be a shame. Kam places a kiss on Mason's cheek before joining us in the pool, while Emily joins the boys.

Seeing them all couple-y sends me back in time when I had that. I mean, Paul and I were never over-the-top with our PDA. But he always made sure that he was within distance of me. Maybe that was his way of keeping a claim on me so no one else could have me. I shake myself out of that time and splash Emily to bring her into the pool. She bends down and hands me her drink before pulling her dress off.

"You're not subtle," she tells me as she slides into the water.

Kamryn snorts and I hand Emily her drink back when she's submerged in the pool. "Sweetie, when have you ever known that to be a trait of mine?"

"Fair point. So what do you think?" Emily asks with a touch of nerves to her question.

I look around Emily and ogle her boyfriend much longer than I should. She splashes me and I return my gaze to her with a smile. "I can see why you fell for him. But there's something about him. I can't put my finger on it." I snap trying to guess what it is about him.

"It's the eyes," Emily says.

"The eyes," we sing.

"How's work, Sarah?"

I look at her and take a healthy sip of my drink.

"That good, huh?"

"We're doing damage control right now. One of the hockey players needs a PR makeover. Jeff stated that since my schedule is so light, thank you Mason, he suggested a babysitter. And guess who has to do the babysitting?"

Emily's mouth falls open. "You?"

"I sometimes hate my job." I mock pout into my drink.

"But you're the best publicist I've ever had," Mason interjects as he and Adam join us in the pool.

Holy shit. Tattooed and pierced? Emily being incredibly cagey about him makes sense and splashes me yet again when she sees who has my attention. I can't help it if my best friends date hot men.

"What?" I ask innocently.

"Get your own single dad," she taunts.

The laughter that spills out in the pool relaxes me.

Adam kisses her on the cheek and pulls her into his arms as we all wade further into the pool.

Funny enough, I thought Jeff was flirting with me when I first started. And my fairy tale mind took me to a place where I imagined dating my boss. I very quickly imagined our illicit hookups in his office. But that was squashed after working with him for a good few months when I learned how messy he was. Jeff is now the older brother I never had and his kids are the nieces and nephews I knew I wouldn't get from being an only child. Now my fairy tale's involve my new client which is possibly worse than my boss.

The rest of the day is filled with drinks, food, and so much laughter my stomach cramps. Having friends is temporary. But having a chosen family is forever. And that's what this small group is.

6

RILEY

"Hold for eight, Riley," my pilates instructor, Mischa, coaches. "Seven, six, core tighter, four, eyes forward, chin up, and one. You can relax now."

I let out a groan as I rest my body. I started taking pilates classes in college with Momma. At first I scoffed at it because I'd never seen a man take a class, but then after a few classes I realized just how much it helped me on the ice. Especially with my balance. Now I incorporate it with my team training and have even gotten some of the rookies and vets to join in on a few classes.

Mischa walks me through two more sequences on the reformer and then runs me through a cool down. Despite my reputation, okay that's totally warranted to some level, I'm respectful to the women in my teammates lives. Mischa is firm and it's something I see in her husband, Coach Anderson. When hockey is going to the wayside, I can always count on the Anderson's to hopefully set me right. They're the ultimate successful, fit couple. Not that I need a fit couple to be the blueprint. Mischa and Coach Anderson both played volleyball and hockey in college, respectively. How they met was through a blind date and have been together for fifteen years.

I sit on the reformer and take small sips of water as she wipes down the other machines and gathers up equipment from class. It's a small class as she only takes on five per round, but she's effective and worth the price we pay.

"Any plans for today, Riley?" Mischa asks over the coffee-house music that's playing through the speakers. Some can argue that Mischa's husband is why she's so successful. And while that may have been true in the beginning she's earned herself a well-deserved spot in the fitness community on her own. Her classes book out a month in advance and have waitlists ten, sometimes twenty, people deep.

I close the cap on my water bottle and stand up. "Momma and Pops are having a barbecue later this afternoon so I'm headed there."

When I feel turned around, that's when my routine and behavior fall apart. It's been like that since my parents passed away. But as I got older my routine was only possible with structure. College classes, conditioning, practice, games, and repeat. This past year was the first time my routine was less structured since college and for that my reputation hit the lowest it had ever been. I made a poor choice with the company I kept and that led me to needing a new publicist and agent.

"Oh my god, please bring us a plate," Mischa begs.

"Only if you let me take Kylie out for ice cream." I bargain with her and slip on my tennis shoes. Because as soon as I utter the Anderson's, Momma will immediately put a container aside for them. In the year that I've been with Columbus, the Anderson's have taken me under their wing. I was rowdy my first month playing and when Coach texted me his address for a more personal meeting, things shifted. I slowly felt myself come back down from the air of arrogance that formed around me. Yes, Momma and Pops are in the same city, but Mischa and Coach understand this life better than them. And when their oldest, Kylie, dogpiled me that first day, I unconsciously knew that I'd have to display some sort of maturity where they were concerned. Did that always work? Clearly not considering the situation I'm in.

"Deal," she says over her shoulder and wiggles her eyebrows. "Jared and I could use the alone time."

"Yuck! You expect me to look him in the eyes now?" I joke, but also cringe, as knowing this about my coach is a step too far. The guys and I may say some outlandish things in the locker room, but coach talk is strictly off-limits.

Mischa's laughter fills the studio as we walk to the front desk to look over my training schedule and her class times. One of the perks of Mischa teaching is that Coach gives her our practice, travel, and game schedule for the whole season so I can pick my classes before they're on the schedule for the public. Mischa's are the only classes I'll take. Not because the others aren't effective, but because she doesn't fawn over us athletes that come in. And as a former athlete herself, her workouts are tailored to our specific needs.

"Three classes a week? Are you sure?"

"It's off-season and I have nothing but time."

Mischa looks at me like Momma does when I'm over-doing it. "Fine but just make sure you're taking your days off seriously."

"I promise Mom," I tease and quickly duck out of the studio as she throws a pen at me.

My laughter fades as the summer sun bounces off the downtown buildings, adding to the late-June heat, while I walk down the street to my car. The downtown area is bustling with groups of friends headed to brunch and fami-ly's strolling the area with their little ones to the splash pad that's a street over. A twinge of jealousy at the friend groups and families hits because I wonder if I'll ever have that.

My parents were the best example of love. Combine them with Momma and Pops and I saw first-hand how their friendship and love was impenetrable. I grew up around love and people in love. I grew up wanting that. And despite my parents being gone, I still want that. But, again, it leaves me wondering if I'll ever have that.

I shake off the jealousy and sorrow when I get to my car and my phone buzzes with some rental listings from my realtor. He's someone I went to high school with who is the only one I trust when finding me a new place. In this case, a second place located in Cincinnati based on the amount of events that Sarah has lined up for me.

> Sam: A few lofts have been put up for rent. You'll find one-bedroom and two-bedroom units. I wasn't sure what style you wanted so both are included.

> Me: Thanks. I'll take a look later today.

My drive home takes about ten minutes. Sasha and Pixie rush me when I walk through demanding a second meal, despite them getting fed a little over an hour ago. They say the way through a man's heart is his stomach, but that also applies to women no matter the species. I bypass the kitchen, much to their loud protests, and head to my bath-room to get ready for the barbecue. I think about the new future and the way my career should head. At twenty-three I feel neither successful nor unsuccessful. I just feel settled. Like I've already plateaued. And it's not a good feeling for a hockey player who has yet to reach his peak. I know I have more to give than what I'm currently giving. And I'm hoping with this change on the professional side, that settled feeling will disappear.

An hour later and I'm dressed in olive green cargo shorts, a white graphic tee and some worn Nikes, ready to head out the door. I feed the girls, because I'm a sucker, I scoop my keys out of the bowl and make the walk to my car.

"Momma? Pops?" I ask when I walk into the house through the garage.

"Kitchen, honey," Momma calls out.

I hang my keys on the hook by the door to the garage and walk in the direction I heard her call out from. Momma is at the kitchen island scooping out what looks like cookie dough and my mouth starts watering. A bowl slides to the left and it's a cup of cookie dough.

"Thanks, Momma." I say gratefully with a kiss on her cheek and lean next to her against the counter. I tower over her at 6'3" with her petite 5'4" but the height difference is even worse when I'm in my skates.

My diet is strict during the regular season but the off-season, while it's still strict, I let go of a small part of that control. Cookie dough is my number one weakness and Momma always sets a bowl off to the side for me when she bakes a batch.

Momma has her hair in box braids with gold cuffs placed throughout as beads on the end of her hair clack as she rolls out dough balls and places them on the baking sheet. With the summer heat and today's guests, she's in a long dress that comes down to her hot pink painted toenails.

Where I turn red as a lobster if I'm out in the sun for too long, that's not what can be said for Momma. Her rich bronze complexion from her time already spent out by the pool emphasizes the garden of tattooed flowers on her left arm. I guess you could say I got the love of ink from both Momma and Pops as most of their tattoos are older than I am.

"What's new?" She asks without looking up from her scooping out the dough.

I pop my finger out of my mouth and chew the dough before answering her. "Sam sent me some rental listings for Cincinnati."

That gets her attention and she looks at me with alarm. "What do you mean?"

"Sarah, my publicist, has me lined up for events to attend there. Some of them don't end until late and instead of driving back home tired, it'd be better to stay somewhere familiar instead of wasting money on a hotel room so much."

Unconsciously, the accident scarred me. I have a perfect driving record, take my car in for regular maintenance, I don't speed too bad, if I talk on the phone it's with Bluetooth, and I never drive if I'm too tired. That was the number one thought running through my head when the apartment listings were coming through.

"Doesn't she know you live here?"

"Mm-hmm. I see her strategy but until it starts working, I have the right to reserve judgment."

The more I think about these events, the more I doubt they'll actually work. Sports fans are notoriously loyal to their teams. So having an athlete from Columbus infiltrate their space in Cincinnati is cause for worry. I hang out in the kitchen keeping Momma company and finish my cookie dough before heading outside to join Pops by the grill. The smell of charcoal greets me when I step into the backyard.

"Hey, Pops," I greet as I walk up next to him.

He swings his arm around my shoulder and presses a chaste kiss to the side of my head. Pops has done that since before my mom and dad passed away. Once they became my legal guardians, he promised to keep showing the affection he always showed me. Like I said, I thrive on routine and Pops showing me this affection is part of that routine. Some would say he's the bald version of Denzel Washington. Only with a lot of tattoos covering every inch of visible skin.

"How's the off-season treating you? You have a new agent?"

"Publicist, but until I have a new agent she'll be my temporary agent as well." I say and bring a chair closer to the grill, lowering my body into it. My muscles are screaming a bit from the pilates class this morning. "I met her, my publicist, earlier this week."

"A she?" Pops asks with mild curiosity and raised bushy eyebrows focused on me.

I guess you could say I had a lot of "girlfriends" in high school. If "girlfriend" is classified as making out under the football bleachers and copping a feel with a new girl every week, then sure. That surely didn't let up in college but I was more intentional about my hookups so I know the reason Pops is giving me that look.

"Yep." I pop the *p*. "She's firmly off-limits, so you don't need to worry about me screwing it up. But I almost doubted her ability until I saw her client roster."

Noise coming through the open windows of the house filters out to us, signaling guests arriving. Pops hovers his hand over the grill to make sure the temperature is right before placing some burgers and hot dogs on the grates. Once he closes the lid, he turns to me.

"Don't let your Momma hear you say that," Pops warns.

"I know."

He looks up and into the kitchen with warmth in his eyes anytime he looks at Momma. It's almost sickening how in love they still are. Most relationships fizzle out after a few years. But not these two. With thirty years together, they've countlessly proven to me that a relationship with the right person can be long-lasting. "Who's on her list?"

"Mason Brooks, Nate Holloway, and Conrad Spencer." I rattle off.

Pop lets a whistle fly. "That's some list."

"Agreed," I say and trail off as some of Pops's friends come strolling out of the house. I like their friends. They rallied around us when I lost my parents. But I think they're still unused to me being a professional athlete. And name dropping big names would only give me a headache when I have to field denial after denial about if I can score tickets to any of their games.

The day passes by in a blur of conversation, corn hole, and more food than I usually eat in a day. Afternoon turns into night and I start to say my goodbyes to my parents and their friends. Momma packs up two to-go boxes, one for me and one for the Anderson's. With another round of thirty-minute goodbyes, I'm in my car and headed back to my condo.

Evenings when I come home to a quiet condo, I wish I had someone there to greet me. I see some of the veterans on the team with their long-term girlfriends or wives and families waiting for them with open arms. It's never both-ered me as much, because I'd rather spend time playing the game I love than be hurt by someone who claims to love me when all they want is to get to the top. And I know Momma and Pops would love to see me in a stable relationship. But until that person comes along, the one who doesn't want just my name to get them places, I'll gladly settle for hockey, my family, my cats, and fantasizing about my publicist.

7

SARAH

I lie in bed and stare at the ceiling fan. Round and around until my heart rate comes back down. Some mornings I wake up in a panic. It's sleep induced panic attacks brought on by my high functioning depression diagnosis. The freak-outs when I would wake up were easier to hide from Paul as we both agreed that living together before marriage would ruin us faster. But unfortunately, the occasional sleepovers caused them to flare up more often than not.

I'd like to say I've gotten better. I've been seeing a therapist for about a year after Kamryn suggested I see someone to deal with my deep failure of not getting Liam signed and my general failure of thinking I could make it in the sports world so early. Have I been told time and time again that it wasn't my fault? Of course. But being told something and actually comprehending it are two different things. Still lying in bed, I do my best to focus on the whirring of the blades pushing air around my room while I slowly come back to my body.

My alarm clock blares, causing me to jolt, and I turn my head to the offensive noise before throwing my hand out and shutting it off. My attention goes back to my ceiling fan and like a true millennial, I've never turned it off so dust has been mysteriously collecting since I bought my house a year ago. That gets added to my never-ending list of things to do around my home. *Dust your ceiling fan.*

With the salary I get, it more than allowed me to afford a home so soon after I moved up here. I live right on the outskirts of Cincinnati in a converted three-bedroom brick townhome. The fourth bedroom was originally on the other side of my closet, so during the renovation, I had the contractors remove the wall to create a closet that Carrie Bradshaw could only dream of having when she lived in her tiny apartment. One of my weaknesses is shoes. Very expensive shoes. So with the expansion I made sure that my closet had a shoe wall. Most people tried to talk me out of converting the fourth room for the "resell" factor. As it stood that was not my issue and I figured that *if* I meet someone I plan to spend my life with, we'll eventually move into a bigger house and I'll get another large closet.

I turn my head again and check the time on the clock, realizing it's past time for me to get up. It's the fourth of July and it's set to be a long day. All of my clients, apart from Nate, will be in attendance at the block party that occurs every year off of Ivy street. It's a way for my clients to get seen and to be seen as normal people, despite the heavy bank accounts that set them apart. And a way to interact with owners of small businesses that keep the city alive.

Whipping off the covers, I roll out of bed and walk into my bathroom and turn on the shower. With a little help from my parents before Paul and I broke up, I was able to redo the bathroom to my liking. I wanted a space that was bright and airy, but also a touch of girly while incorporating my favorite color, dark blue. Okay, my favorite color is also red, but having that in my bathroom would not have worked with my red hair. So we settled for dark blue with pink accents and gold handles paired with a dark wood vanity and a white marble top counter. The flooring is also heated so that when the temperature is closer to my age, I'm only freezing my tits off.

I go through with my shower and proceed to get ready for the day. The last time I checked the weather it said it was in the high-90's, so I wrap myself and my hair in a towel, then stroll into my walk-in closet. As I get further removed from my relationship with Paul, I find myself grateful that he never moved up here. I would have had to sacrifice my version of Carrie Bradshaw's closet and that would have made me insufferable. And now when I think of letting any man into my space, I get the heebie jeebies from thinking about it. I love my space and I love what I've created here. But it would take a special man for me to change things around.

I find the wedges I want to wear today and riffle through my dress collection before settling on a white eyelet dress with a corset bodice, thin straps, and a flowing skirt that falls past my knees. Most redheads stay away from wearing white as it washes them out or their freckles spread like crazy. I'm the opposite. My hair gets lighter and I take on a light tan, oddly enough. So I love wearing white as it gives me a glow that I can fake when I'm less than glowing after a morning wake-up call like the one I had.

While blow drying my hair, I hear the distant chiming of my phone with what I know to be an incoming text. Retying the sash on my robe tighter, I shuffle back into my bedroom and sit on my unmade bed, snagging my phone off the charger in the process.

> Riley: Reporting for duty.

> Riley: *1 attached image*

I snort, very unladylike, as I see him in a full American flag outfit. My gaze snags on the way the shorts mold to his thick thighs and down to the very appealing thigh tattoos peaking out from the edges of his shorts to the rest of the ink covering his legs before I quickly close out of the picture and think of a response.

> Me: Why are you texting me?

Really, Sarah? That's the best you've got?

> Riley: I wanted to show you that I'm ready for my first event.

> Riley: Is this not the type of picture you want?

> Riley: I can send you something else...

I'm about to respond *No* when another picture comes in. This time of two cats. Huh. I did not peg him as a cat dad.

> Me: I'll see you at 11.

> Riley: Yes, ma'am

I can't ignore the tingly sensation that rolled through my body at Riley calling me ma'am. *You have to,* I tell myself. Putting my phone on the nightstand again, I head back into my bathroom to finish getting ready. I pull my hair up in a high ponytail and curl the tail part of my hair. To accessorize, I add a star-patterned bow and some ruby earrings. I keep my makeup light with a tinted moisturizer and some mascara. I complete the look by slathering my arms and chest with sunscreen before sliding my dress and shoes on. Taking a look at myself in the floor length mirror I have set up in the corner of my room, I survey myself from all angles and deem myself ready to be surrounded by the public.

I THOUGHT I timed myself perfectly. But I'm running late. Again. I preach the importance to my clients on being early, but sometimes time slips away from me. Luckily I find a parking spot by Kamryn's office and walk in the direction of the block party. Pulling out my phone I send a text to one of my usual hookups. The need to use someone to get my mind off of Riley is stronger than ever. And I think I know just who to text.

> Me: Any chance you're free tonight?

> Eric: Anytime after 6, I'm all yours.

> Me: Great. I'll swing by after the block party.

I love sex. Admitting that out loud to those who only sleep with their significant other garners me a lot of odd looks. But I didn't have to worry about satisfaction with my ex. It was a mutually beneficial relationship.

I'm pulled from my thoughts when boisterous crowds tumble out of the nearest bar. Excited chatter and patriotic colors end up walking towards the block party while my feet carry me to our agency's booth.

Patriotic pride surrounds me. As much as I don't love going overboard, I can admit that holiday's bring the best of

Cincy together. Give me a hotdog with ketchup and that's about all my spirit can withstand.

"Sarah!" I hear my voice boomed from the right side of the closed-off street.

Turning my head, I see Mason and Jeff standing near each other. I maneuver my way towards them. My heeled wedges cushion my steps as my dress swishes around my knees with every step. I pop my sunglasses on top of my head when I get closer to our tent area.

"You still haven't paid up for the baseball series," Mason greets as soon as I'm in earshot.

"As soon as you lock down my best friend, I'll pay up." I respond and pop a chip from a bowl into my mouth. I stop mid-chew when I see the look on his face. "Shut up! You're gonna propose soon? When?" I don't know how I didn't see it coming.

Mason surveys the crowd walking by our tent and I realize I should do the same. Two of my four clients are here. With Riley's enthusiasm I figured he would be the first here.

"In the fall. She's preparing for Nina to come out so that's when I'll do it," he tells me.

Nina graduated the same year Kam and I did. I didn't have any classes with her so I only knew of her. But Kam did, seeing as they were both Fashion majors. I don't know all of what happens in Kam's line of work, but if she's working with Nina then that means they're working on something incredible. I'm one of the few people from college Kamryn kept in contact with from our class. After Liam died, the majority of our group blamed her and that sent her on a downward spiral. She did her best to push me away but I had my hooks in her. Kam couldn't get rid of me if she tried. Me taking the job up here to be near my bestie was also a factor.

"You're hiding something. What else?"

"I'm hopefully surprising her with a house. I've been looking for a while but nothing has fit. So fingers crossed something pops up in the next few months."

"I'm happy for you both," my voice drips with sincerity.

"Thanks, Callahan. Anyway, I'm gonna get to mingling and I'll see you in a few hours."

"Later." I wave him off and watch as the crowd swallows him whole as they welcome their former quarterback with open arms.

I see Jeff is engaged with his clients, so I pop my sunglasses back on and head out into the crowd. My senses pull me towards a candle booth with no other reason than I love the smell of them. I make a mental note to come back with my wallet and buy a few of the larger candles. My feet drag me further into the party. Music sounds from all around, friendly conversation takes place in large clusters, face painting stations are set up at every other booth, and I witness business collaborations happening right before my very eyes. This is what I love.

"Fancy running into you here," a smooth voice that sends tingles down my spine greets me.

Riley.

"I was wondering where you were," I muse, still not making eye contact with him, as I smile at a mom and her daughter painting butterflies on canvases.

I stiffen as our arms brush when he brings them up to cross them over his chest. "I knew you missed me," he gloats.

"Don't flatter yourself. It's my job to know where my clients are." I deadpan and resume walking through the crowded street. I know Adam's restaurant is here with a booth, but I don't bother stopping by as it's Dylan's birthday and they're out celebrating as a little family.

"I got an apartment in the city," Riley tells me when he catches up to me.

"Good for you? Why are you telling me this?"

"Well, boss lady, as you know I don't live in this city, and you have me attending *soooo* many events here, I took the liberty to find a place to crash instead of driving home exhausted."

Okay, his reasoning is more mature than what I would've guessed for someone his age. But I don't tell him that as I feel Riley is the type to need constant reassurance in the form of an ego boost.

"Again, why are you telling me this?"

I noticed it's gotten quieter the longer we walk. I slow down and turn to see we're on the outer edge of the block party. Away from prying eyes.

"Because you, as my publicist, probably need the details on where I'm living," Riley responds with a grin.

We both stop walking and I finally turn to face him. When we met, it was easy to be influenced by the lights and the alcohol at the club. And then again when it turned out he was my new client I was able to hold some power. But in this light, I can't help to notice his inky, dark blue eyes that sparkle with excitement and how the sun highlights the golden strands in his dark blond hair. His leather and berg-amot scent wafts towards me as a gust of wind blows through the street and it claims itself as my favorite scent. How he manages to tower over me, despite the inches these wedges give me. But Riley isn't wielding any sort of power over me. It's like he's making sure I know I'm in control. It's hot and something that I like that he's giving me.

Stop that, Sarah.

"I really don't. And anyways, you're supposed to be mingling with fans and getting the sports world to love you."

Riley props his hands on his waist and looks towards the crowd. Unease flashes across his angular face before he quickly turns the charm back to me. *It's a mask.* He was so confident and assertive the night we met and I assumed by the reports that he was a wild child through and through. But now I'm seeing something different.

"I'd rather get to know you."

"There'll be plenty of time for that, Jones. Now go mingle. I'll see you before the day is done," I tell him and give him a pointed stare before he stalks off.

I'd still like to think the reports on Riley are wrong. In fact, as I think over our last interaction, I know they're wrong. But why? Why does he wear a mask? I stand corrected that he reminds me of Liam. They're so similar it's scary. I don't want a repeat of what happened with Liam to happen to Riley. Although based on Riley being in the NHL and Liam not making it to the MLB, they're miles apart. But maybe, just maybe, he'll prove me wrong and show me that the man I met all those months ago is the true Riley.

LATER THAT NIGHT as I sit on my couch with a glass of wine and *Grey's Anatomy* playing in the background, I try to think about why I couldn't go through with sleeping with Eric tonight. He's my go-to for a no strings attached hookup. But for the rest of the block party, Riley found effortless ways to always be in my line of sight. Everywhere I turned he was in my path. Maybe he did it on purpose? I can't deny that seeing him in that patriotic getup was pleasing to the eyes.

Most men would look ridiculous wearing something like that. But not Riley.

"Ugh," I say aloud to a room of no one. Maybe I need one last time to get it out of my system. That has to be it. But how? I technically work for him. If I quit for at least twenty-four hours, that won't really be wrong. Would it?

"Stop that," I say out loud to myself. You're not messing your future up for sex. No matter how good the sex with him was.

I just need all mind separation from him. Yeah. That's it. Out of sight, out of mind.

8

RILEY

I look like a penguin. Like a rare, all-black penguin. That's what runs through my head as I stare at myself in the mirror in the hallway of my small apartment. All the email for this event said was that it's "Black Tie Not Optional" so that forced me to pull out my best suits. I went with an all-black James Bond appearance but I still manage to appear like myself, what with the tattoos creeping up the side of my neck and the hair that refuses to stay combed back no matter how much pomade I use falling over my forehead.

Luckily I don't have to worry about getting cat fur off my suit. I made the choice to leave the girls at home with Momma going over to check on and feed them. I'm lucky to have parents who will check on my girls when I'm out of town. If you can classify as being in the next big city over from where you live out of town, then sure. I've never voluntarily visited Cincinnati. But the more I'm here, the more I like it. *I wonder why that is*, I ponder.

It's been a month since my first event and I hate to agree with Sarah's plan that it's helping my reputation amongst

78

sports fans. Tonight we have a benefit to not only gain sponsors for the teams in Cincinnati, Columbus, Cleveland, and Akron; but to gain and keep our current fanbase. It's said that fans stay loyal to the teams they grew up watching. Like a sort of bloodline that they need to keep pure. But with the performances of all of our teams unfortunately on the downslope, we need to do whatever we can to reignite the spirit. And if I can get some new fans out of these events, then I'll continue parading in said penguin suit.

Thank goodness some of my team will be there tonight to hopefully help my schmooze some big money players. My being vocal on the ice does not translate to off the ice.

Baby Pucklings

Me: *1 image attached*

Max: Thanks for the new lock screen photo

Me: Dick.

Logan: I didn't even know you owned a suit.

Me: I've worn suits to the arena before.

Noah: Not suits that'll make the girls throw on a white dress and say "meet me at the altar" 🐧

Max: 🤯 Did Noah make a joke?

Me: I'm leaving.

Logan: See you there, buddy.

Looking at the time, I pocket my buzzing phone and swipe my keys off the counter before heading out to my car. I could have ordered a car service, but I want the option to leave early. Plugging the address into the GPS, I make the short drive to Hotel Cincinnati. I did some research on the space (closet nerd) and found that this is a relatively new boutique hotel.

What should be a fifteen minute drive to the hotel turns into an almost forty-five minute drive due to the Friday traffic. Whoever decided that the cocktail event needed to happen an hour before the main event, should be arrested.

When I finally pull up to the hotel, the valet comes to greet me. He gives me a ticket when I climb out of my car and make my way inside. This hotel is spectacular and if Momma were here she would fawn over everything. I make a mental note to try and book her a room here for Mother's Day.

The lobby is littered with patrons in fancy dresses and three-piece suits. Couples not much older than me and couples decades older than me flit from one side of the room to the next and it hits me that I've never seen so much money in one space. I've never been in the wealthy crowd myself. And despite the money I make from hockey, I'm still that young boy who'd rather be at home with his cats than schmoozing it up with the rich and elite.

I make my way through the crowd with hopes of finding an open-bar. I don't want to get too loose, but maybe a little liquid courage will lighten me up. Sarah didn't specify what tonight would entail besides getting more sponsors to open their wallets and support our teams. When I spot several people with champagne flutes and tumblers that must indicate I'm headed in the right direction.

"Riley!" I hear from the right of me, stopping my quest for the bar.

With my height, I tower over some of the guests and see

my guys huddled in the corner waving me over. I scoot past guests as I make my way to my team.

"How long have you been here?" I ask when I reach them.

"About twenty minutes," Logan tells me and takes a sip of his drink. Of all the guys on the team, I'm closest to Logan. We started at the same time in the league playing in different positions and moving up at the same speed, but never once playing on the same team. When we both got drafted to Columbus it took us about a day to mesh together on the ice and when it came time for the game that made us an unstoppable duo.

The guys fall into small talk while I continue to take in the space. We've not even gone into the banquet hall and if it's anything like the lobby, we're in for a long night. A wave of auburn hair catching my attention on the other side of the lobby by the bar, my saving grace, and I excuse myself to head over to Sarah. I hear the tail end of her ordering a French 75, the bartender is about to turn away when I interrupt, "I'll take one of those too."

I lean one arm against the bar and see Sarah stiffen next to me. While she avoids eye contact, I give myself permission to check her out. Her hair is in what Momma calls a low bun with pieces framing her heart shaped face. The dress she's wearing is a deep maroon that's backless and ends right above the curve of her back. I get a sniff of the sweet vanilla scent of her perfume and have to control the inner beast because the scent mixed with her natural body odor does something feral to me. The bartender sets our drinks in front of us and I watch the flex in her bicep as she picks up her glass takes a sip from her drink.

Sarah looks over at me expectantly and I follow suit. My

head rears back at the flavors hitting my tongue. "Is that gin?"

"Can you not handle it?" She asks as a smile graces her burgundy painted lips.

"Oh, I can handle it," I play back. "I'm just surprised. I didn't peg you for a gin girl."

"There's a lot you don't know about me."

I open my mouth to question what she means when someone announces it's time to head into the banquet hall. I'm not sure what all is about to entail so I down my drink in one swallow and place the empty back on the bar top.

"Are you nervous?" Sarah gently asks.

I blow out a breath and turn, placing my back against the bar. "I'm not the biggest people person. So these events you have me going to are pushing me out of my comfort zone."

She finishes her drink and places it on the bar next to my empty glass. Sarah places her hand on my arm in a comforting gesture and my eyes laser in on the contact. "For what it's worth, I think you can charm the pants off just about anyone."

My eyes move up to hers and I can't stop the smile from forming. "Like I did with you?"

"There you go ruining a sweet moment between us," she scolds me with a laugh and then turns serious. "Riley, I know our working relationship is just beginning and we don't know each other all that well, but I am here for anything you might need."

I place my hand over top of hers and give it a soft squeeze. "Thank you, Sarah."

"You're welcome."

With a final squeeze to her hand I shove my hands in my pockets and walk off towards the banquet hall. My retreating form burns from her stare. I will myself not to trip over air and make it into the banquet hall. All I have to do is schmooze enough people and then I'm free to leave. How much time do I have left?

THREE HOURS later as I'm standing outside at the entrance and I groan out a long exhale while I wait for the valet to bring my car around.

"It wasn't that bad," Sarah says as she walks down the short flight of stairs.

My voice gets stuck in my throat when I see the shoes she's wearing peek out from the thigh high slit of her dress. "For a shy guy like me it was like pulling teeth."

A soft laugh breaks through the noise from the hotel and I want to ask her to repeat that so I can record it and listen to it over and over.

"What are you about to do?" I ask but shouldn't as it's clear she's trying to keep respectable boundaries clear between us.

"I'm planning to head home and soak my feet. I love heels but I don't think I'm made to wear them for the long-term," Sarah explains. "My Uber should be here soon."

Be bold, I tell myself. "Cancel it. I wanna take you somewhere one of the locals at the block party suggested."

She eyes me with skepticism, wary of crossing the line between professional and personal. "Riley..."

"Just as friends–acquaintances. I promise."

A beat passes before she's pulling up her phone and canceling her Uber. At the same time the valet brings my car around. I move to open the passenger door and Sarah thanks me before I'm rounding the car, tipping the valet, and sliding into the driver's seat.

"This isn't where you take me to a frat party, is it? Because I did that in college and I hung my hat up six years ago."

A laugh barks out of me. "I promise no frat parties. Although I would like to see photographic evidence of that."

"Over my dead body," she jokingly threatens.

A comfortable silence takes over in the car as I make the short drive to a small wine bar. It turns out the block party proved very useful for getting to know the locals. Some were generational families who've owned restaurants since long before I was born.

I park a little ways down the street and get out of the car, rounding the back to the passenger door to help Sarah out. She hesitantly puts her hand in mine and uses me as leverage to get out.

"Where is it you're taking me?" she asks when I've moved her to the building side of the sidewalk, with me on the street side.

I hover my hand on the small of her back as I lead her down the concrete path. "I met this couple at the fourth of July event and they own Memories Wine & Jazz Bar. They said I could come by anytime and that I always had a table."

"I knew going to the event would work out for you," Sarah gloats.

"Is this where I get on the ground and kiss your feet? Because I have no problem getting on my knees for you." I move around her and open the door after saying that.

She gives me a scathing look before walking through the door. I stop right behind her when I enter and the heat from her body soaks into mine and I have to tamp down the urge to wrap my arm around her and kiss her temple.

This space is a moody person's dream. Black and white tiled floors with botanical wallpaper. The black marble-top bar is paired with a dark wood bottom and is occupied by a few couples as sommeliers dressed in black whip up drinks. It's a place where I could see myself occupying frequently when I'm in the city.

"Take a seat anywhere," one of the sommeliers instructs from behind the bar.

I survey the space from over top of Sarah's head. The patio is open and for a summer night, it's strange to find the space bare. The owners did mention that they have live music a few times a week and I was hoping we could catch something. Unfortunately it looks like we were a little too late.

I step around Sarah and grab her hand as I lead us to the patio. The outdoor area is spacious with several tables and loveseat couches for more intimate gatherings. I lead us to an isolated area before settling at one of the loveseats.

"Oh. It's a little cold out here," Sarah says when she settles in her seat.

She's not wrong. The breeze from the water blows in and with no buildings to act as a barrier cool air whips right in and bounces off the building. But I'm used to the cold, what with spending most of my time on the ice. I take my suit jacket off and rest it along her back. Making sure that it's secure, I turn and make sure the patio heater is turned on as well.

"Better?" I ask.

"Mm-hmm," she murmurs without making eye contact and I can't help but gaze at her with a smile on my face. "This isn't a date."

"Didn't say it was," I respond and pull my phone out to scan the QR code that's on the table in front of us.

We order our drinks and for the rest of the night, we talk. As friends. Because that's all Sarah will give me. But I understand it as she technically works for me now. Our talk doesn't squash my hunger for her. No. It slowly burns it until I'm ready for the next hit she can give me.

Sarah is unlike any woman I've met before. When she talks about something she's passionate about, her whole face lights up. When she laughs, not a fake laugh to get me to move on, but a real laugh. One that starts in her belly and lights up her whole body. It makes me want to take an ice pick to the brick wall she's put up to keep us firmly in our place. And when I drop her off at home later that night, I make another promise to myself to abide by the rules to get my reputation in shape.

And hopefully get Sarah to see me as more than a screw up.

9

SARAH

It's an early September morning in Columbus. My steps are cushioned by my white Air Force Ones as I walk through the lobby of the arena. I decided to tone down my outfit, which I'm now grateful for, as the chill from the rink skirts over my face when I make my way through the tunnel. I pull my three-quarter zip CSU sweatshirt tighter around my body and am grateful for the jeans I chose to wear that are covering my legs. I also brought my laptop to hopefully get some work done for my other clients. But with the chill in the arena I doubt my fingers will allow me to type a thing.

Today, Riley is working at a Little Blades camp as per his reputation rehabilitation. Although, now that I've gotten to know him a little more, maybe it wasn't his reputation that was the issue. But simply those who weaseled their way into his life and caused him to veer off track. It's easy for that to happen when you're no longer in the safe and constructed bubble of college. The real world exposes the sharks from the sea turtles. And I think that's exactly what happened with Riley. Because the more I get to know him, the harder it is to find anything reckless about him.

Laughter and the sound of blades cutting through the ice is now a new soundtrack to my life. I was never too interested in hockey growing up, it also wasn't a popular sport in Charleston, so to be surrounded by it now puts me in an entirely new environment that I'm determined to get comfortable with. I'm in awe and today it's my job to take some pictures and videos of him with the kids. Not fawn over the sport or who's on the ice.

I spot Riley easily on the ice and lean against the opening as I watch him get chased by a few of the little ones. The action brings a smile to my face and I whip my phone out to take some pictures and videos. I keep the main focus on him. His carefree smile and laugh that echoes around the ice. I alternate between ground level and at the highest point of the arena I can go to get the bigger picture of this sport he plays. My attendance eventually doesn't go unnoticed as an hour later, the sound of skates gliding through the ice gets louder. I look up from my phone in time and see Riley, looking larger than life, with a smile that spreads from cheek to cheek, getting closer to me. Before I put my phone away, I quickly snap a photo of him and lock my phone.

My neck tips back as he stops inches from me. He's in his element here. Not schmoozing with sponsors to make sure Ohio's professional teams stay funded, relevant, and supported. But on the ice is where I see he shines the brightest.

"I'm not sure which I like seeing you in more: your Louboutins or Nikes."

"Luckily, you don't have a say in what I wear." I tell him and I look past him at the kids trying to shoot the puck in the net.

"Yet." Riley says with a wink and I narrow my eyes at

him. "So what do you think?" He asks and moves to the side to allow me an unobstructed view of the ice.

"Definitely a different ball game," I say and bite my cheek to keep from smiling.

Riley snorts at my wrong terminology. "Rink, babe."

"That's what I said," I tell him and I try to keep a straight face as he drops his head in defeat. I don't ignore that my heart skipped at his simple pet name for me. "Anyways, I've already gotten some good pictures and videos for your Instagram. Do you have a website?"

"Nope."

"Okay. I'll get to work on that and see if I can get some action shots from your team photographer. I've also got some feelers for brands who want to work with you."

"Already?" Riley turns and looks at me with shock covering his face.

"Why is that so surprising?"

He shrugs although I don't miss the guarded expression. It's clear his last team never built him up. Athletes have fragile egos and if no one is there to feed them praise, they wither away. Not even the sport they love will be enough to save them.

"Hey, why don't you get through this and then later we can go through the brands who are thinking about working with you and your dream brands to work with." I don't physically reach out to coddle him. Because when I touch him, no matter how platonic, my mind eats up that contact.

"Are you sure? You don't have anywhere to be?"

"Nope. I'm all yours today." The moment the words leave my mouth I want to take them back. But the grin on Riley's face replaces the disbelief from earlier and I consider that a win.

"Famous last words." Riley says and this time I do reach out to shove him and watch as he glides away.

With a soft smile and a shake of my head, I walk up to the stands and find a spot away from the parents to get some work done.

~

A couple hours later, a whistle causes my head to shoot up from my laptop. Looking around, the arena is practically deserted. I pack my laptop up and walk down to ground level to meet Riley.

"Are you done for the day?" I ask him as I resume my earlier position at the opening to the ice.

"Yep."

"Why are you still dressed out?"

"Have you ever skated before?" Riley asks, completely ignoring my question.

"No."

"Do you want to?"

I chew on my bottom lip. On one hand I've always wanted to. On the other hand, I'm scared I'll fall and hurt myself. "I don't have skates," I tell him. The argument is weak at best as we're literally at an ice rink.

"Nice try, Blue. Meet me at the bench." Riley says and skates over to the closest bench.

Blue? That's a new one. But I walk over to the bench anyway and wait for more instructions. Riley joins me at the bench and sits down, patting the spot next to him.

"I guessed on your shoe size." He tells me as he holds up a worn, rental pair of skates.

I look at the size and hum my approval.

"I know. No need to praise me for my correct guessing."

"God, you're full of yourself." I say as I drop down on the bench.

"And you're stalling. Nikes off. Skates on."

I narrow my eyes at him, but do what he tells me. When I've tied the last string, Riley stands up and walks to the opening to the ice. He holds his hand out to me and, wobbling over to him, I tentatively take it. He steps out onto the ice, but I freeze like Bambi as if my wobbly steps don't already represent the tiny deer when he first steps on the ice. I'm not afraid of anything, really. But falling on my ass in front of a professional hockey player would take embarrassment to new levels.

My grip on his hand tightens when I place a foot on the ice.

"Now the other one." Riley instructs and holds his other hand out to me, wiggling his fingers. I place my freehand in his and wait. "Now I want you to bring the other foot out, but have it land sideways with your toes pointing out."

I do as he says and my grip on his hands tighten when I'm on the ice with both feet.

"Good girl. Now straighten your foot up."

My body warms from his praise and slowly, I straighten my foot up and stand up straight. My grip on his hands is still deathly strong, but he doesn't seem to mind. I keep my eyes on my feet because I'd rather them stay under me than above me.

"Before we move, I'm gonna need you to bend your knees a little. It'll help you stay balanced." I bend my knees a smidge and feel my body get less tense. "Just like that, Sarah. Okay, I'm going to move and pull you with me. Okay?"

"Mm-hmm," I respond as I watch Riley's feet while the cold air whips through my hair.

"Weave your feet in and out, like me." He demonstrates.

I try to do what he does but my legs won't cooperate. "Nope! Can I just stay like this?"

I expect him to scold me and bark an order at me to move my feet like him. But, he doesn't.

"Yeah, Blue. You can stay like that," Riley responds with a lightness in his voice.

We continue going around the rink. I let Riley lead me through circles around the rink and I almost slipped a couple times, which almost cut off the circulation in his hands. Yet, he still didn't seem to mind.

"Okay, I think I'm done for the day," I tell Riley after about thirty minutes. My grip on his hands is still firm. And the little voice in the back of my head is still worried that I cut off the circulation in his fingers. But still he never complained.

"Are you sure?" He asks as if I need a minute to think about getting off these death traps he calls skates.

"Positive."

He leads me over to the bench and shows me how to get off the ice. I unlace my skates and groan in relief as one skate comes off and I start wiggling my toes.

"You stomp around in three-inch heels and skates are what gets you?" He questions while resting his elbows on his knees.

"Hey, now," I start and take off the other skate, repeating the motion of wiggling my toes. "I could walk circles around you in heels. I could walk backwards in heels. But trust me that both are medieval torture devices."

Riley snorts and I look over to see him looking at me and shaking his head. I raise my eyebrow waiting for him to say something.

"I'm gonna go get changed and then we can go through

brands." He stands up and holds his hands out for my skates.

"Sounds good. I'll meet you in the lobby."

I watch Riley round the bench with my skates in his hands and head into the tunnel. I finish tying up my shoes and grab my bag, before heading out to the lobby.

My phone buzzes right as I reach the front.

Emmy-Lou: Dinner tonight?

Me: Maybe…

Me: I'm in Columbus for work.

Emmy-Lou: If I didn't know any better, I'd say you were dating someone.

Me: He's my client.

Emmy-Lou: Yeah. And Adam was my student's parent.

Me: Our situation is 100% different.

Emmy-Lou: For now.

Shaking my head, I put my phone in the back pocket of my jeans right at the moment Riley strolls down the hallway with a duffel slung over his body.

"Are you hungry?"

I look at the watch on my wrist and realize I haven't eaten in hours. My stomach responds before I have a chance.

Riley's laugh at my expense is a far cry from the man who sulked into my office those months ago. "I know a couple of places. I take it you don't want to work at my place?"

I give him a look like, *be serious.*

"Okay." He holds his hands up. "Follow me."

Riley and I walk out of the arena. Our cars are one of the only few left in the lot, so it's easy to see one another's cars. The late summer heat has heated the inside of my car and I pull off my sweatshirt before falling into my car. With how nice it still is, I hit the button to roll the top down and wait for Riley to lead the way to food.

10

RILEY

Thank goodness I put my sunglasses on as soon as I got in my car. I almost swallowed my tongue when Sarah took off her sweatshirt. I'm intimately familiar with what's under all of the clothes. But the innocent reminder was enough to make me want another go with her. Here. In the parking lot in broad daylight.

And despite feeling more at ease with her than anyone I've ever spent time around, that's a no-go as we both know the consequences if we do cross the line. But the more time we spend together, the more I want to ignore the main reason we're in each other's lives. Which is my career and what I need to focus on.

I adjust myself and start my car, pulling out of the spot towards the exit. I watch in amazement as Sarah drops the top on her BMW and pulls her hair back. Her sunglasses slide on her heart shaped face and I can see her gaze fixated in my direction, silently waiting for me to make a move. Pulling out of the lot, Sarah follows behind me and I think of what brands I want to work with so that I'm not coming to this work-lunch empty handed. To be honest, I never gave it much thought. Would it be food related? Hockey related? I just don't know. I always assumed my publicist would put me with the first brand that reached out regardless if I aligned with it.

When we pull into the restaurant's parking lot I get out and round the front of my car as I wait for Sarah to gather her things. I don't expect the place to be too crowded. But as it's still summer break, and lunchtime for those in office jobs, you never can tell. I move around Sarah and open the door for her and I follow in closely behind her, very reminiscent of that night at the jazz bar.

"Hi, welcome to Evan and Cody's. Just two?" The hostess greets and asks us.

"Yes, please," Sarah responds.

The hostess grabs a couple of menus and rolls of silverware before she motions us to follow her. As we walk towards our table, I see we've garnered the attention of a few of the patrons. I'm not overly known as I'm still in my rookie contract. But even die-hard fans would recognize rookies.

She sets our things down then backs away from the table. "Your server will be right with you." She tells us before heading back up to the front.

We slide in on either side of the booth and get settled in. Sarah grabs for a menu and opens it up without a word.

"I hope you're not vegetarian. If you are, I think they have a few safe options," I tell her as I grab my own menu.

"I grew up in the south eating pork rinds. I think I'll be good."

"What are those?" I crinkle my nose because those just sound odd.

"Deep-fried pork skin." Sarah laughs when my face turns to pure mortification. "They're an acquired taste, that's for sure."

Our server comes over, interrupting us to take our drink orders. I look at Sarah over the top of my menu. Her furrowed brow as she thinks of what to order is a common look when it's aimed at me, but one I like seeing on her nonetheless. From what I've gathered, she's always on and so sure of what she wants. Side effect of her job, I'm assuming. So to see the quirk, whether she deems it one or not, is refreshing.

"So what other weird foods did you grow up on?" I ask her and look back down at my menu as if I wasn't staring wistfully at her. A balled-up straw wrapper hits me on the forehead and I jump a little at the trash hitting me. "Hey."

"I'll have you know, boiled peanuts are not weird foods." Sarah says as she points a finger at me, but with a smile on her face.

"I'll take your word for it," I say as I continue looking through the menu.

She sets her menu off to the side, a clear indication that she knows what she wants and turns her gaze on me. "So should we get to the nitty gritty of the brands you want to work with?"

I decide on what I want to eat and then set my menu on top of hers. I cross my hands and place them on the table in front of me. "Cologne, naturally. Every man needs a brand they reach for. I personally am hoping to work with Tom Ford one day. Maybe a cat food brand because I am a Cat Daddy after all."

"You having cats was not on my bingo card." Sarah says as she types the information in on her phone.

"I like all things pussy," I tell her.

"You were doing so well." Sarah claims through a laugh as she drops her head onto the tabletop.

I like making her laugh. If it makes our working relationship run smoothly, then I'll make her laugh as much as humanly possible.

Our server comes over to take our orders and once again, we're alone. Only not really. Sarah keeps looking over my shoulder and I can only assume that we've gathered more attention. My assumption is confirmed when I peek behind me and see phones all pointed towards us.

"That's not going to bother you, is it?" I ask and now I'm kicking myself in not recommending we just eat at my place. Although, I understood her refusal.

"I'm used to it. Happens when you're best friends with a successful fashion designer who's also dating the former Cincinnati quarterback and you decide to all have dinner on a Friday night after a playoff win."

"Yeah, how did that happen?"

"I've known Mason since high school. Then Kamryn and I were roommates and sorority sisters through college," she explains to me and then realizes something. "This is very date-like talk."

"Hey." I hold my hands up. "I'm just trying to get to know my publicist better."

"Mm-hmm," Sarah responds.

Our server comes back out with our food and to refill our waters. We talk about her job and what I like about hockey. I don't tell her how I got into hockey as that's probably too deep for lunch. By the time we're done eating, apart from my cologne and cat food brands, we've gotten no actual work done.

"This work lunch was a bust." I say as I sign off on the receipt. I refused to let her pay. Momma always said that if I offer to take someone to get food that I need to pay.

Sarah looks at her phone and huffs. "I guess you're right."

We come to a mutual agreement to handle everything by email. I have a pre-season skate coming up and she has baseball games to attend. It will also be easier for us as my thoughts continue to stray to NSFW activities. I slide out of my side of the booth and hold my hand out to her when I move to her side to help her out. As we walk out of the restaurant, hushed whispers and the sound of cameras going off reach my ears. When we finally reach outside, we both let out a sigh of relief.

"Well that was some exit," I say.

Sarah snorts as she gets her keys out of her purse. "So our next event is your first regular-season game."

"Yep. I'll make sure to set you up with some team gear." I say, leaning up against her car.

Sarah drops her bag in the passenger seat and faces me, mimicking the same position as the one I'm in. The amount of comfort she shows towards me is one of understanding. Our eyes lock and every moment since we met is reflected in her eyes as I'm sure it's the same when she's looking at me.

She looks like she wants to say something. Instead, with a deep breath, Sarah pushes off her car and grabs the handle. "Well, today was good. Seeing you in your element on the ice, helps me to understand you a little better. I'll see you later, Riley."

I watch her get into her car and make my way around to my door. When I'm about to open it, my phone vibrates in my pocket. Pulling my phone out, I see Logan calling me.

"Hey, man. What's up?" I ask.

"What's up? How come you didn't tell us you were dating the redhead from the charity event?"

I rear back. "What are you talking about? I'm not dating anybody."

"That's not what sports channels and gossip blogs are

saying," Logan says. "Check your phone. I'll talk to you later."

Slowly pulling my phone away, I see my messages icon with a double-digit number. Tapping on it, I click on Logan's name and the headline makes my jaw go slack.

'Bad Boy Hockey Right-Winger Dating Mysterious Redhead'

I tap on the article and it doesn't report on anything reputable. But there is a grainy picture of us from when we went to the jazz bar followed by one from today. Today's picture caught Sarah's head thrown back in laughter and me staring at her like a lovesick fool. I'm about to rush back to Sarah's car, if she hasn't already left, but stop when I see her already resting on the side of my SUV with her own phone in her hand.

"I take it you just saw the article?" She asks and waves her phone in the air.

"Yeah. Here you are helping me with my reputation yet you're getting dragged into it."

"This does seem like something you'd talk to your publicist about," Sarah jokes.

"How are you joking about this? Wouldn't this blow back on you?"

"It's a coping mechanism and probably. I just need to tell my boss it's not what he thinks it is if he sees this before I have the chance to explain." She says and leans back on my car.

I look at her unabashedly while she does her thinking to hopefully get us out of this new mess fans have created. I'm about to offer a solution when she beats me to it.

"If your being seen with me makes you be seen in a positive light, why don't we run with it?"

"Huh? I thought you were all about not fanning the

flames? Now you want to fan them? I'm confused," and I really am.

"You're already being seen better by the fans, your team, and even sponsors just from the handful of events I've had you do. But if news gets out that you're also in a committed relationship, then you'll also appeal to younger families and the sponsors who've been married for decades."

When she says it that way, it makes sense. "So we date?"

"Fake date," she tells me.

Why does the idea of fake dating make me happy but also sad? "Fake date, huh?"

"Just for the season. And then we part ways in April. Both me as your publicist and as your fake girlfriend."

The thought of not having Sarah in my life next spring makes me nauseous. But the thought of being able to date her for six months has me holding my hand out to her.

"Deal," I say.

"Deal," she says as her hand meets mine and our eyes lock.

There is no denying that Sarah and I have chemistry. I feel it every time we lock eyes or brush up against each other and tension fills the air. But if I only have six months with her, then I'll use that time to convince her that we can last longer than that.

11

SARAH

Idiot. Idiot. Idiot.

I pace the floor in my office and think about the idiotic way I opened my mouth and suggested fake dating Riley. I mean, sure he's cute. Okay I'm lying to myself. He's fucking handsome. But he's also younger than me. And I'm his publicist. So there's that. I could have used my brain and said I would put out a statement on his social media accounts denying any coupling happening between us. But I didn't. And now I'm in this mess with Riley until April.

I yawn for the tenth time in thirty minutes as my lack of sleep is finally catching up with me. I've been up since before the sun trying to get the story of Riley and I being linked killed before either of us has a chance to figure out what it is we're supposed to do. While the story was taken down, there is no guarantee that people didn't screenshot that article or the photos of us.

A knock on my door causes me to jump.

"Yeah?" My voice comes out squeaky and I clear my throat.

Jeff pops his head in and his brows furrow in confusion when he sees me in front of my window. "Everything okay?"

And the cause of my pacing stands in my doorway. I can only hope he's been too busy with his own clients, managing those of us who work for him, and being a father to have had the chance to read the article. If it's any inclination that he did see it, maybe he's waiting for me to fess up? Because if he did, he would've stormed into my office the first chance he got. But if he didn't see it, then I have a chance to take the lead on where Riley and I go from here.

You know where you want to go, my evil twin says.

"Yep. Perfect." I lie with a smile.

Jeff regards me as he knows I'm lying, but accepts what I tell him regardless. When he closes the door I continue with my pacing and thinking. Pacing and thinking. Over and over until I stop in my tracks. Then it hits me. I scramble to pick up my phone from my desk and pull up Kamryn's contact.

"Hey," she picks up and answers on the third ring.

"Hey. I have to ask you something that might be intrusive." I start and resume my pacing. Anything to keep from sitting still.

"As opposed to the last ten years of our friendship?" She says with laughter in her voice.

"Fair," I start and take a deep breath.

"Sarah? What's up?" Kamryn asks when I'm silent for longer than usual.

"When you and Liam were test driving your friends with benefits relationship, when did you realize you had feelings for him?"

A deep breath is released into the phone. "Wow. You weren't joking about being intrusive." I hear a heaving breath on the other end of the line and I just know she's tipped her head back in her office chair to gather her words.

"I always had feelings for Liam. You know that. But if I had to pick the exact moment, I think it was the week before I met Mason. Liam ghosting me helped me to move on faster though. Why do you ask?"

"I'm being linked to a hockey player," I tell her.

"The one you're supposed to babysit?"

"That's the one."

I hear tapping and assume she's looking it up. "Oh, he's hot."

"Kamryn," I whine.

"I'm sorry," she laughs into the phone. "Okay, what's the issue?"

"He's my client, he's younger than me, and instead of putting myself in save-mode I suggested we fake date."

Silence. And then laughter. Kamryn's laughter is so loud that I pull my phone away from my ear and wait for her to compose herself.

"Okay. I'm sorry. Really, I am. Fake dating. That is– Let me ask you something. If he wasn't your client, would you be hesitating?"

"No."

"What about his age? If he were older than you would you be hesitant?"

"No. But you wouldn't even know he's younger than me unless you looked him up or asked him."

"Looks like you have your answer, Sarah Jane. The other question is, what are you going to do?"

There's my best friend. "Well, I told him we give the fake dating thing six months and then go our separate ways."

"Six months?" She questions skeptically.

"Is that a long time?" I ask, now fearful that it's too long to keep up a charade. "That's when hockey ends," I tell her.

"No. The timing doesn't really matter. But, Sarah, I'm

worried about you falling for him." She tells me. "And I know you haven't told me everything that happened with you and Paul, but know that I'm here. When you choose to love again, and I hope you do because you have so much love to give, I want you to remember that love should be freeing."

I snort into the phone. "You don't have to worry about that." Paul ruined me for any future relationship I planned to have. So me falling in love is nothing anyone should worry about.

"Okay." I hear the skepticism in her tone again and then hear noise from her office and a muffled voice in the background. "Damn. I have a meeting to get to. But, we'll talk later, okay?"

"Yeah."

"Oh, and I want to be the first to know when you're no longer "fake dating," she says with a teasing lilt to her voice.

I snort into the phone at her optimism. "Never gonna happen. Love you."

"Love you," she says and then hangs up.

Walking over to my computer, I pull up my calendar where I have all of my clients schedules laid out. None of them have anything pressing that I can't handle from home. Just a few emails and a phone conference. Decision made, I pack up my things and stop by Jeff's office before leaving.

Knocking on his office door, I pop in. "Hey, I'm gonna do some admin work from home."

He looks up from his laptop. "Okay. Everything okay?"

"Yeah. I have to work through something that I can't do here," my tone is even as I explain it to him.

"Why don't you just work from home the rest of the week?"

"Are you sure?"

"Positive," he tells me and surveys me carefully. I hope he comes up empty. "Are you sure everything is okay?" Jeff asks me again.

No. "It will be." I say and leave him with a parting smile.

MY TO-DO list is down to this final task. I look over the contract one last time and fire off the email to Riley. I'm not sure why I didn't think of a contract before I opened my big mouth. I'm meticulous in my job. Contracts make me horny. But making this sporadic deal with him scrambled all rational parts of my brain. My email pings with a check-in from Jeff and soon I'm back in the trenches of brand negotiations and mapping out my travel schedule for the next year.

I'm walking out of my home office an hour later when I hear the rumble of a motorcycle echoing down my street. I don't think much of it as my neighbors drive all sorts of cars. But it's my doorbell ringing that halts me in my trek to the kitchen and I freeze like a deer in headlights. I could be a sensible adult and hide. Because I'm not expecting anyone or a delivery from one of my many late night shopping excursions. And I'm a millennial who doesn't answer the door for anyone she's not expecting. The doorbell rings again followed by a knock on the door and I cautiously make my way to the door. Checking the peephole, I see Riley on my front stoop with a helmet in his hand.

"Hey." I say after whipping the door open.

The late September air chills me, but my body burns as his eyes track over my body from my scrunchy sock-covered feet to my shorts that barely cover anything to my exposed midriff to the messy bun and finally meeting my eyes. In my hide-from-the-doorbell panic, I forgot I was dressed in clothes not appropriate to answer the door in.

"Hi," Riley finally says after a hard swallow.

"Is there a reason you're at my house?" He only dropped me off at home once, and that was at night, so his memory is impressive.

"Yes. No. Fuck. I got your email while I was at a pitstop and figured it would just be faster if I read and signed it in person," he explains. "I went to your office, but they said you went home for the day. So I came here."

"Huh. Okay, then. Come in." I hold the door open wider and he steps inside. He's the first man in my house since Paul and it's doing trippy things to me.

"Nice house." Riley says after I shut the door.

"Thanks. The contract is in my office. Follow me." I hurry up the stairs and listen as Riley sets his helmet on the floor and toes off his boots, with the unexpected soft stomping as he trails up after me.

My office is as feminine and moody as you can get while still looking professional. A huge light oak desk sits in the middle of the room with an area rug underneath to hide the cords. I have two matching oak bookshelves flanking me with the window to the right of my desk that overlooks the backyard. The walls are covered in a dark floral print wallpaper that makes the space dramatic and romantic. I completed the space with a rust colored loveseat with deep set cushions on the opposite wall with a couple of throw pillows and a blanket.

Riley whistles when he completes his perusal of my space. "Why would you ever work in an office?"

"I need to get out of the house sometime," I tell him with a smile and pull up the contract. "Here. You can read through and then use the trackpad to sign."

Riley takes the seat I vacated and looks over the contract. I curl up on the love seat couch that's on the opposite wall and scroll on my phone. I catch up on social media posts and respond to texts while he reads the contract I've drafted up.

The contract is straight forward.

1. PDA in public, but we keep it to a minimum

2. We don't launch our relationship on social media since this is all a facade

3. No falling in love

The last one is for both our benefits. But six months should be enough time to fake it til we make it. And hopefully by the end, the public is no longer focusing on who he's dating.

"Done," Riley says.

"Perfect. Will you hit save and then I'll file it."

I hear the light clicking of the mouse and then Riley is standing up and coming to sit next to me. With him on this couch this love seat has all but shrunk. I'm all too aware of him and his body heat sinking into me. Warming me from the close proximity when he should just leave.

"Are you worried you'll fall in love with me?" Riley asks.

I look up from my phone and the smile on his face is disarming. If I were a hopeless romantic, I would say yes. But I'm more optimistic than anything.

"No. That's more for your benefit than it is for mine." I tell him, tucking my phone into the side of the couch and giving him my full attention.

"And why would I be the one to fall in love with you?"

I know he doesn't mean it in a rude way, but that stings a little. "Because you're younger than me. And for some reason my incredible charm gets people to do just that. Also,

I don't do love. At least not anymore. So it'd really be you doing all of the falling."

His eyebrows come together with a furrow. "So you're saying that in a few years my charm will do wonders?"

"No. And anyways, what are you doing on a motorcycle so close to the season starting?" I turn my body to face him and rest my arm on the back of the couch.

"I like the freedom that a bike gives me. And since it's so close to the season starting, I wanted one last ride before I put it in my parents garage. Have you ever been on one?"

I shake my head quickly and his eyes crinkle with a smile.

"My offer still stands if you want to ride," Riley says and with those words the air is suddenly charged. I always knew the chemistry I felt with Riley wasn't a fluke. And in this moment it is undeniable.

For me, it's so easy to put us in the Athlete and Publicist category. If he were anyone else I could lose myself in him and never come up for air.

"I think you should go," I whisper. His innuendo continues to hang heavy in the air and the longer we stay locked in each other's stare the easier it is for me to forget about our roles. I could lie and tell him we need to practice for PDA. We don't need practice, but the longer we sit on this couch meant for two, the easier it would be to just let my walls down. To give in to whatever this burning chemistry is between us in a single breath.

Riley moves.

I move.

Our lips crash together and Riley wraps his hands around my waist and hauls me onto his lap. I feel his hardness pressing against my clothes-covered clit and gasp. Riley uses the moment to slip his tongue into my mouth. Our tongues tangle and I lift up, scooting closer and sitting on his erection. His hands slide up my shirt, he groans when he realizes I have nothing underneath and tugs my body closer to him. My hands slide into his hair and I pull hard on the blond strands. Breaking the kiss, I kiss down his neck and lick into the divot at his neck. My hands fall to the bottom of his shirt and I pull the material up his body until his chest is exposed and the material bunches around his neck.

"Off." I say through heavy breaths.

Riley takes off the shirt that I'm cursing and tosses it to the side. I can finally see him in daylight. The tattoos that cover his chest are done with precision and a kaleidoscope of colors take over his body. My hands trace the designs and I watch in delight as his abs constrict with my feather-light touches with goosebumps following in a trail. I move forward to kiss his chest. Trailing my lips across his chest and flicking a nipple with my tongue. His groan vibrates through my body and hits my clit as I continue to move down his body. I slide off the couch and move my hands to the button on his jeans. Riley lifts his hips when they're loose and I slide them down until they're bunched right around his knees. His cock springs free and I wrap my hand around his length, rubbing my thumb across the tip and smearing the pre-cum that's beaded on the tip.

I hold eye contact as I lean forward and lick up the cum that's leaking from his cock. Sucking the tip into my mouth, I use my hand and pump him from root to tip. Never breaking eye contact, my other hand slides down my body and slips into my shorts. I'm soaked and my fingers slide right into my opening. I moan around his length as I pump and curl my fingers inside of my pussy.

"Pull your fingers out," Riley pants. "Show me how wet you are."

I whimper around his length as I do what he says. The emptiness is noticeable and I squeeze my thighs together to try and relieve the ache.

"Fuck, you're dripping." Riley says and grabs onto my wrist. Wet heat envelops my fingers as he sucks them into his mouth. Cleaning my juices off the appendages. The next thing I know, I'm pulled from his length and straddling his lap. "Enough with this. My cock hasn't been in your pussy in way too long."

I wrap my hand around his cock and Riley pulls my shorts to the side. Rubbing the blunt head through my opening. "You mean this pussy?"

Riley's head falls to the back of the couch as I continue to tease us. "Yes," he groans, "stop being a tease and give us what we both want."

"Since you asked so nicely." I lift higher on my knees and line him up at my entrance. Slowly. Oh, so, slowly I lower on his cock as he fills me up. I coat his length little by little until I'm sliding down his cock and full of him. I throw my head back as he fills me and give my body a few seconds to adjust to the stretch before I'm rising on my knees, leaving the tip of his cock buried inside me and sliding back down.

"Oh, god damn, baby. Your pussy was made for my cock." His head falls to the back of the couch again and I clench around him as his words slide into my soul.

"Eyes on me." I tell him as I place his chin between my fingers and fix his gaze back on me.

His eyes burn into mine and his hands slide up my torso, ripping my shirt off. I fall forward, my hands falling to the back of the couch, caging him in as I ride his cock like a mechanical bull. My nipples are so hard and my breasts ache from the pleasure. Riley cups my breasts in his hands, his thumbs tease my nipples and he pulls one between his lips causing me to whimper. His eyes hold mine as he pulls a nipple between his teeth and lightly tugs. I feel the tug down to my clit and I speed up my movement.

"Play with my clit," I whine. Riley delivers and his hand slides between us as he pinches and rubs my clit. Over and over until I explode. I ride out the wave of ecstasy as my orgasm hits me.

I slow down my movement and weave my hands into his hair. My hips slow and roll as I trail my lips down his neck. Sex with Riley is the best I've ever had. I won't tell him that though. His ego is at an all time high and I don't need to add anymore ammo.

"Hold on tight, baby." He warns before he grabs my hips and ruts up into me. Chasing his own release. I kiss the underside of his ear and tug on the lobe with my teeth. That sets him off and he explodes with a roar. I feel the warmth from his cum as his orgasm hits. My hips continue to work him through his release and I feel his cum slide out between us. "Fuck," Riley whispers against my head.

I sit back and look at him confused.

"I didn't use a condom."

"Oh. Well I have an IUD and I haven't been with anyone since you." I tell him, almost feeling shy about the fact that he's the last one I was with. But what I don't tell him is that I tried to sleep with other guys to chase the high that he ignited in me. We didn't use a condom the first time, which was risky business and it took a lot of trust for us to be bare together.

"Same," he tells me.

The longer we hold eye contact, the more I feel him hardening inside of me. I quirk an eyebrow at him. "Again?" I ask incredulously.

He leans forward and kisses and licks along my neck.

"You expect me to not have a reaction after telling me you haven't been with anyone since me?"

"Okay, caveman." I moan out as I reflectively roll my hips along his length.

"Nuh uh." Riley says and gets up, keeping my legs locked around his waist. "Where's your bedroom?"

"End of the hall." I tell him and kiss along his jawline.

12

RILEY

I speed walk down the hall as fast as I can while still buried inside of her. When I reach her room, I tuck her pelvis closer to mine and gracefully climb onto the bed. With a smacking kiss on her lips, my cock slips out of her heat as I slide down her body. In our lust for each other, I forgot her shorts were still on. I swiftly pull them off her body and toss the offensive material over my shoulder. With her finally bare, my fingers replace my length and I settle between her thighs.

Sucking her clit into her mouth, I curl a finger inside of her. Sarah's breathlessness and her body's response to me is the biggest turn-on. Knowing that this is what gets her closer to an orgasm is a win in my eyes. My mouth replaces my fingers and I lick at her opening. Our release mixes together and the taste of us drives me feral. I wrap my arms around her thighs and eat her like I haven't had food in days. Her thighs clamp around my head as I tongue at her opening the way I would kiss her.

"Riley!" Sarah shouts when my tongue curls inside of her. Her reaction spurs me on and the pressure of her thighs squeezing my head harder encourages me more. I add my fingers back to the mix and curl them inside of her and flick my tongue over her stiff clit.

I know she's close. I pull my mouth from her and move my thumb to her clit. "Come for me, Sarah." I tell her and latch my lips back to her opening at the same time she lets go. She floods my mouth with her release and I do everything to drink up her essence. I'm addicted.

To her taste.

To her smell.

To her.

I continue to lick and work her through her release until Sarah pulls me up and fuses our mouths together. Her tasting herself on my lips is the sexiest thing I've experienced and I don't miss the sound of her moaning as she does. I line myself at her entrance and slide into her still fluttering cunt and thrust home. I wrap an arm under her thigh, hooking it over my shoulder and sliding deeper as my pace increases. Sarah slides her hands down my back. Pulling on my lower back and meeting me thrust for thrust. I break our kiss and look down at where our bodies meet. My cock tunneling inside her pussy is enough to have my balls draw up.

I stop suddenly and sit back on my heels, taking Sarah with me. I cradle her in my arms and bounce her on my cock.

Sarah throws her head back on a silent scream as my cock hits her g-spot.

"That's it, baby. Let go and let me hear you. Come all over my cock," I coach her as she lets go, screaming my name. My second orgasm follows her and I work us both through our release. Her body goes lax in my arms and I gently set her down, my cock slips out of her heat and I watch as our release spills out of her. That's hot and almost makes me want another go.

"Okay," Sarah pants out and stares up at the ceiling breathless. "That's one thing we won't have to fake."

I snort and roll off the bed. "Do you have any towels?"

Sarah gets off the bed, in all her naked glory, and walks past me into her bathroom and through to what looks like a massive closet. She comes back with two towels and sets them on the vanity.

"Bathroom is all yours."

She makes to walk out but I snake my arm around her waist, dragging her back into my space. "Where do you think you're going?"

"To let you shower alone."

"Nice try, Blue." I release her and turn on the shower. Turning around, I see her surveying me like I'm an undiscovered creature. She's probably confused by the nickname I've given to her. But I plan to keep that name under lock and key for the time being. I put my hand under the water to feel for the temperature and when I feel it's warm enough, I grab her hand and drag her under the spray with me.

Sarah is reluctant and stiff at first, but then she loosens up. She grabs the bar of soap and runs it under the water to suds it up. Rubbing her hands together with the soap and then running it over my body, I watch in amusement with her concentration. Her brows scrunch in concentration and her bottom lip disappears as she tucks it between her lips. I breathe raggedly through her thorough washing of my body and have to think of literally anything when she drops down to her knees to wash my legs and my cock which twitches in her hand. When she's done, she places the soap on the shelf and maneuvers me under the spray.

Once I see all the soap has run off my body, I return the favor. Her body has curves that I love gripping onto but is tone in all of the right places. Kneeling I kiss her stomach and I make sure to pay close attention to between her legs and don't miss her flinch.

"Sorry." I tell her as I continue washing her. Although the caveman in me likes the thought of her a little sore. When I tap her on the ankle, she places her hands on my shoulders and hands a foot to me. I marvel in the muted pink on her toenails being a stark contrast to her vibrant personality. When I've finished washing her, I carefully switch our positions and move her under the water to rinse all of the soap off.

I can't resist pecking her on the lips before I turn off the water and reach for a towel. Stepping out, I dry off my body as fast as I can, wrap it around my waist and then grab the extra towel for Sarah. I turn around and dry her off, then wrap the towel around her as well. I hold my hand out for her and she takes it, letting me help her unnecessarily out of the shower. I peck her on the cheek and leave her to get dressed.

When I walk back into her office, my clothes are scattered all over the place. Weirdly, my phone managed to stay in my pants and I open it up to a few texts from the guys asking to go to dinner. It's around four and I could make it back in plenty of time. I've done everything Sarah needed me to do, so I have no need to stay. But I want to stay. Why do I want to stay?

Shrugging on my wrinkled shirt, I make my way back to her bedroom and find her in the bathroom with a white silk floral robe covering her body. I lean against the doorframe and watch as she lathers her body in lotion. I like watching her in silence. It's as if I get the unfiltered, peaceful version of her that she chooses not to show to the rest of the world.

"Hey," she says when her eyes flicker to me in the mirror as she finally notices my presence.

"Hi," I return a smile at her. "I've gotta head out."

I watch for any sign that she wants me to stay but I detect nothing. She's good at remembering what we are, or what we're not, and it seems that I need to follow suit. Or maybe she's not good at it and has to constantly remind herself that we're nothing but a contract.

"Okay. Well, I guess I'll see you in a couple weeks for your first game." Sarah tells me as she turns around to face me. She looks so delicate that it completely disarms me.

"Sure." I say and walk forward, invading her space and backing her into her vanity counter. She looks up at me with a renewed fire in her eyes. The shades of blue in them drowns me and makes me want to never come up for air.

My mouth fuses to Sarah's for a hard and toe-curling kiss. Her hands find my waist and she rises to her toes to deepen our kiss. And just as fast, I rip my mouth from hers, leaving her in the bathroom holding onto the vanity and breathless.

Hopping down the stairs with renewed energy, I shuck on my leather jacket, toe on my boots and snag my helmet from the chair in her foyer. I don't hear any sounds coming from upstairs and I figure she's still trying to figure out how to breathe. Opening the front door, I lock the small lock and head out to my bike.

That contract was right to stipulate that we not fall in love.

Because I might already be halfway there.

~

"WHAT DO you mean you don't want to go out?" Noah whines when I tell them my after dinner plans.

I went right to the restaurant from Sarah's house. I was hopeful that the drive back to home base would help gather my thoughts. Only the farther I got from her, the more I wanted to turn around and spend more time with her. *You're fake dating, Riley. Remember that.* But now all Noah talks about is going out to hopefully get laid and that's the last thing that's on my mind. No. The only thing on my mind is a redhead in Cincinnati with eyes so blue, I could paint them and keep discovering new shades of blue.

"What I mean is that I'm beat from my drive. Take Logan." I tell him and take a sip of water. The truth is that while I'm tired, I'm also still wired from today. But I need more than an hour on a traffic-filled highway to take it all in.

"I don't wanna go out," Logan says with a mouth full of chips from next to me.

"Sorry, buddy." I tell him and turn my attention back to a pouting Noah. "What happened to what's-her-face from last season?"

"She moved."

"You need more than one backup." Max says from next to him and takes a pull from his beer.

Logan shakes his head and takes a drink from his water. We're the only two not drinking tonight. Once September rolls around I go cold turkey. Not that I have a problem or anything, but I don't perform my best after a couple of drinks. I learned that the hard way my rookie season. While going into my second season, I know the training and practices won't get much easier. But it's better to stay on top of my game when I'm not dragging my ass to practice after having one too many beers. So I'm already putting myself in that focus mentality. Thinking of the game makes me wonder if I can convince Sarah to come up here for a few days to get the true hockey training experience.

I'm nudged in the side by Logan and look at him like he's crazy. "What?"

"What's up with you?"

"Nothing." I tell him and shake my head. It's definitely not like me to get hooked on someone I'm not really dating. But Sarah manages to rewire something in my brain to where all I think about is her. It's funny how I went from aloof months ago, to wanting to impress her with everything I do.

"Nuh uh," Noah starts. "That's a lovesick look you've got on your face."

"I don't have a "lovesick look" on my face," I tell them defensively which raises alarms.

"And you're defensive." Max notes.

Assholes. "I might have met someone," I confess to them.

"That redhead you were with?" Logan asks.

Yes. "No. You guys don't know her and I'd rather not spill anything. Not until I know she's not in it for the money." That stings even me saying because I know Sarah isn't fake dating me for the money. It's clear that she has her own money judging the way her house exudes wealth.

"Well, I'll be damned. I never thought I'd see you settle down so soon," Noah says.

"Dude, I'm only twenty-three. I'm too young to officially settle down."

Although the idea doesn't completely terrify me. The dating apps are horrible and if I do meet someone, it turns out they only want to be with me because I'm an athlete. I'm not in the headspace to fund anyone's lifestyle. And dating someone who doesn't have a stable job seems more like a headache than anything.

Looking at the time on my watch I realize I need to head out. Fishing out my wallet, I throw $100 on the table to cover more than my share. "I'm gonna head out, guys. I've got a pilates class in the morning."

Scooting back from the table, I fist bump the guys and make my way out of the busy restaurant. I acknowledge a few fans and take some pictures before bee-lining my way to my bike. The drive home doesn't take long and my girls greet me with enthusiasm. Not just for my presence but for food as well. I feed them and shut off the lights, before heading to my bedroom for the night.

As I stand under the stream of water, I reminisce on all that today entailed. I have six months to be the best fake boyfriend and client. And by the end of those six months, I'll hopefully convince Sarah that we don't have to end.

13

SARAH

The music floats out of the surround-sound speakers of the studio. Flashing lights from the photographer's camera flicker in my peripheral. Nate is finally in town from his stretch of road games and today was the only day to get his brand shoots done. Since he's on the more shy side, he asked me to join him. As I also help him get photos for his social media team, I take some behind the scenes photos and videos.

They wrap an hour later and I watch as Nate slowly dims.

"Are you okay, buddy?" I ask when he drops in the chair next to me and I pass him his shirt.

"Yeah. Just ready to be home." His point is emphasized with a massive yawn while he shrugs on the shirt I handed him.

"Oh, come on. You're supposed to be the life of the party. Not ready to rot on the couch." I tell him as I hand him his jacket next.

He gives me a pointed look and I bite back a laugh. He's never been like that and I love teasing him for it.

Nate stays with me as I pack up my things before I'm off to Columbus for a few days to get the lay of the land. But I won't deny that my heart jumps at being in the same city as Riley for a few days. *Stop that, Sarah.*

We part ways in the parking lot and I check my phone again before getting on the road. I know Columbus is over an hour, but for some reason the anticipation is killing me.

Riley: Hey, boss lady.

Riley: What time are you headed here?

Me: Boss lady? I expect that as a nameplate.

Me: I'm headed there now. My hotel is ready for check-in.

My phone rings with a call from Riley.

"What's wrong with texting?" I ask in lieu of a greeting.

"What hotel are you staying at?"

I pull my phone away and pull up the email. "Hotel LaRoux. Why?"

"No reason," he says. "I'll see you soon."

He hangs up before I can respond. "Stupid, arrogant, young hockey player." I mutter to myself and start up my car.

Getting out of the city on a Wednesday is easier said than done. I hit construction traffic and then get stopped at every traffic light. But finally, after two song lengths I'm on the way up north.

"W‍HAT DO you mean you have no record of my room?" I ask the concierge. I try not to come off too angry as he's just doing his job. But, seriously? I have my confirmation email on my phone.

"I'm sorry, miss. I'd book you another room, but with all of our sports teams playing this weekend, we're completely booked."

If he was lying I would know. But unfortunately he's not as I checked the schedule for this weekend so I knew what I was getting into which is why I booked my room so far in advance. "Okay. Thank you, though."

I do the walk of shame back to my car with my suitcase in tow. Pulling up my phone I do a quick search of any hotel with availability for the rest of the week. Nothing within twenty miles.

"Why the long face?" A voice asks in front of me.

I stop and drop my head back, groaning loudly. "Did you do this?"

"Now what kind of boyfriend would that make me if I made my girlfriend stay in a hotel when I have a perfectly good condo you could sleep at?" Riley asks as he invades my space bringing his familiar cedar wood and leather scent mixed with what smells like sweat.

I right my posture and come face to face with the blond devil himself. "The fake kind."

"No fun in that. Now let's go." He says and takes my suitcase from my hand before moving towards my car. It's then I notice him in workout clothes with a light sheen of sweat covering his body.

"Where's your car?" I ask even though I already know the answer.

Riley looks over his shoulder at me with a devilish grin. He taps the trunk of my car, motioning for me to pop the trunk. With an annoyed breath, I do what he wants and wait for what's next. Riley rounds the car to the passenger side and nods at me, waiting for me to join him on that side.

"I'll drive," he says as I make my way over to him as he opens the door and holds his hand out for the keys.

"You're like an overeager puppy." I tell him as I drop them in his hand and slide into the passenger seat.

"You love it." He leaves me with a smile as he closes the door and rounds the car to the driver's seat. I watch in amusement as he squeezes into the seat and moves it back.

I don't admit to myself that I like someone taking charge.

I don't admit that Riley showing more effort than Paul is something I like.

I don't admit.

I don't admit.

I. Don't. Admit.

Riley effortlessly backs my car out of the spot and pulls onto the main road. I try to memorize landmarks but everything blurs as he navigates the streets with ease. I revel in not having to think for the first time ever and the next thing I know, we're slowing down and turning into a parking garage. My head turns in Riley's direction but he firmly ignores my look.

I open my mouth multiple times to ask where we're at, but I use my brain and deduce that we're at his place. He pulls into a spot next to his behemoth of a Range Rover and silence falls over us as he parks and turns my car off.

"Home sweet home." He announces and slides out of the car without waiting for my snarky retort.

I'm slower to get out as my senses are all out of whack. But when I do, I see Riley waiting impatiently with my suitcase.

"Yes?" I ask.

He holds his hands up in front of him as his only response and I suspect it's to hold his tongue. Riley walks towards the elevator bank and I can't help but follow closely behind. The elevator opens instantly and we file in. Taking up opposite sides of the car, I can't help but flashback to our first time in an elevator.

"So what's the plan for this week?" I ask Riley as the elevator rolls up. It's also to hopefully distract my mind from us and elevators.

"Well, we have our first preseason game tomorrow evening. I usually hang out at home before heading to the arena. But you're free to explore the area." Riley tells me as the elevator stops on his floor.

"I might stick around here so I don't get lost."

"Okay. If you want, I can be your tour guide the day after," Riley assures me.

I smile at his back as he opens the door to his place. "Thanks," I tell him as he holds the door open for me. The high ceilings and open living room greets me as I walk out of the foyer. "Wow. This space is incredible." Movement out of the corner of my eye surprises me. "Oh, hello," I say and squat down.

"That's Sasha," Riley tells me as she comes to sniff my fingers.

She nudges her snout under my fingers and demands pets. Her white coat is freshly brushed and she looks up at me with the bluest of blue eyes. "Can I pick her up?"

"Mm-hmm."

I put my hands around her body and rise with her in my arms. She's a lot lighter than I thought and her purr-box is immediate when she's in my arms. Kamryn and Emily's cats are the only ones I've been around and I adore them but I've never been able to commit to adopting a cat of my own. I stick my nose in her neck and walk forward with Riley trailing behind. His living room opens to a view of downtown slowly coming to life. A big dark blue sectional takes up most of the space but it's not overwhelming. He has throw blankets and pillows in a variety of neutrals that add warmth to the big room with a huge flat screen TV taking up the opposite wall. It's not what I expected from him but surprisingly this space fits who he is. Or what I know of him at least

Riley sets my suitcase and weekender bag by the TV. The sound of my luggage brings my attention to Riley. His gaze is unfocused yet focused on me at the same time.

"What?" I ask when his gaze starts to make me squirm. I place a kiss on Sasha's head and set her on the couch.

He shakes his head and heads into the kitchen. Which is even more impressive considering he's in a condo. A huge black marble island separates the space, a stainless steel french door refrigerator with a matching stove and microwave complete the set and beckon to be used. The warm wood cabinets give the space a masculine and homey feeling. Off to the right I see a dining table big enough to fit eight sat on top of a dark blue and maroon area rug.

"Riley, your place is stunning."

"Thank you. I don't have the biggest eye for design. So with the help of my interior designer and my Momma, we got this place up and running in under a year." He tells me as he slides a glass of ice water to me.

"Thanks." I take a sip of water to cool myself down. Why is it so awkward with him? *Work mode*, I tell myself because it's my safe zone. "So I started your website."

His eyebrows fly to his hairline. "Already? I thought these took months to do."

"You were easy." I say as I move to my bag and pull out

my laptop. I walk back over to the island and stand at the end.

"My new slogan," Riley jokes and stands to the side me at the island. I take him through what I did and how I did it. Some may think it's not necessary for a hockey player to have a website. But when his career is done, Riley and his fans will have some place to look at that highlights his career. It's also a great reference point for if he ever decides to do camps.

"Do you like it?" I ask and turn my head to look up at him now completely terrified that he's going to reject the whole thing.

"It's really good. At first I was skeptical. Because why does a hockey player need a website? But I like it."

I turn my head back to my laptop and bite my lip to hide my smile. I don't admit that I need praise for my work. But growing up as an only child, it paved my need for some type of acknowledgment.

"Good." I tell him and shut my laptop. "What do you normally do before games? I mean, I know this isn't an official season game, so I'm not sure how your routine works."

"Am I the first hockey player you're working with?" He asks as he backs up, realizing we're a bit closer than we should be.

"Yeah," I say, a little shy and look over at Riley.

His soft smile brings heat to my cheeks. "How about I make us dinner and I'll give you a crash course on the sport."

"Okay."

Riley pushes off from the island and moves towards the fridge. "You're not allergic to anything?"

"Nope," I pop the *p* and see him turn back to the fridge, but not before seeing his cheeks lift with a smile. While he busies himself with fixing our dinner, I slide off the barstool and move to my suitcase for a change of clothes. When suddenly it dawns on me so I turn back to face the man who canceled my room. "Hey, Riley? Where am I sleeping?"

The blond behemoth purposefully refuses to turn around in a timely manner. But I'm used to waiting. So that's what I do. With my hip popped and my arms crossed, I wait for Riley to turn around. When I see he can no longer fake being busy, I brace myself for whatever excuse he's planning to sell me as he turns to face me.

"You see," he starts and I can actually see the thoughts forming in his head. "I have two rooms. But the second is unfurnished and has the cats litter boxes and other things for them in there."

"Are you saying you have a dedicated full room for your cats?" I squint my eyes at him and before I can rationalize anything normal, I beeline to the other room. Ignoring Riley's protests behind me, I push the door open and come to a screeching stop at the threshold. Riley slams into me from behind and steadies me with a hand on my waist.

"I'd say I could explain myself, but this is explanation enough." Riley fails to adequately explain.

It's like Petsmart threw up in here. Two dog beds raised on platforms, cat towers on either side of the beds and in the middle, toys everywhere, and scratch posts spread out with some running up the walls.

"I don't know if I should laugh or cry," I breathe out.

"Laugh, please." Riley tells me.

I finally turn and face him. He's got Sasha on his shoulder and it's too cute that I can no longer be horrified by the room that I'm in. "Okay, if this is their room then where do I sleep?"

Riley exaggeratedly sniffs the air and all but sprints out

of the room. "Oh no, I need to go check the food and make sure it doesn't burn."

"Riley Theodore Jones!" I call after him. "Please tell me I'm not sleeping in your bed." Sasha joins her sibling on the couch and I do a double take. The eyes of the Maine Coon follow my every move as if I'm about to strike her owner. I turn my focus to the mountain of a man who's at the stove ignoring me.

"If you were my real girlfriend you'd sleep in my bed anyways," Riley says like it's a matter-of-fact thing. Which to be fair, if I was his girlfriend I'd be in his bed.

"Well, I'm not." I stomp my foot.

Riley turns his head towards me, amusement taking over every inch of his face. "Did you just stomp your foot?"

"I did."

"Brat."

I raise a perfectly shaped brow at him.

He sighs and holds his hands out in front of him. Which he tends to do a lot around me. "You can make a pillow barrier if you're worried about not being able to control yourself in a bed with me."

"Asshole," I mutter and zip my suitcase back up and roll it into his room. In my ire, the second I step into his room my shock level keeps growing. Bad reputation or not, Riley has a cozy bedroom. I take a look at his nightstands and choose to set up camp at the empty looking one, deciding this will be the side that I sleep on. Taking my lounge clothes out of my suitcase, which just consists of shorts and an oversized sweatshirt, I head into the bathroom to change.

"It's so hard to be mad at him with a bathroom like this," I say aloud.

Riley playing schemer has made the lines blurry. I know

he knows what he was doing. He has mischief written all over his persona. I'll show him who's the one who can't control themselves. If he wants us to play house, then he just met his match.

14

RILEY

Besides the sound of the Italian sausage sizzling in the pan, it's too quiet in here. Normally it's the girls getting into something and me having to clean it up later. But now that Sarah is here, my suspicions are leveled up to a thousand.

Was it a jerk move to cancel her hotel room without any warning? Yes.

Was it a jerk move to want her in my space without consulting her? Also, yes.

In the short time, everything has been better with Sarah around. The voices that have been demanding more from me have quieted. To be better. To push myself. To not let down my loved ones. They all quiet when she's around. I can breathe a little better knowing she has my back and it shocks me because I didn't expect to get so comfortable so fast with her.

I sense her before I see her. It's weird. But what I don't expect is her to come up behind me and wrap her arms around me. Uh...what happened in the time she chewed my head off to when she changed her clothes? An epiphany doesn't happen that fast, does it?

"Not that I dislike you wrapped around me like a fanny pack, but why *are* you wrapped around me?"

"I figure we should get used to touching each other in non-bedroom ways since we'll be around other people this weekend. And you just flinched." Sarah tells me and points out my body's reaction to her touch, but I don't buy the reason.

"Well your hands are colder than the ice baths I take," I use as an excuse. Which that's what it is.

"You should feel my feet," she teases.

"I'll pass," I tell her and my body finally unclenches with her wrapped around me. "So how does us in public work? And what's our story?"

"What do you mean?" Sarah asks and I feel the loss of her body heat as she comes to stand next to me.

I look over at her and my eyes zero in on what she's wearing: short shorts that show off her toned legs and a Cincinnati football sweatshirt with scrunched gray socks on her feet. My eyes travel up her body and I meet a smirking Sarah who raises her eyebrow at me. If that's what she wants to play, then let the games begin.

"I know you've seen *The Proposal*. They needed a story to convince people that they all of a sudden started dating and fell in love. But without the engagement for us. Unless you want to wear a mini ice rink on your finger." I say teasingly and wink at her.

She crosses her arms and leans back against the counter. "No. I'm not wearing a ring until it matters."

Huh. She's hiding something. And maybe right now, it's not my place to ask. But hopefully one day she'll let me in.

"So what's our story then? Because we can't use the club

as our meet cute." I turn my attention back to the boiling pasta water and check the Italian sausage to ensure it's cooking through.

"First, I'm shocked you've seen *The Proposal*. And second, that you know what a meet cute is." I hear the amusement in her voice but I don't take the bait.

I pull the strainer out and place it in the sink. "My Momma is a rom-com and romance book fan. And despite Pops and I's protest, we endured monthly marathons when I was growing up and we always let her choose."

With the pasta al dente, I save some water and pour the rest in the strainer. I do all of this while Sarah watches. And if it's one thing I know I'm exceptionally good at, it's cooking. Yes, I get meals delivered once the season really amps up because I'm short on time after practices and games, but it's nice to cook. And I have this big kitchen that should get used more regularly. Showing my skills off to her is another way I hope to win her over. *Yeah, I'm so screwed.*

"You sound close to your parents," Sarah observes from her spot at the counter.

I move back to the stove and work on assembling the pasta. I take a deep breath and let it out, preparing myself because she'll find out regardless. I might as well tell her my whole story now. "They are some of the most selfless people in my life. I don't know where I would be if they hadn't adopted me."

"You were adopted?" Sarah asks hesitantly after a beat of silence.

I plate our finished dinner and walk our food to the dining table. Sarah follows and takes the spot on the right and I grab us silverware before taking the seat next to her.

"I was ten years old when I was in a car accident with my Mom and Dad. I survived, but they didn't. Momma and Pops were my godparents and my parents best friends. Unfortunately they could never have kids of their own so it was an adjustment when I started living with them. I was a sophomore in high school when they eventually broached the topic of legally making me theirs. I don't know all of the legalities of what it took, but by the time school ended I was officially a Jones. At that point I had already considered Momma and Pops mine but this legal-ness of it made it more final. Neither of us had to worry about the what if. Like 'what if' my Mom or Dad had a relative they knew nothing about and they tried to take me."

"I'm so sorry." Sarah says and places a hand on my arm. It's a mix of pity and comfort and I'm not sure if I hate it or just want more of her comfort. "May I ask why you didn't keep your last name?"

"I love my parents. Both sets. And I could have chosen to hyphenate. But I didn't. My mom and dad will always be my parents. But Cassie and Dean raised me, saved me, and comforted me when I needed it the most. Taking their last name wasn't about erasing my parents memory...what little I do remember about them. Maybe one day when I have a family I'll name one of my kids with that last name."

The side of my face burns with Sarah's gaze but I avoid it and shovel pasta into my mouth.

"So that's my big back story," I say after I can't take the terse silence. "What's yours?" I take the focus off of myself, but I know one day we'll have to dive deeper into it.

Sarah retreats and takes a bite of her food. I do the same and wait for her to gather her thoughts.

"My best friend's boyfriend died in a car accident. And when it happened I felt like a failure as he wanted me to help him look desirable for scouts. I was originally on the path to become a sports agent—which is why I stepped in so easily for you, but when no one knocked on the door, he spiraled and crashed his truck into the back of an eighteen-wheeler. And then my ex cheated on me when I got a job here and told me the girl he cheated on me with was pregnant. Oh, and that as soon as he landed back home he was proposing to her."

"What the fuck," I say, completely dumbfounded as my fork clatters inside the bowl and I quickly pick it back up.

"I know. My mom likes my ex like he's her own and never fails to mention it to me when she sees him around town. She thinks I should give him another chance."

My forks clanks on the bowl-plate again from complete horror and disgust. "I–I have half a mind to fly to...wait, where are you from?"

"Charleston," she tells me.

"Right. I have half a mind to fly to Charleston and give your mom a piece of my mind."

Sarah stabs her pasta and toppings, which I imagine is how she reacts when her mom calls. "She is a hard-headed woman. I haven't talked with her since the day you came to my office."

"What a damper to your good mood." I deadpan.

She snorts into her glass of water. "You could say that."

"So back to our story. What is the plan?"

We both finish our meals in companionable silence and then Sarah turns in her seat to give me her full attention. "Are you a farmer's market kind of guy?"

"Can't say that I even know where one is around here."

"Okay, same. I was just trying to make it cute." She tucks her leg under her and my eyes track the movement of her sweatshirt rising up on her legs. "What about making it fitness related?"

"We can do that. I usually do Pilates a few times a week and throw in a run every now and then."

"Pilates?"

"Yeah. Do you have any complaints?" I ask with a teasing tone in my voice.

"None. Okay, we'll say we kept running the same trails and you decided to man up and ask me to run with you one day."

"Man up?" I ask with a smile threatening to break through.

"That's what I said," Sarah teases and scoots around in her seat. "And then you were captivated by my charm and sweat and asked me out the next time we ran into each other."

I snort and gently boop her on the nose before getting up to take our dishes to the dishwasher. I put the leftovers in a container and set the pot and pan in the sink to soak.

"Do you need any help?" Sarah asks as she stands up from the table.

"Nope. Go sit your cute butt on the couch."

"Fine," she says with a huff. "But just so you know, I hate being told what to do. I'm only doing it because I've been dying to plop on your couch."

I shake my head with a smile and watch as her ass sways on the way to the couch. Thank goodness doing the dishes will allow time for Little Riley to calm down. I watch as Sasha makes her way to the redheaded beauty on my couch and drops in her lap. Traitor. At least Pixie is more wary of her so I don't have to worry about her feline betrayal.

"So you help him get the puck into the goal?"

I pulled up an older hockey game to teach Sarah about the sport. She's picked up on it fairly quickly and I like that she's not blowing smoke up my ass by feigning interest.

"Mm-hmm," I try to keep my focus on the game and off of her. But I like watching her face when something happens. The genuine excitement lifts her eyes and cheeks as she smiles bigger than I thought possible.

"I thought football was a violent sport," she observes as a guy is slammed into the boards.

"Please. Like they could take a hit like we can."

Both sports are equally as tough. But hockey is a lot more dangerous than football. All it would take is a skate going into something it shouldn't and unfortunately it's game over for us.

Sarah turns her attention to me. "Have you broken your nose?"

"Once in high school and then once my first game with Columbus."

"Any other injuries I should know about?"

"You can do a thorough search of my body if you really want to find out." The last word just leaves my mouth when a pillow crashes into my face. My laugh travels up my throat and out into the open. I pull the pillow from my face and come face-to-face with a scowling Sarah. Clearing my throat and tossing the pillow to the side, I lose the remnants of my laughter. "Any other injuries? Well, besides my broken leg when I was a kid and the broken nose, no other injuries that I know of."

Sarah narrows her eyes at me and turns back to the old game. We sit in comfortable silence through the rest of the game. She asks me necessary questions about how my position works, subs, face offs, penalty boxes, and hat tricks. We watch one more game until I see her start to fade.

I turn off the TV and stand up, holding my hand out to her. "Let's go sleepy-head."

She looks at my hand like it's covered in needles before placing hers in mine. I pull her up and send her off to my room. I finish up the closing down of my living room and kitchen, feeding the cats, and when I've done everything as thoroughly as I can, I realize I can no longer avoid my room. Shaking out my hands, I walk towards my bedroom. I've never had anyone stay the night who wasn't one of my teammates when they decided to crash. But they slept on the couch and my worry was non-existent with them. So having Sarah in my room, sharing a bed with her, freaks me out.

I shut off the last light and stroll into my bedroom as carefree as possible. My steps falter when I see her tucked in on the free side of my bed. I tell myself to not think of it as her side of the bed. But it's hard when I see Sasha once again cuddled in the crook of Sarah's arm as the blue light from her phone illuminates her face.

"If I were a jealous man, I'd say something about my cat velcroing herself to you." I tell her as I close the door to a crack.

Sarah shifts her eyes to me and smirks as she leans down to kiss Sasha on the head and pull her closer. "Good to know your masculinity is firmly intact."

I pull my shirt off and exaggerate the stretch of my body. When it's off my body I toss the fabric at her head and head into the bathroom to brush my teeth and empty my bladder.

As I crawl into bed, I try to pay attention to if she's nervous. Either Sarah has an incredible poker face or she's completely unaffected.

"Riley, your tenseness is clashing with my aura. Relax," she tells me as she continues to scroll but I stay plastered to the edge of the mattress. "Have you never shared a bed with a woman?"

I brush her off and scoff at her insinuation while I fluff my pillow.

She lets out a breath and I hear the tapping on her phone from her manicure. "Fine. Walk me through your game day routine."

"What do you know about game day routines?" I ask and turn my head towards her although the pillows we're both lying on blocks half of her beautiful face.

"Are you forgetting what I do for work?" She asks and I hear the quiet thump of her phone being set on the night-stand next to her.

I scoot more onto the bed and slide down into the covers more before placing my hands behind my head. "Silly me."

"So, your routine. Spill it."

I feel the bed shift as Sarah turns on her side towards me. Sasha stretches out and I give the cat a lethal scowl earning a snort from the beauty next to me.

"Let's see...I usually do a light yoga sequence to stretch my body, drink a protein smoothie, play with my cats, and yeah that's it." I finish quickly.

"You're lying," Sarah calls me out. "What else?"

I cover my face with my hands and groan into them.

Sarah pulls my hands away from my face and I feel Sasha run across my legs and jump off the bed with a *thud*. "Tell me."

"My mom's favorite singer was Faith Hill. So every game day, I pull up one of her albums and blast it through either the speakers here or if we're traveling, my headphones. It's silly and my parents have been gone for more than half my life. But it makes me feel closer to her somehow." I avoid looking at Sarah as a light sheen of tears forms in my eyes.

No one's ever asked me why Faith Hill is who I listen to. I figured most don't care for sob stories. But being able to tell Sarah is freeing.

"It's not silly, Riley," she starts, voice soft. "I think missing someone and loving them unconditionally isn't something you can just stop. Time is a bitch at best but what keeps the people we love alive is the memories we have with them."

I swallow hard and blink my eyes fast to push away the tears. I don't know what to say to Sarah. Because her saying those things validated every feeling I've felt since my parents have been gone.

The bed shifts again as Sarah moves closer. "When my ex came to see me, I finally let go of the breath I had been holding onto since we went long-distance. I felt I was always floating outside of my body. And when he showed up to my house, it was like our time had finally come. This was the moment that I had been waiting for. But that relief was cut short when he dropped the bomb on me. And I decided then and there that I would never love someone so freely like that again. So you are lucky that the love you still feel for your parents is so strong. Because not every kid gets to have that with their parents without conditions."

"What a pair we are. The boy who loves freely and the girl who guards it."

"That's not a bad thing. And I *can* love. I love my best friends. I love my job. I love Cincinnati..." Sarah lists and falls on her back to look up at the ceiling. "But something about loving someone in the eternal sense again scares the shit out of me." The last few words come out as a whisper. "I realized that I needed to love myself in ways that neither my ex nor my parents ever could. What I was doing was always living up to their expectations, their set rules. Then when I was finally miles away from home I realized that love from them was suffocating me. It's when I was finally here that I concluded that I actually don't know what love is and that I won't love someone until I can finally love myself the way I deserve."

I turn my head and see her blinking back her own tears. Holding my arm up, she takes the silent invitation and scoots closer, molding her body to my side. Her body tenses, movements choppy and body tense, until she lays her arm over my stomach and rests her head fully on my shoulder. Sarah's leg soon follows as she throws it over my own. Another part of my pre-game routine I failed to tell her is that sex is off the table. The sexual frustration mixed with the adrenaline from the upcoming game fuels me to where after the game is when I need to blow off steam. So to have her curves molding to my angles is a battle I never thought I'd have to fight.

The tips of Sarah's fingers trace over a spot on my chest and I sense her wanting to say something. "I was diagnosed as manic depressive last year. Bipolar as most people know it as. My therapist seems to think it's PTSD brought on by my need to always be perfect and fear of failure." I feel wetness on my chest from what I'm assuming are her tears and run my hand up and down her back. "Well, I did fail. And on top of that it brought out OCD tendencies. I'd wake up from nightmares screaming and in a cold sweat. My ex told me to get over it. Like it was so easy."

"So you two never lived together?" I ask softly. Hearing that she's been suffering and with no support makes me want to rip her ex to shreds.

"We had the occasional sleepover and that's how he discovered my nightmares."

What idiot makes someone feel bad for something they can't control when unconscious? I know after my parents died, I couldn't sleep for months. And as a child I chose not to be a burden to Momma and Pops for taking care of me. But Sarah, the man she was dating, made her out to be an inconvenience.

"If a nightmare happens and you're with me, I promise to let you know you're safe." Her arm tightens around my waist. "You're safe with me, Sarah."

I continue to run my hand up and down her back and when her body loses the last of the tension she was carrying, I sense her deep breathing as she slowly falls asleep. Her warm vanilla scent surrounds us and I soak it in. I throw my other arm out and turn the side light off. Kissing Sarah on the top of her head I stare up at the ceiling until sleep takes me.

15

SARAH

I wake up hot. No. Scratch that. I wake up sweating. Riley's body melts into mine. Our bodies are flush. One of our hands are intertwined and his other hand curves around my midsection as if he's afraid I'll fall off the bed despite us both curled in the middle. No inch of space left untouched. His breathing is still deep and steady and I do my best to not alert him that I'm awake.

I need to reinforce, to not only him, but to myself that this thing between us is fake. But last night threw me for a loop. Him telling me his pre-game routine and how he carries his mom with him. To me telling him about how love will never be in the cards for me. It shifted. We shifted and I need us to straighten back up.

"Why are you thinking so loud?" Riley's rough morning voice startles me.

I start to move, but he tightens his hold on me. I'm about to answer his rhetorical question when I feel his impressive morning wood wedged between my cheeks. My nipples tighten and my breath stutters. I know Riley can sense the change in me if evident by the small shift in his hips.

"Good morning," I say and try not to move my body when I speak. In order for us to adhere to the fake part of our relationship, sex needs to not be the main focus. We already know we're good at that part.

"How did you sleep?" Riley asks.

"Surpris–" my voice is cut off when his hand that's wrapped around my middle slides under my tank. His fingers lightly trail up my torso and to my pointed nipple.

"What was that?" He asks as he circles the pointed tip.

"We should stop," I say weakly as I push my chest into his hand.

"We won't go any further than this. But this is for you." He tells me, voice thick as he diverts his hand to the waistband of my pajama shorts. "I'll stop if you want me to."

"Don't stop," I breathe out.

I'm already wet and Riley meets no resistance as he moves a finger over my clit and down to my entrance. I roll my hips and his finger slips easily inside of me giving him my answer. "Fuck, baby you're soaked. Keep talking or I'll stop."

Riley nibbles on my earlobe causing a stuttered breath to spill free. "I slept surprisingly well. But you do snore." That earns a pinch to my clit. "Oh, fuck."

"What else? What are you excited to see?" Riley asks as he continues to bring me to the edge. He adds another finger to my entrance and curls them as he circles my clit with his thumb.

"I...hockey, ice." He expects me to form a complete thought?

"What else and I'll let you come," he licks a trail from the crease in my neck and dips into my ear. His fingers massage my inner walls. Never moving any faster than a leisurely pace. He groans when I clench around his fingers.

"You playing," I say as a sheen of sweat forms on my forehead.

"That's what I like to hear. Now come for me Sarah." Riley orders as he pumps his fingers in and out of my pussy and rolls my nipple between his thumb and pointer finger. My body tightens and with the curl of his fingers I let go. Moaning his name as my orgasm flows through my body. Riley works me through my climax and slows down the thrusting of his fingers. When the last of my orgasm fades he pulls his hands from the waistband of my shorts and kisses the side of my head before rolling out of the bed and into the bathroom.

Huh. I try not to think too much about what just happened. Or what didn't happen. Namely Riley not getting his finish. So I fall back on the mattress and stare up at the ceiling and listen to the faint sound of the shower running through the closed bathroom door. Is he taking care of himself? If so, why not let me do it for him? Maybe this is his way of putting that line back in place? But, if so, then he wouldn't have touched me to begin with. Sasha jumps up on the bed and finds her spot by laying right on top of me. Her presence is a welcome distraction to what may or may not be happening mere feet away from me.

"At least you like me," I tell her as I give her some head scratches. The vibrations of her purring soothes the dark thoughts that tend to sneak in my mind uninvited. I won't call him a trigger, but Riley walking away brought those unwanted thoughts in.

It's a weird thing. Depression. It sneaks in when you least expect it to. But I never considered myself to be depressed. Because what's so bad in my life that my mind went on shutdown mode? I mean besides the baseball fail-ure, the cheating boyfriend, and nonchalant mom. Really, what is so wrong that the waves of sadness wash over me at unexpected moments? I could be celebrating huge contracts or my clients teams winning the big game. But out of nowhere, that dark, heavy cloud of feelings will come and crush whatever strides I've made to not be sucked back in.

I have Kamryn to thank for pushing me to finally talk to someone about my buried feelings. I remember that day last year so clearly. Sitting at a bar with my friends and realizing that we were missing a crucial part of our group. That was a low point for me. It was the point where I was wondering *why* and *what's the point* every single day. Most days I woke up crying and then pasting on the happy-go-lucky face to everyone else. It was the need to no longer being afraid to fail that I finally started making bigger strides at work. But the cycle would continue to repeat itself until Kam told me she didn't want to lose me. The self-deprecating jokes and focus on the past were what finally clued her into knowing that I wasn't fine.

Yet there was never a day when I told myself I was done with life. I was just so tired. I was tired of feeling like I wasn't succeeding as fast as my friends. I was tired of feeling left behind. I was tired of feeling stuck in the past with no way forward. But I would never and could never tell my friends that. They have been through too much for me to just dump on them. And being a burden to someone is the last thing I want.

The door to the bathroom opens and I quickly wipe the tears off my face and go back to petting Sasha.

"What time do you have to be at the arena?" I ask and hope that my voice doesn't hold any of the leftover emotion.

I hear a drawer open and look over to see Riley with his back to me, riffling through it and pulling out some briefs. He drops his towel and I get a good look at his glutes as he pulls the briefs on. Picking up the towel off the floor, he turns and runs it over his hair.

I give him a pointed look and watch as his face transforms. That damn mask I saw the first time we officially met. What happened to the man who gave me an orgasm less than twenty minutes ago to the man standing in front of me in just his briefs?

"I don't have to be there for another few hours." He finally responds and tosses his towel into the hamper that's in the corner of his room. "I'm gonna make some breakfast. Do you want any?"

"Just coffee," I tell him.

Riley just nods before snagging his phone off the charger and heading out of the room with Pixie following close at his heels. I shouldn't worry too much about his sullen mood, right? It is a little odd he's not as chatty since that's been his M.O. since we met. Maybe this is also part of his pre-game routine that he left out.

I listen to him clanking around in the kitchen as the murmuring from the TV floats this way. Should I get up and shower? Join him in the kitchen? That's what a girlfriend would do. But we're not real. This could just be another way that I'm reinforcing it into my brain.

Snagging my phone off the nightstand next to me, I open it to multiple texts from my girls.

Kamryn: Mason has extra tickets to today's home opener. Anyone wanna go with us?

Emmy-Lou: Sure. I still know absolutely nothing about football. But Adam is working and Dylan is with his grandparents.

Jax: If I can finish this brand project, count me in.

Kamryn: Sarah?

Emmy-Lou: Hello….!

Jax: Maybe she's still sleeping?

Kamryn: She's a machine. She never sleeps.

Kamryn: If you don't respond in the next ten minutes I'm driving over to your house.

I look at when she sent the message and realize it's been ten minutes. I scramble to reply.

Me: I'm not home.

Emmy-Lou: This is why we should share our locations.

Kamryn: Where are you?

Me: Columbus. Riley has his first preseason game.

Jax: And where exactly are you staying?

Me: In Columbus.

Emmy-Lou: Don't make us repeat Jax's question.

Me: At his condo. Bye!

I turn my phone on silent, kiss Sasha on the head, and head into his spa-like bathroom. I'm not sure why I'm antsy for this day. It's not like I haven't been to the games of my clients. *Yeah, but you've never fake dated any of them.* Conscience is a bitch. I hop in the shower. Taking care to make sure my hair doesn't get wet. But what surprises me is seeing some of the products I use at home lining a shelf. Riley was in my shower for barely five minutes. No way he cataloged everything that quickly. *Don't read into it.* I go about washing my face and body, then plucking a towel off the rack and wrapping it around my body.

My toiletries are on a corner of the bathroom vanity so I go about getting somewhat ready: brushing my teeth, doing my skincare, brushing out my hair, and rubbing lotion all over my body. I come out of the bathroom to a Columbus Blue Jays tunic type of jersey shirt/dress laying on the bed. Looking towards the door, I expect Riley to be leaning against it, but I still hear him puttering around in the kitchen. Since the game isn't for another few hours I throw on another lounge set I have in my bag and head out into the kitchen.

Riley is at the stove manning breakfast with Pixie watching him from the kitchen island. My steps are quiet, but that could be because he has the TV on. So when I slide up behind him he jolts a little before relaxing and I'll blame it on my hands being cold despite roasting my body in the shower.

"Thank you." I tell him before placing a kiss on his back and walking over to sit on a barstool.

I watch his back flex as he plates the food and slides one in front of me. I quirk an eyebrow at him as this is the opposite of what I'd eat on the weekends.

"Humor me. Because coffee is not a meal and it's going to be a long day."

I take the offered fork and we eat in comfortable silence. When all of our food is gone, I lean back on the chair and have a stare-off with Pixie. "I don't think she likes me very much."

Riley snorts into his water glass. "She's just protective and wary of other people."

"Not like Sasha," I point out.

"I call her my Little Walmart Greeter. She knows no fear."

"So I guess we should talk about the game?"

"Yeah. I put your name down under me. So you'll be escorted to the friends & family box after you head to will-call."

"What? Riley you don't need to do that," I protest. I assumed I'd be sitting on the floor. But that's what happens when we make assumptions.

"My Momma and Pops would whoop me if I didn't have you sit with them."

"Excuse me?"

His wide ocean blue eyes meet mine before instantly shooting up to the ceiling. "Huh...did I not mention my parents coming to the game?"

"No. That was conveniently left out."

It's not that I'm against meeting a boyfriend's parents. But, again, to not only remind myself, we're not dating. And me meeting his parents is serious business.

"Look, I know this thing between us has an expiration date. But you can't expect to never meet my parents. Whether you stayed as my publicist or as my fake girlfriend, it was going to happen," he tells me and that explanation slowly brings me back down to earth as if he was thinking of us as more than what we're contractually stated. Which he's right. I would have to meet his parents. I've met my other clients' parents. But under this circumstance is not how I wanted that to happen.

"I don't want people in your life to get hurt," I confess. "That includes you."

"Hey," he starts and turns me on the barstool, putting my legs between his spread ones. "I am going to be fine. I know what this is and I know what this isn't. You don't have to worry. We just need to keep up for public appearance sake."

"Okay. So touchy-feely in public and distant behind closed doors. Got it."

Riley nods and stands up from his stool, placing a kiss on the top of my head and taking our plates to the sink. When he does things like that, it makes me wonder if he knows the rules that are in place. Because while his words say one thing his actions say something completely different.

I bring my laptop to the bar and get to work on emailing brands for Eli. While he may not love being in front of a camera, the camera loves him. I also send him some of the pictures the photographer sent over from his shoot. With his off season looming closer and closer, I do want him to take a break from the spotlight. But that doesn't mean I stop working for him.

Me: Tell your mom and sister I miss them.

Nate: Mom wants to have dinner when she's in town.

Me: Just let me know when.

Most publicists and agents are against mixing business with pleasure. But I find in doing that my working relationship with my clients gets stronger.

"Hey, Riley, did you get a new agent?" I ask him without looking up from my screen.

"That's what I've been forgetting. No. Also none have been the right fit for me."

I look up at him and see his furrowed brow. What I'm beginning to slowly learn about Riley is that he wants specific people on his team.

"Let me see if Mason's agent is looking for another athlete. Is that okay?"

"Really? I mean, his agent is legendary." He looks like a kid in a candy shop at the suggestion of Mason's agent possibly representing him.

"Yeah," I say with a smile. "I can reach out to him next week. But for now you're stuck with me."

He shuts the water off and dries his hands on the towel that's hanging on the stove. "It's better than being agent-less and not knowing if the front office is making moves without me knowing would be terrifying. I could be jobless right now and not know it."

I pick up my phone and look back at Riley. "Well I haven't gotten any ESPN notifications, so you're good for now," I joke.

"Funny," he volleys back and looks at the time on his watch. "I have to get ready to head out. Do you need the address?"

I shake my head slowly. "I can just look it up."

He nods and heads to his room to get ready. I turn my attention back to my laptop. With Mason coming to the end of his career, Nate in the playoffs, and Marcus in preseason training, my calendar is so far organized. Despite them all playing around the same months, I still have a moment to breathe. So maybe I should pick up a short-term hobby? It couldn't hurt. I get to looking up workout classes in Cincinnati when Riley walks out of his room with a duffel in his hand. He strolls over to where I'm still camped out on my barstool and looks over my shoulder.

"Nosey much?" I ask and close my laptop a little.

Riley whistles nonchalantly on the way to the refrigerator, the sound of it opening breaks up the sound of my heart beating louder than I thought possible. I must be out of shape. *You're sitting down.* I shut my inner voice down and watch as Riley grabs an electrolyte drink from the fridge and turns to meet my expectant stare.

"So, I'll see you after the game?"

"Yep," I say, popping the *p* in a way to hopefully cover up the breathiness in my voice.

What's the protocol? We just stated that in private we keep our distance. But why does it feel like second nature to give him a hug and kiss goodbye? It seems Riley is having the same mental war but decides nothing is better.

"Okay. Well I'll see you later." Riley says and walks back over to his discarded duffle bag.

"Score a touchdown." I joke and turn back to my laptop with a smile on my face.

Riley leaves with a chuckle and the door closing, leaving me with his cats, sends my heart into my throat. I can do this. I can get through six months of being his fake girl-friend and come out completely unscathed. I can play the doting girlfriend and not get attached. I. Can. Do. This.

16

RILEY

"Is that too tight?" Evan, the athletic trainer, asks while taping up my ankle.

I flex my foot and roll my ankle around. "Nope. It's good."

He finishes wrapping and hops up from his spot.

"Thank you." I tell him and head back over to my locker. Locker is stretching it. It's more of a small open coat closet. I dress out and put on my skates, checking my phone before I lace up and head out to the rink for warm-ups.

Even though this is a preseason game, the fans usually come out in massive groups to watch us play. It's always better this way. Seeing the fans get pumped for hockey. They love it just as much as we do. And that always energizes us to play better.

I join the guys on the ice and drop down to do my stretches. Even though we do these stretches daily, my muscles still pull tight and I groan when I stretch out my groin and hamstrings.

"Girlfriend here?" Max asks.

"What?" Logan and Noah ask at the same time.

I curse Max in my head for ousting me. "She should be here soon and she'll be sitting with Momma and Pops," I move into a hamstring stretch but don't hear anything from them. "What!?" I ask when I notice them looking at me.

"Back it up. Girlfriend? How is it that Max knows but we don't?" Noah questions.

"I didn't tell him. How do you know?" I point my question to Max.

"My cousin works as a valet at Hotel LaRoux and saw you with her in the parking lot. He wasn't sure since you never said anything. But this just confirmed it."

If I had my phone, I'd send a quick text to Sarah that we've been spotted. "Yes, she's my girlfriend. No, you don't know her. And no, she doesn't have any siblings."

Logan drops down into the splits. As our goalie he needs to be more limber than the rest of us. "She's meeting the fam already. That's a pretty big step."

"Is that wrong? I've never had a girlfriend during the season, so I have no clue how to navigate it." Spilling my guts on the ice before a game, definitely isn't the smartest move. But I'm not lying when I say that I've never dated anyone during the season. So navigating when to meet the parents is new territory for me.

"Well," Max starts. "My older sister hid her now husband when they were dating for months. I mean, it helped as she was out of state for college. So coming home to introduce him to us wasn't exactly convenient."

"Huh," I start as I gather the rest of my thoughts. "Well, I think she can handle herself."

At least I hope she can. Because if it were me and I had to unexpectedly meet my fake girlfriend's parents, I'd probably freeze like a deer in headlights. But Sarah is tough. She has to be for the job she's in. And that's exactly like what our relationship is. A job. Suddenly the idea of us faking doesn't seem so appealing with the way I think about it. It's clinical and straightforward. Two things I never would have classified myself as.

The guys and I finish up our stretches and jump in with the rest of the team to do light shooting and defensive drills. After a while, our coach whistles for us to head back to the locker room to dress out for the game. Coach gives us a pep talk. If "Don't get your asses kicked" constitutes as a pep talk, then I guess that's it. When we're dressed out, we all waddle back out to the ice for our roster call.

I'm usually able to block out the noise during this time. Sometimes the crowd calling out or heckling us ruins my focus. But not this time. Last season I probably deserved the call out. This season not so much. The roar of the crowd fuels me and I take a moment to let my eyes wander over those in the crowd.

Noah taps me on the helmet before skating over to Max and doing the same. He skates to center ice and readies for the face off. In the blink of an eye, his persona changes from the Noah I know off the ice and the Noah on the ice. He's one of the best centers I've worked with and he's quick. Quicker than your average hockey player. My adrenaline is pumping through my veins and it's as if the game starts so fast that by the time I breathe, we're up 1 goal.

My line retires for a couple of plays before we're switching back out in the second period. Florida came out with a fire lit under their asses. Even with this being a preseason game, we've been fighting to gain possession more than we've needed to. Noah manages to get control of the puck before he drives down the ice and with a flick of his wrist, the puck sails into the back of the net.

"GOOD GAME TONIGHT, GUYS," Anderson says from the middle of the locker room. "We have some things to work on, but for the most part we're just about regular season ready."

We all pound our sticks on the locker room floor and cheer.

"Settle down, settle down. Next preseason game is in three days so no practice tomorrow. But, I want you all to do something light to move your bodies. Sitting around and letting yourself get sore doesn't do any of us any favor. Now hit the showers."

We all move at once. I set my stick in my locker and unlace my skates to the chatter of Max and Noah making plans.

"Are you sure we can't convince you to come out with us?" Noah asks.

I groan involuntarily when I tug my jersey and pads off. "Positive. I've got a girl and parents to get to."

I walk towards the shower with their teasing quips in the background. Calling Sarah my girl makes the fake feel not so fake. But it needs to be. It's fake. We are fake. As much as I drill it into my head, I can't help but want to screw the rule we set in place. Because every touch, every glance, and every moment spent together blurs the fake to where it feels real. I hurry through my shower, but make sure I'm extra clean and once I'm dry, I throw on some street clothes of black jeans, a gray hoodie, and some black Timberland boots.

"I'm out." I say to the guys after I roughly towel dry my

hair. Tossing the towel into the hamper, I sling my duffel bag over my shoulder and make my way to the box seats.

Look, I'm nervous. I know I shouldn't be. I'm just going to meet my fake girlfriend who's been hanging out with my parents for the last few hours. *Shit!* I speed walk down the hall and head towards the elevator. I mash the button several times, even knowing that it won't get here faster. As soon as the car lands and opens, I press the number '3' and close the doors. My fingers tap in rapid succession against my thigh as the car swiftly takes me to the top floor.

I exit to the right and follow the murmur of animated conversation and muffled laughter until I reach the family box. I was hoping that most of the other WAGS would be gone, but it seems they're all waiting around as well.

"Honey," I hear a familiar voice callout. I see Momma waving her hand and make my way to them. My steps falter when I see Sarah donned in the shirt I purchased for her with thigh high black boots and a three-inch heel.

"Good game, Riley," Pops says with a kiss to the top of my head.

"Thanks, Pops. Hi, Momma." I say, and greet her with a kiss to her cheek.

"The team is looking great," Momma tells me when she steps back. Sarah points to the chair behind her and I set my duffel next to her purse.

I nod in agreement. "We have some things to work on. But overall I think this is going to be a good season." I turn to the spitfire next to me and focus on the twinkle in her eyes. "Hi, baby."

A flush comes to her cheeks as she meets my gaze. "Hi."

I snort and wrap my arm around her shoulders. My lips fall to her temple and my heart slows down with her back in my arms. I angle my head to speak low into her ear. "You look hot as hell. And the boots? God damn, baby. I almost had to walk back out into the hallway."

I hear her breath hitch and she wraps an arm around my waist and slides her free hand into the front pocket of my hoodie. A throat clearing pulls us out of our small bubble.

"Sorry," I say, facing my parents. "I see you three have already met." I slide my hand into my hoodie pocket and hook a finger around one of Sarah's.

"Mm hmm. Your Momma showed me all sorts of pictures of you as a kid." Sarah speaks up and traces the palm of my hand with her fingers sending shivers down my spine.

I narrow my eyes at her and turn my attention to my parents who are wearing twin amused faces. "Did you two see Mischa and the kids?"

"Yes. We're having them over for dinner tonight. So we should probably head out soon," Momma looks at Pops and I know she's silently warning him that they can't stay for more than five minutes. Pops is a certified yapper once he gets warmed up.

He lets out a sigh. "Momma's right. Sarah, it was so lovely meeting you," he tells her.

She untangles herself from my embrace and moves to hug him. "It was so amazing to meet you, Dean."

"Get this boy out of his shell, would you?"

"Oh, please. I can never get him to stop talking," Sarah retorts.

Pops whispers something to her that has her looking at me in confusion. Her smile dims just slightly as she nods her head and Pops kisses her on the cheek.

Sarah steps over to Momma. "Cassie, you are an actual doll."

"Come over to the house and we'll bake one day."

"You've got yourself a deal," Sarah says, and moves in to hug Momma.

I'm a pool of emotion that I'm not sure which to pick out. Sarah and my parents bonding that fast during the game is not something I expected. Maybe I should have let my parents know that the relationship I'm in is fake. Because knowing them, even if I introduced her as a friend, they'd still play matchmaker. My parents finally say goodbye to me and after an extended goodbye to a few of the other parents in the box, they're finally out of the door.

"I thought you were nervous to meet them?"

Sarah wraps her arms back around my waist like it's the most natural thing in the world for her to do. And to the others still lingering in the family box, it is. "I was. First off, you should've shown me a picture of your parents so I knew what they looked like."

"I thought about that as we were warming up. And by then it was too late," I start and move a piece of hair out of her face and tuck it behind her ear. "But it seems they found you regardless."

"They did and I like them a lot. Which scares me," she admits and rests her chin on my chest.

"It will be fine." I reassure her and kiss her on the tip of her nose. I look around the box and realize it's mostly cleared out. "Let's get out of here."

I move around her and grab my duffel and hand Sarah her purse.

"So I think I finally have a grip on hockey." She says, taking my offered hand as we walk out into the hallway.

"Oh yeah?" I ask and press the door for the elevator. "Was I in the sin-bin?"

"I said *think*, smartass. I still have a long way to go in

terms of being fluent. But I'm hoping that sitting with your parents will help me learn the sport better."

The elevator opens and we file inside. Sarah takes one side and I take the other after pressing the button for the ground floor. I finally get to take a look at her without my parents in the vicinity. Starting at her thigh high black stiletto boots, to the Blue Jays shirt dress that stops a couple of inches above her boots, and to the black purse that hangs off her shoulder and her softly curled hair. She plays the role of a WAG perfectly. And I thank divine intervention that the guys weren't up in the box with me.

"I wanna take you somewhere," I tell her as the elevator descends to the ground floor.

"Do I need to change?"

"Nope. But we are going to drop your car off at my apartment." I push off the wall and hold my hand out to her as the doors open. Sarah takes my offering and weaves her fingers in between mine like she's done it for months. Whether it's for anyone from the game who's still lingering or if holding my hand is as natural as breathing, I don't question it. Turns out our PDA is more for the lingering team and puck bunnies. Murmurs follow us as we walk out to the parking lot and I have no doubt a picture of us will end up online.

"Where's your car?" I ask Sarah as we near mine in the lot.

"About that. I maybe, kind of, sort of Uber'ed here." She tells me and swings our arms back and forth.

"Oh, did you now?"

"Uh huh. How weird would it look if we drove home separately? I just saved us both the rumors."

We make it to my car and I open the door for her. "Get in ya goof."

She sneaks a kiss on my lips before she steps onto the running boards and I smack her on the butt as she's sliding in. I leave her with a parting wink and head around to the back to toss my duffle bag in. I slide in the driver's seat and start up my car. The sun is just setting as I peel out of the parking lot and head east towards the lake.

About halfway through the drive, we stop and pick up chopped salads before continuing on our trek.

"Favorite food?" I ask, when I get off on the exit towards the lake.

"Easy. French fries," Sarah answers with no hesitation.

I quickly look over at her and turn back to the road with a smile on my face. "Okay. What kind of french fries?"

"Brace yourself, Riley. Because this is one of my favorite topics."

I shrug my shoulders and roll my head around like I'm preparing to head into a boxing ring. "Alright I'm ready," I say through our mutual laughter.

"I love bar fries. You know the ones with the sort of flaky outside? I love those the most. Waffle fries hold a lot of dip, so I don't count those out. A crinkle cut fry that's crispy on the outside and fluffy on the inside is so good," she stops when she sees me looking at her for the tenth time in the last four minutes of her rambling. "What?"

"Oh, nothing. It's just nice to find you have flaws," I state jokingly.

"Take that back!" She lightly swats at me.

"Look, I'm not judging. But I think it's cute."

"Cute," she scoffs. "So, I like french fries. I'm sure you like something that's at an almost unhealthy level."

I think hard about something that isn't hockey related. "Hmm. Do cats count?"

"Riley, I've seen that cat room. So I know your obsession is strong. But no. That doesn't count."

I flip the lever for the turn signal and pull into the lakes parking lot. Several other cars are parked out here so I'm glad I wasn't the only one with this idea. I find a spot that's got the best view of the horizon and shift the car into park.

"Hmm. I can't say I have any unhealthy obsession like you do. Although, fries, I could obsess over them with you."

"Paws off, buddy," she jokes and dishes out our food. "What are we doing here anyways?"

"Have you ever seen the Northern Lights?" I ask and shake my salad container to distribute the dressing evenly.

"No," she sighs wistfully and then shakes up her own salad container. "But it's always been a bucket list goal of mine to cross off."

"Well, you're in luck. Reports are saying that we'll be able to see them."

"Really?" Her face lights up as if I told her I was bringing the moon to her.

"Yeah. I figured it would be something fun to do. And since we're friends...?" I trail off and look at her.

"Yeah, we're friends." She says with less conviction.

"Perfect. Since we're friends, I figured this would be a fun thing to see together."

"Touché." She starts and opens up her salad.

We eat in companionable silence with the windows partly rolled down to let the early October breeze float through the car. I smile as I watch kids running back and forth along the lakeshore. A pang of jealousy hits as I realize my childhood was stripped away the night I lost my parents. I'm sure I don't laugh as freely as I used to. In fact, I can't remember the last time I felt free. Shaking my head, I swiftly finish the rest of my food and place my empty container in the plastic bag it came in. Sarah follows suit not long after.

My dour mood is thick in the car and I hate it. I continue looking out at the water, adapting my breathing techniques from the doctors.

"Riley?" Sarah asks quietly. "What's wrong?"

"I don't know. I was just watching those kids running and it hit me that I didn't get that as a kid." My honesty hits her.

Sarah shuffles around in her seat until her boots are off and she's turned towards me with her legs crossed. "Tell me more about your parents."

"Dad was a history teacher at the local high school. It was his favorite thing to talk about, next to hockey and my mom. But history was his number one and his dream was to eventually teach at the local university. That's how much he loved history and he wanted a bigger way to spread that love. My mom owned a yoga studio and it came in really handy for her when I started playing hockey. Dad was always chewing gum to try and quit smoking and mom always smelled of fresh roses and clean laundry. Those were three of my favorite scents and I–I can't remember the last time I had those scents hit my senses." My brow furrows when I realize it's been over a decade since I had them around. "I just miss them. Their warmth, their presence, the way they made everyday an adventure. Whether it was drop-offs at school or heading to hockey practice. I'm always hit with the what-ifs when I wonder what my life would be like if my parents were still alive. But then I'd never have gotten to know Momma and Pops the way I have."

We sit in the front seats not saying a word. Because what is there to say?

"I was right last night," Sarah says from beside me. I look

over and see her observing me with her chin propped on her fist.

"About what?" Last night is a blur. And add on the game, I have no clear distinction about what we talked about.

"About love. The love you feel for your parents is evident in the way you memorialize them."

Sarah and I share a look. Whether it's about love, loss, or life, I feel she understands in a way no one else in my life does.

"You know I was wary about you being my publicist," I confess.

"Why? Afraid I'd throw myself at you? Or because I'm a woman."

I cringe. "A little bit of both. No offense."

"After being in this line of work for a while, I unfortunately got used to it. I mean, I shouldn't. The men who think I can't handle male athletes are the ones who are crying at the end of the day."

"You are quite the ballbuster," I joke.

"For a good reason," she defends.

I'm about to agree with her when we hear commotion outside. We both turn in that direction and my eyes grow wide while I hear a gasp from Sarah. The lights have appeared in the night sky and we both fumble to get out of the car for an unobstructed view. I've never seen anything like this. And the *oohs* and *aahs* from up and down the shore express the same sentiment. Sarah and I stand next to each other, leaning against the front of my car, as the lights flow in front of us. I peek over at her and see the most blissful look on her face since the first time we met. The colors lightly bounce off her face and her joy is this tangible thing that I want to hold onto forever.

"Bucket list item crossed off?" I ask while fully looking at her.

"Yeah," she sighs dreamily while still looking up at the lights. "I've never seen anything more beautiful."

"I have."

She turns to me and playfully rolls her eyes. But I don't miss the blush that rises to her cheeks. Sarah turns back to the lights and I don't miss the way she crosses her arms over her chest. It's then I realize she's only in her boots that she put on fast and her dress from the game.

"Do you want to go back in the car?" I ask.

"And see the lights through the window? No way," she protests. "I'm fine out here for a bit longer." She tells me and I don't miss her chattering teeth.

I shake my head and pull her in front of me and wrap my arms around her. Her body shakes from the chill and my body heat mixes for the first few seconds before she twines her hands around my arms.

"Better?" I ask when she's breathing steadier.

"Yeah. Thank you." Sarah tells me and rests her body back against me with her head falling back to my shoulder. Even in her heeled boots she barely comes to my chin and I like that I can dwarf her in size. It's like I can be her protector no matter what.

We stay like this, locked around each other watching the lights as they dance through the sky with cheerful laughter from kids still running along the shore. Soon, families disappear one by one until only us and a few couples are left. Exhaustion slams into me and I can't hold back the yawn that escapes from my throat.

"Are you ready to head back?" I ask.

I peek around and see her eyes at half-mast as well. "Yeah. Let's go." Sarah steps away from me and wanders to the passenger side. I follow closely behind and beat her to the door to open it for her. She gives me a tired smile, before climbing to her seat. I round the back of the car and see the last car pull out of the lot.

Today was a whirlwind. And as I drive home, I hope that coming out here tonight was another tick in the 'pro' column to why Sarah and I could be a good match. The adventure and ease at which we exist together is why the fake dating doesn't feel fake anymore.

17

SARAH

"Surprise!" and "Congratulations!" are thrown out when Kamryn and Mason walk into Sotto's that night. I rush to my bestie and hug her with all of my strength.

"I can't believe you two are finally engaged," I cry.

We all knew this was going to happen. The girls and I helped Mason set up his proposal at the house he recently bought. Not only was the house a surprise, because Kamryn is tough to get anything past, but the engagement was something that I predicted in college.

"You all are masters at keeping things from me," Kamryn points out. I know that's a subtle dig at the way Emily hid Adam.

"I thought we moved on from that?" I question quietly.

Emily and Adam hit a rough patch recently and have taken some time apart. It's been hard seeing her fall back into her shell, but I know for a fact they'll find their way back to one another. It's just that Emily needs to work through her own baggage before she finally hands herself over to him.

"Sorry. We have," Kamryn says. Mason comes over and I

give him a hug as well. They share a look that they seem to only know what that means and suddenly I'm nervous.

"What?"

"We know it's early." Mason starts and wraps his arm around Kamryn's waist. "But, we'd like, actually we'd love, for you to be the one to marry us."

"What?" I ask again as tears form.

"Sarah, you've been our number one champion for ten years. You're the only person we could think of to see us get our happily ever after."

"Yes. I would love to," I say through my tears before I'm engulfed in a hug from my friends.

"We'll talk about the date later. But you marrying us would mean the world to us." With a final hugging squeeze, they move on to celebrate with more friends and family.

I take a moment to compose myself before wandering over to the open bar and snag a glass of champagne.

"I see they asked you?" Emily asks as she slides next to me at the bar.

"You knew?"

"Of course I did. It was only right that you marry them off." She says with a smile that doesn't quite reach her eyes.

"Are you okay?"

She shakes her head and looks at me with glassy eyes. "No. But I will be."

Emily backs away from the bar and I watch as her retreating form is swallowed by Kamryn and Mason's guests. I feel for her. And while I understood her reason for breaking things off with Adam, I'd never seen her more alive than with him. Granted, I didn't know her during her James phase. But Emily blossomed during her time with Adam.

I watch on with a smile as Mason drags Kamryn to the makeshift dance floor. Which is really just the center of the basement space the restaurant set up for us. When I had my slip about Liam, it wasn't that I thought they should be together. Far from that. But more than that he should've still been alive. Do I think Kam and him were end game? No. I always knew her and Mason would end up together it was just a matter of how.

The harp from the speakers begins before the hauntingly beautiful voice of Florence Welch pours from the sound system. She sings about the sun, the moon, and the stars. And if that isn't a poetic representation of Kamryn and Mason's story, I have no clue what is.

"So I hear you're dating a hockey player." One of Mason's former teammates, Mac, says as he sidles up next to me.

I choke on my drink and wipe my chin with the back of my hand. Thank goodness for smudge proof liquid lipsticks. "Where did you hear that? Hi, Shannon."

"Hi, Sarah," she responds. "The way my nosey husband meant to start, was that there is a very cozy photo of the two of you floating around from seeing the Northern Lights."

"What?" I exclaim rather loudly and turn to the married couple.

Mac whips his phone out and shows me the picture. My mouth drops open. It's of us looking up at the sky. The colors dance over each of our faces. Riley's arms wrapped solidly around me with my hands curled around him. We look...NOPE! I can't even say it. I hand Mac his phone back and give a quick bye before heading to the enclosed patio. I pull out my phone and see texts from Jeff.

Jeff: *1 attached image*

Jeff: Anything you want to tell me now?

Me: Can we talk Monday?

Jeff: Sure.

I guzzle down the last of my champagne and open the next text from Riley. He's been on an away stretch for games these past couple of weeks, so I haven't seen him since that night. The space has been good for us. It's helped me get my head back on straight and I've managed to finagle us back to athlete and publicist. Out of sight and out of mind works better than I could have hoped.

Riley: At least we photograph well.

Me: Not the time for jokes.

Riley: I know. That's how I cope.

Me: Let me put on my publicist hat and I'll talk with you sometime next week.

I don't wait for Riley to respond before I turn my phone on airplane mode for the rest of the evening. Tonight is about love. And as I dance and drink while my best friends make-out all around the room, I don't think about the shit show that will be at work on Monday. I think about love.

"DATING?" Jeff booms.

I have never seen him angry. Okay, that's a lie. But it's never been towards me. So I sit on the chair in front of his desk as he paces back and forth, stomping like his feet are made of bricks.

"If it counts, it's fake."

He halts and turns his angry glare onto me. "Sarah, you

already have everything stacked against you in this line of work. What made you think that this was a smart plan?"

"I was thinking it was going to help him," I speak up.

Jeff quirks a bushy eyebrow at me. "Explain."

"It happened after that day trip to Columbus, for that camp he was doing?" I look at Jeff and he nods his head as if jogging his memory. "We went out for lunch and some fans recognized him. All of a sudden, a couple gossip blogs were running stories of us dating. I managed to kill any of the stories that were floating around, but..."

"Okay. I still don't see how that got you to here."

"Sponsors tend to dish out more money for teams and players who are responsible. With Riley looking not so responsible because of his last agent and publicist, we decided that if it looked like he was in a committed relationship, then the sponsorships would flow." I sit back in my chair with a huff.

"So you're doing it for money?"

"No. We're doing it so Riley doesn't get kicked off of the Blue Jays before he's well into his signing year. Jeff, his reputation was terrible. He had no sponsorships because his fuck-face agent and publicist were only in it for the free things he could get them. Now, his jersey sales are climbing through the roof and I have so many brands emailing me for a chance to work with him that I can barely keep up. Trust me when I say that this is for him."

I am passionate about my job. But I'm even more passionate about my clients thriving outside of their job as an athlete.

"You care about him. Don't you?"

"I care about all my clients. Don't turn this into something it isn't." *Thud, thud, thud*, goes my heart behind my ribcage. I'll admit that deep down I like spending time with

Riley. My first impression of him was based on the articles. But now that I've gotten to know him, he's so much more than that.

"Okay," Jeff says skeptically.

"Don't worry. Besides, I drew up a contract that our arrangement ends in April." The calendar faded to November in the blink of an eye. My heart thumps a steady beat at realizing we only have five months left of our arrangement.

Jeff gives me a look, but doesn't press any further. With my "dating" news out of the way, he loops me in on some new agents he's thinking of bringing on. He fills me in on what his daughter, Zoey, is up to as she prepares for her middle school choir concert and how Frankie is begging him to start baseball. And as I sit, watching him glow with pride, it makes me wonder if being hard to love and closing myself off from wanting love will stunt any personal growth I'm wanting to make.

I GLARE at my therapist from my seat on the couch. While I don't have the same one as Kamryn, they do work in the same building so we'll sometimes cross paths. But, luckily today is not one of those days.

"So you've talked about this," she checks her notes even though I know she knows his name, "this, Riley. Have you talked to him about your aversion to love?"

"No. Because this thing between us is fake."

"Was this your idea or his?" She asks me with raised eyebrows.

"It was mine. Why does that make a difference?"

"Why don't you tell me. There seems to be a lot of questions going back and forth between us. But have you told Riley your true aversion to love? Because despite the obvious reasons you two are tip-toeing around, whatever it is you're doing, he seems like he would be all in."

"I don't want to open myself up to love again, because that makes me too vulnerable. Opening up to love, means it would be so easy to get hurt again. And I don't think I can do that."

"Think or won't?"

"Ugh." I drop my head to the back of the couch and swallow hard. "Won't."

"Sarah," she starts and sets her iPad on the table in front of her. "Courage and joy are two of the most vulnerable things you can be. And you are both of those everyday. In your job, with your friends. So why not love?"

"I have been loved with conditions too many times to count–" I stop talking when tears clog my throat. "I see the love my friends have with their significant others. I see the love my clients have for their sports. And it's all free. It looks easy. In my experience, love was neither of those two things."

"So you're wondering when love will come without conditions?"

I nod my head. Too at a loss for words on what to say.

"You know what I think?" Lindsay asks rhetorically, but I shake my head and shrug my shoulders because I know she'll tell me anyway. "I'm telling you this as a friend and not a therapist. I think that you're so conditioned to thinking that love is connected to pain when in reality, it's the most freeing intangible thing you'll ever feel. You say you're scared of being vulnerable, but this, coming to therapy is one of the most vulnerable things that anyone can do. Why not take that next step in admitting that somewhere along the way, Riley crawled over that twelve-foot brick wall you reinforced with steel and instead of him convincing you to deconstruct it, he's helping you reinforce it with him inside? When will you realize that this thing between you two may no longer be fake?"

"He's my client. I can't even think about crossing that line."

"Haven't you already?"

She's right. Without even knowing who Riley was last year, we already crossed a line. But we flat out swept it away when we got into this arrangement. Things with Riley may no longer be treading on the line of fake. But I have no clue if what we're doing is considered real.

After my session I drove to Whole Foods to pick up wine and junk food. Well, whatever Whole Foods considers as junk food, and some ice cream. When I get home, I change into my loosest and comfiest clothes and camp-out on the couch. To punish myself, or treat myself, I pop on *No Reservations* and begin my self-imposed rot marathon.

18

RILEY

"Thanks, Mischa. I'll see ya next week." With a lift of my hand I stroll out of the studio and head to my car. The cold November air whips through the buildings and hits already bundled up patrons. Me included. I pick up my pace and basically jump into my car and start it up. Checking my phone I see no messages. Which is weird because Sarah and I are supposed to have a meeting in a few hours so I expected something from her.

Something has been off with her and I'm running through every scenario wondering if it's something that I did. We have the next two days off from hockey so it makes my decision to head to her much easier. I pull out of the lot and speed home to get showered and on the road. I'm not sure what this visit will entail, so I pack an overnight bag just in case.

> Me: Hey, would you mind coming over to feed the girls tonight?

> Logan: No problem. Is everything okay?

Me: Thanks. And I have no clue.

I'm lucky that Logan lives a couple floors down from me, so I don't have to worry about giving him an access code. And we both have spare keys to each other's places so that's another worry off my plate. Once back in the garage, I toss my bag in the passenger seat of my Range Rover and decide to give Sarah a courtesy call. It goes right to voicemail and that sets off an alarm bell in my head.

I get to her office an hour and a half later and I have to tell myself not to sprint inside. The receptionist is busy typing away when the elevator opens to her floor but stops when I park in front of her desk.

"Hi, is Sarah here?" I ask as charmingly as possible.

"I haven't seen her. But she does get in before me, so you can head back and check."

I push off her desk. "Thank you."

The office is a little busier than the last time I was here. So I'm able to see the layout with more occupied cubicles with phones ringing, the tapping of keyboards, and the sound of the printer spitting out paper.

I round the corner to Sarah's office but stop short when I see her lights off. Fishing my phone out of my pocket, I call her again. And again it heads straight to voicemail.

"Riley?" A moderately built man in his mid-thirties asks.

"Yeah," I say hesitantly and finally place him. "Jeff, right?"

He nods. "I think she took a sick day. I've tried calling her as well and got nothing."

I try not to let my panic show. "Okay, thanks." I pivot to leave, but he stops me.

"Would you mind coming into my office?" Jeffs turns to his large corner office without waiting to see if I'll follow. I don't want to. Every muscle is screaming at me to head to Sarah's house. But I do what he says. Because like it or not he's Sarah's boss, which kind of makes him my boss. "I know about your arrangement with her."

The door closes and I wait for Jeff to round to his desk chair. "I don't know…"

"She already told me. But not because she wanted to. I saw the pictures and she explained everything to me."

"So you know that we have a deadline?" I question as I lower into the seat in front of his desk.

"I do. I also know that you're the first guy she's attempted to date since her asshole ex screwed her over."

"Fake dating," I correct him.

He steeples his hands in front of his lips. "Are you trying to remind yourself of that?"

As a matter of fact, I am. But I don't justify my need to respond. The truth is that the night we saw the Northern Lights, I knew I wanted to say to hell with our fake dating and actually date.

"You know, we've never needed HR to step in. Because I never thought one of my agents would date a client. But even with the arrangement you two have going on, I've never seen her happier. When I met Sarah, she was content, if not a little heartbroken despite still being with her ex. But when you came into the picture, it was like I didn't even recognize her. So while I've never needed a meeting with her or any of the other agents, I don't have an issue with you two together. And if that's the way you two choose to go then we would need to give you a new publicist. Because paying her while dating her doesn't sit right with me."

I survey him while he talks about Sarah. I don't see any lust or longing hidden in the depths of his brown eyes. Just care. He may be one of the first people to show her love because it's clear her parents never did. At least not in the way that it counts. But it doesn't stop me from checking. "Do you care about her?"

"Not the way you do."

I furrow my brows and will him to continue.

"Sarah is like a little sister to me. Bothers me like one too. But, no. When I hired Sarah, I had just buried my wife and was learning how to be a single father to two kids. She saved the three of us whether she likes to take credit or not."

"I'm sorry for your loss," I tell him. I lost my parents. But he lost his wife. His kids lost their mother. I don't know how anyone can look so put together and be as successful as he is. Sarah taking care of them is the kid of person she is whether she realizes it or not.

"Thank you. Well, I'm sure you want to check on Sarah?" I nod my head and his smile is warm. "She keeps her spare key under the mat in front of her door." My look of shock and horror has him laughing. "I know. I've told her that's the worst hiding spot and the first place anyone would check to easily break-in. So maybe you can be the one to drill it into her head."

"Maybe." I say and stand up. "Thanks."

"No problem."

My stride is steady, if not a little hurried, as I let my legs carry me out of the office and to my car. Even though I was at Sarah's house a couple of times, I still remember how to get there. And fifteen minutes later I'm pulling up and parking at the curb. Her cars in the driveway lead me to believe that she's fine. But another part of me tells me she's not. I knock soft but firm and wait for her to answer the door. After a few minutes of waiting for it to open, I look under the mat, and sure enough a key is there, so I let myself inside and make sure to lock the door and set the key on the entryway table.

"Sarah?" I call out. Nothing. I stroll down the hall to her living room and find it empty. Taking my shoes off, I climb the stairs to her office. Again, nothing. My feet lead me to her bedroom and I see a human-sized lump in the middle of her bed. The blinds and curtains are shut leaving the room dark despite the sun on maximum brightness today.

I pull off my jeans and shirt, because outside clothes in bed are gross, and lift the covers to her sleeping form.

"Riley?" She croaks out in a whisper.

"Hi, baby. What's wrong?" I ask as I pull her closer to me.

"Migraine," is all she says. And she must be out of it because she doesn't question why I'm here. She just burrows herself into my curled arms and lets out a pitiful whimper that hits me right in the chest.

I run my hand along her back and massage her head and neck. She doesn't push me away or tell me to stop. After a while, her body goes boneless as she falls asleep. I continue with my ministrations until sleep takes me as well.

HANDS RUNNING up and down the side of my torso arouses me from my nap. I turn my head to Sarah's blue ones and my lips lift in a small smile. "Hi."

"Hi."

"How's your head?" I ask.

She winces as I speak but I don't take offense from it. "Still pounding." Sarah whispers and breathes deeply.

"What's wrong?" I'm instantly on alert and search her face for more signs.

"I get really bad nausea too."

"Sounds terrible," I joke.

She does a short laugh then stops. "Don't make jokes." She tells me and buries her face back in my neck.

"Do you want some food? I can make chicken noodle if you have the stuff for it."

"I don't have any food."

I kiss the top of her head and untangle myself from her. "Okay, then. You go back to sleep and I'll run to the store. Soup makes everything better."

I leave her with a soft smile on her face and a pang in my chest where she belongs.

THE STEAM and mouth-watering aroma from the chicken noodle soup invades my senses. I didn't bother going back upstairs when I got back from the store. My plan is to take a bowl up to her room and feed it to her. Because I doubt she's had much of anything today if evidence of the bags under her eyes were any indication.

I'm scooping her soup into a bowl when I hear a noise from the hallway. Sarah's lifeless body trails into the kitchen, surprising me.

"Hey, sleepy. I was gonna bring your food to you."

She shakes her head gently and drops into a seat at the kitchen table. "I wanna eat down here with you."

"Okay."

I sit next to her with a big helping in my bowl and a smaller helping in hers. Her movements are cautious as if she's scared to move too fast to aggravate her head. She looks so fragile in this moment. It makes me remember that underneath the shark-like persona she presents at work, she's still just a girl. Well, a woman.

When I finish my soup, I push my empty bowl away and pull hers in front of me. Her protest dies on her lips when I drag her onto my lap. I hold the bowl in my far hand and scoop up some soup with the other and bring the spoon up to her lips. We continue like this. Me feeding her and her willingly letting me help her. When her bowl is empty, her body sags against mine and I stand up, carrying her to the couch.

I cover her with a blanket and wait for her face to relax. "I'll be right back."

"Hey, Riley?" Sarah asks.

"Yeah, baby?"

"Thank you."

"You're welcome." I kiss her on the forehead, out of comfort and to see if she's got a bit of a fever and head into the kitchen to clean up. Once I'm done, I check on Sarah before heading back out to get my bag and to call Momma.

"Hi, Riley. What's up?"

"What do you do for someone who has a migraine?" I snag my bag off the passenger seat and head back inside at a brisk pace. We're told we won't get snow, but I highly doubt that as the temps have dropped faster than usual. Back inside, I set my bag on the landing and go over to Sarah's front room to continue talking with Momma without disturbing her.

"Do you need me to bring over some medicine?"

"No. Besides, it's not for me. It's for Sarah." I tell her to reassure her.

"Poor thing. Is she drinking enough water?"

"I think so? I made her some chicken noodle soup and had her drink some Powerade to get her electrolyte levels back up."

"You're too good for her."

"She makes me want to be good," I announce.

"Well, honey, I think you've done all you needed. Just let it pass through her body."

I let out a breath. "I will. Thanks, Momma."

"Anytime, Ry. Love you."

"Love you too." I hang up my phone and set it next to Sarah's spare key. I walk back into the living room and look at her passed out form. Not wanting to disturb her, I lift up her legs and place them in my lap when I settle on the couch.

My efforts are futile as Sarah wakes up again. She sees where I'm at and gingerly moves over to me and curls into my waiting arm. "I've never had this," she says so low I almost don't hear her.

"Have what?"

"Someone to take care of me when a migraine hits. Paul, my ex, always told me to take some medicine like that was the cure all to him. And my parents would laugh it off and say I was begging for attention," her voice is tight and monotone. Like these people in her life stripped her of her joy before she even realized what was happening.

"You have me now," I tell her, my voice strong with conviction. I hate that she's had to deal with this pain by herself.

"But for how long? Riley, this is supposed to be fake." Her voice cracks on the last one and it's enough to crack open my heart and spill everything to her.

"Baby, this isn't fake for me. Not anymore. I know it happened fast. I know we were supposed to stay on our respective sides of the line. I don't want to use the word 'fake' anymore. At least not when it comes to us."

Sarah traces a pattern on my free hand and I hear the wheels turning in that gorgeous head of hers. "But, you're my client. I technically work for you. If that's not a conflict of interest, then I don't know what is."

"Do you want to talk about this now?"

She lets out a breath. "I think the not knowing how to move forward will drive me insane."

"Alright. I talked to Jeff today when I went to your office looking for you. Funny, but he was the one who said he was fine with us dating. But that it would be in the best interest of our relationship that I should be given a new publicist."

Sarah nods but stops with a hiss.

"Baby, we can talk about this tomorrow. You're in pain."

"No. I wanna keep going."

"Okay, stubborn woman." I say and kiss the top of her head. "He didn't demand I get a new publicist. But he did point out that our relationship would look weird if I was still paying you. So I have to give him an answer soon. And it depends on you."

"Me?"

"Yes, you."

"I want to say yes, Riley. So bad," she starts and I feel wetness seeping through my shirt. "But I'm so scared. I swore off relationships and love. And being with you makes me more vulnerable than I ever wished to be again."

"Let's not put the cart before the horse, okay? One day at a time. But if you do decide that a full-blown relationship and love is something you want, let it be me. Okay?"

She looks up at me through cloudy eyes, "Okay."

"Let's go up to bed. You're exhausted."

"You're staying?" She looks at me as if no one has ever put her first.

"Of course I'm staying."

19

SARAH

Faint scents of cedar wood and leather blanket my body as I come out of sleep. Riley's arms are locked around my stomach and his head rests against my back. His deep breaths almost lull me back to sleep. But my bladder is begging to be released and if I don't get up I'll have to order a new mattress.

I try to unwind his arms, but he locks them tighter. "Where do you think you're going?"

"Bathroom. I have to pee."

Riley loosens his grip and I slip out effortlessly. I use the bathroom and brush my teeth while looking at my reflection for the first time in over twenty-four hours. I could use a shower too but I want to get back to Riley. As soon as I exit the bathroom, Riley is switching places with me.

"I have an extra toothbrush underneath the vanity," I tell him through the closed door.

His responding grunt is enough of an answer for me. I slink back into the still warm sheets and check my phone. Dozens of messages greet me and I conclude I'm too tired to respond to any of them. So I turn my phone all the way off right as Riley finishes up.

"Hi," he greets me when he's back in my bed.

"Morning."

His bed head hair falls in his face and I push it back. My hand falls to the angular curve of his jaw and my thumb traces the full bottom lip.

"Do you remember yesterday?"

"The dull headache is a reminder. So yes."

"Anything else?"

"You mean about us dating for real? It rings a bell." My smile matches his and I love that I get this unguarded version of him.

"We'll take it slow," Riley promises.

"Does slow include breakfast? Because I'm starving."

His silent chuckle shakes the bed. "Yeah, baby. I can feed you."

"Okay," I whisper barely loud enough for me to hear. The fire that burned bright the night we hooked up is alive and well. "Kiss me first and then feed me."

"You're bossy," he tells me but zones in on my lips.

Our lips meet and my breath hitches. Riley's hand cradles my neck and angles my head as he deepens the kiss. His tongue teases at my bottom lip, begging for entrance. When I open for him our tongues tangle, but he doesn't take it further than this. And all too soon, he's backing away and pecking my top and bottom lip.

"We're going slow," he reminds me.

"Mm hmm," I agree.

Riley gets up and tosses a pillow at my face before heading downstairs. I decide to brave my phone again and turn it back on. More messages filter in and I start from the latest to the newest. Most of them are wondering where I'm at while I was held up in darkness. Yesterday's migraine took a lot out of me. And while I'm not back to 100%, as I still have a dull headache, I can at least shake my head without wanting to cry or barf.

Jeff's message is next and I respond with an update that I'm on the mend and will be back in the office on Monday. Do I think us having an office is redundant when our work can be done at home? Yes. But I think Jeff likes the ability to see his employees. Plus it gets him out of the house which is something his kids always push for.

I respond as best as I can to my other clients before I move onto my group chat with the girls.

Main Bishes

> Kamryn: I need a coffee break.

> Emmy-Lou: Wish I could but I'm teaching.

> Jax: I'm in the editing cave.

> Kamryn: Sarah?

twenty minutes later

> Kamryn: Is her radio silence concerning?

> Jax: Maybe she's in meetings?

> Kamryn: Maybe?

> Emmy-Lou: Rain check on the coffee.

> Me: I was in a migraine cave all day.

> Kamryn: Did you use your headache cap?

> Me: No. I just slept all day…

> Emmy-Lou: What's with the … ?

Me: I have good news.

Jax: Do tell!

Emmy-Lou: Spill it

Kamryn: Don't edge us!

Me: Riley and I are dating.

Emojis fill their responses along with "I knew it!" to "We can't wait to meet him"

I let them know I want them to meet him soon and then place my phone back on the nightstand. Flipping the covers off, I change out of yesterday's lounge clothes and slide on a new pair of sweatpants and a new sweatshirt with a pair of fuzzy socks and head downstairs. The low hum of the TV greets me when I reach downstairs, followed by the sizzling sound of bacon as the salty aroma fills my nostrils. I lean against the wall furthest from the kitchen and watch as Riley commands the space like I'm sure he does on the ice. His broad shoulders flex as he does something on the stove and just seeing the controlled strength is close to making me drool.

While I should definitely not combust over someone younger than me, Riley holds himself in a way none of the guys my age did back then. And getting a front row seat to the guy who made headlines months ago shows me that he's like an onion. I'm finding that with every new layer he exposes, I like. I'm finding that every new layer I'm intro-duced to, is protected until it's ready to peel. Does focusing on his age say more about me, than him? Yes. But I'm slowly working through that and realizing that I won't care about his age much longer.

"It smells good in here." I say as I push off the wall and

make my presence known. He looks over his shoulder at my approach and I don't miss the appreciative stare from him that lights up my body even in an oversized sweatpants and sweatshirt combination. One thing he never fails to make me do is feel appreciated for the way I look.

"It's just about done if you want to have a seat at the table." He tells me as he flips the final piece of what looks like an egg white omelet.

Nodding, I silently move to the table and watch as he turns off the stove and plates our food. He must have brought a change of clothes as I'm noticing he's in a pair of plaid drawstring pajama pants that mold to his thighs and pool around his feet. Riley takes the seat next to me and my stomach grumbles embarrassingly loud.

He places a kiss on my upturned cheek and then hands me one of the forks he was holding onto. "Eat up, Blue."

I cut off a piece of omelet and blow it off before closing my lips around the fork. "I'm surprised your culinary skills haven't locked anyone down yet."

"I haven't gotten that far in any relationship for my skills to lock them down." Riley responds and takes a sip of water.

"Why not?"

"Most women are interested in a hockey player, which means quick money for them," Riley tells me.

"And that's not something you want."

"Correct. I saw the love my parents had and the love Momma and Pops have. And I want that. I think I've always wanted it. But that's not something guys admit. Let alone guys at my age," Riley says.

"I think it's refreshing." I tell him and lean over to kiss his cheek.

We finish eating our food and sit back in our chairs once we push our plates forward.

"How's your head?" Riley asks sincerely.

"I still have a dull headache. Which is normal the day after a migraine."

"Do you know what causes them? I'm sorry, I've just never had a migraine like what you've experienced," Riley says.

I bring a leg up on the chair and hook my arms around my shin to keep it in place. "I wish I knew. I've been tested. But I think they're genetic. I don't get them as often as I used to. Occasionally one will come and take me out for the day. All that I do is ride the agonizing wave."

"I'm glad I came over yesterday to try and soothe your pain."

I rest my head on my knee and turn to face Riley. "Me too."

We stare at each other in the morning light of my kitchen. Blue eyes to blue eyes. Calm to calm. And I realize I've never felt more at peace than in this moment with him.

"I told my friends that we're dating."

His eyebrows are covered when they fly to his hairline. "What'd they say?"

"A lot of *I knew it* and emojis depicting excitement for me. They're eager to meet you."

"Did they meet your ex?"

My upper lip curls. "Do you really want to talk about this?"

"Knowing you is knowing some of your past. So yeah, I do."

I let my leg down and instead slide them over Riley's outstretched limbs. His bear paw comes to rest on my knee and seeing his inked skin against my sweatpants is an intoxicating sight.

"Kamryn met him once and she didn't like him all that

much. And now that I'm removed from that time in my life I can see what she didn't like about him. But at the time I was blinded by lust and the attention he gave me that I mistook it for love. He put me on a pedestal and I think that's why our breakup changed me."

"Your reason for not loving?"

"Yeah," I tell him. "My therapist said that I'm vulnerable in my everyday life but when it came to my new feelings for you I refused to acknowledge that part of my vulnerability."

"I'm scared too," Riley admits.

"You are?" I ask and look up at him.

"My feelings for you slammed into me out of nowhere. It's almost like hockey was in the way and I made any excuse to have you around."

"Like you canceling my hotel room," I note.

"Guilty." He says with a wide smile.

"Question," I say.

He nods. "I might have an answer."

"Why do you call me Blue?"

"Because of your eyes," he says with no hesitation.

"Most people would have called me Red. But you went for my eyes. Why?"

"Because I feel like they change color every time I look into them. One day they're deeper than an ocean blue and the next they resemble the blue from a crayon."

Swoon. "You're going to be a great boost for my ego," I tell him.

"I hope that's not all I'll be good for." He says and pulls me into his lap.

I rest my arm around the back of his chair and play with his hair. "It's one of the many things I'm sure you'll be good for." He pinches my thigh and I swat at his hand. "How are you planning to tell your friends?"

"Well, they've been referring to you as the "hot redhead from the charity gala", but I think they'll be not as surprised as I hope."

"I do like that nickname," I preen and squirm as Riley tickles my sides. "What are their names?"

"There's Logan, Noah, and Max. Logan and I moved up at the same time in the league. So when we got drafted by Columbus, it took us about a day to mesh together on the ice. Noah and Max were in the same draft class as us, so we all kind of stuck together."

"Speaking of, when do you have to head home?" It's weird that I'll already miss him and I'm quite literally in his lap.

"Later today. I have an early pilates class and then practice later in the afternoon."

"I guess I am reaping all the benefits of your pilates classes." I say as I run my hands down his firm arms and to his forearms.

His teeth are bared as a smile takes up his face and then fades just as quickly.

"What's wrong?" I ask and my eyes travel all over his face looking for something.

"I'm just wondering how this is going to work. Season is about to get underway and you live here. I'll be lucky to make it down here between training and games."

"I'll split part-time between here and Columbus. I'll take a look at your schedule and during the home games I'll stay with you and the away games I'll come back here."

He nods as he considers what I'm saying. "Okay. Look at us figuring out a plan."

I silently laugh. Riley and I spend the rest of the morning talking about life. Hypothetical scenarios that run through our heads, dream vacation spots, local hidden gems that we promise to take each other to, and our hope that this thing between us can work. He makes me laugh. Which is a foreign feeling in a relationship. And it's not my fake laugh. It's the laughter that leaves my stomach sore in the best possible way.

But I don't get my hopes too far up. Love is still something I'm terrified about. Although a simple thing like trying with Riley gives me hope.

20

RILEY

I tap my stick on the ice and wait for Max to pass the puck. The defender of the other team turns his head for a blink and by the time he's refocused, Max is passing the puck to me. I hear the roar of the crowd as I manage to hold possession of the puck and dodge the opposing team. Noah manages to get my attention and I look up in time to pass the puck to him. When he gets the puck, he's swarmed by the other team and I slide in to help him out of the hole.

"Back off Petrov." I snarl as I slam him into the boards.

"In your dreams, Jones." He says and slams me back.

I manage to stay upright and push him back. Noah finds an opening out of the cluster and rounds back to find an opening at the net. Victor turns his fire eyes on me and I duck out of his reach before he can swing on me. I like a fight when it's necessary. But he tends to take it further than need be. I put myself into gear and get back to the middle of the ice and wait for the buzzer to sound from Noah's goal. He's good and our top scorer. Our left winger gets my attention and we both nod.

I look up at the play clock and see less than thirty

seconds and we're up by one. If Noah can score this and our defense holds them off, we keep the streak alive. Bear and I push our way through the cluster to allow Noah a break-away to score. Their goalie is good, but Noah is better. He looks to the top right of the goal and plays the goalie by shooting to the bottom left. The buzzer goes off, the crowd goes wild, and Bear and I tackle Noah.

"Fuck, yeah Birdy!" I scream into his face and knock on his helmet a couple of times before skating over to Logan and hyping up the rest of the line and the crowd. With Noah's goal we've got the cushion to not worry about New York rushing their play. We line back up and Noah faces off. He wins and passes the puck back to Logan who then passes it off to Bear as he loops around the net.

I start my slow skate around our half of the rink and make my way to the bench when the buzzer sounds. We all make our way to the tunnel and head to the locker rooms. Fans clamor for attention and girls call for us to sign any body part we can get our hands on. Their words, not mine. Plus, I already have everything I want waiting for me in the family and friends box.

Max's boisterous voice travels down the hall before he's like an energizer bunny bouncing into the locker room. My skates are already in my locker and I'm in the process of taking my jersey off to head to the showers.

"We're getting lit tonight boys!" Max exclaims as he has his phone's flashlight waving around in the air. The team either groans or eggs him on.

"Gharety!" Coach Anderson barks.

Max yelps and scrambles off the bench. "Yes, Coach." *Kiss ass.* The rest of us snicker at Max's change in voice.

"Shouldn't you be with the athletic trainers?"

He nods quickly. "Yes, sir."

Anderson looks down at his clipboard and looks back up and sees Max still standing in place. "Go."

Max trails off with his tail tucked between his legs. Chatter starts back up and I grab my things for the shower.

"You going out tonight?" Noah asks.

"Mm hmm. Did you not see the texts last night?"

"Yeeeess," he says, lying through his teeth.

I shake my head and move into the showers. The lively chatter is one I've missed. After three straight losses going into our week at home, it was good to end this week with a win. Turning the water off, I dry off with the towel and head back into the locker room.

"Riley, are you headed up to the box?"

"Yep. My parents and Sarah are up there." I tell the guys and pull my shirt on, barely muffling the kissing noises they're making. I ignore them because it's been a great few weeks with Sarah. The away stretch of games are the hardest but we manage to make it work with modern technology on our side. I pack up my bag and stroll out of the locker room to head to my girl.

What I also failed to mention to the guys is that her friends were at the game tonight as well. Not only would it be their first time to meet them, but mine as well. And my nerves are through the roof. Sarah says I have nothing to worry about. But she's biased. Stepping off the elevator, I make the short walk to the family and friends room to madness. It seems everyone had the idea to stay.

I say hi to some of the parents and make my way through the room to my crew. Pops flags me down before I can see anyone else. Sarah is in here, I can feel her.

"Good game, kiddo." He says and kisses the side of my head.

"Thanks, Pop. Hi, Momma." I greet her with a kiss on her cheek.

"You guys looked great out there. But, I'm sure you're ready for some lighter days."

"You have no idea." This home stretch came at the perfect time with Thanksgiving a handful of days away. "Where's my girl?" I ask and try not to be rude.

"She's right there." Momma points to the cluster of people off to the side.

We make eye contact and the smile that covers her face is infectious. Sarah excuses herself and walks into my arms.

"You did great." She praises and wraps her arms around my waist.

I kiss the tip of her nose and revel in the sight of a light blush that covers her face. "Thank you."

She turns her attention to my parents who are looking like they've hit the daughter-in-law lottery. I raise an eyebrow at them as they continue to stare at us.

"Oh, fine," Momma concedes. "We'll see you this week for Thanksgiving?"

"Wouldn't miss it." Sarah tells her and moves to hug Momma. She kisses Pops on the cheek before returning to my side.

Momma kisses me on the cheek, followed by Pops. "She's good for you."

"I know." We wave them off and Sarah secures herself to my waist again. She tilts her head back and I run my fingers through her loose tresses.

"Are you ready to meet my friends?"

I clench my teeth and breathe in. "Yeah."

Sarah leans up and pecks me on the lips. As she turns, she pulls me by the hands to an expectant group. They all quiet immediately and I feel like I'm being judged for standing by Sarah.

"So, this is Riley." She waves her hand towards me like she's Vanna White. "Riley, this is Kamryn, Mason, Emily, Adam, Jax, and Trent." Sarah finishes with a slight sneer at the last guy and curls into my side. *Interesting.*

"It's nice to meet you all. Sarah's talked about you guys a bunch."

"Likewise. Now, Riley. Tell us how you charmed her." Kamryn starts and drags me away from the group.

I look back at Sarah and see she's smiling and shaking her head. "She told you about the stuff from before?"

"Yeah. And while my best friend puts on the biggest front, these past few years have definitely hardened her to where I haven't been able to recognize her. Until you. I haven't seen her happy in a very long time and I have you to thank for that."

"You don't have to thank me," I tell her.

"I do. It was a few months after Mason and I got back together. We were out at a bar day drinking and she got this far away look in her eyes. Riley, I think my best friend was suffering longer than I realized. How I didn't catch that when my first choice was psychology, I'll never know. But with you, she's softer. She's finally letting herself feel. She's the her I met in college."

I look over at Sarah to see her head tossed back on a laugh at whatever Mason is saying. It's hard to imagine Sarah back then with a dark cloud as her only companion.

"Just promise you'll take care of her heart. It's a lot more fragile than anyone knows."

I look back at Kamryn who's got her focus on Sarah and then Mason. Our hearts are the same. Mine and Sarah's. But while mine has been mended by love, hers has been left alone to heal in fractured pieces. "I promise."

THE TABLE in the club is littered with empty champagne bottles from celebrating our win to celebrating Mason and Kamryn's engagement. I have a beautiful red head in my lap whose arm is wrapped around my shoulders and her fingers are playing with the hair at the nape of my neck. I told her slow, but with every brush of her fingers against my skin, it makes me want to drag her to a dark part of the club and have my way with her.

"You're playing with fire, Blue," I growl into her ear and nip at her earlobe. .

"I have been known to have a pyro side," she jokes.

Before we came out, we all agreed to change out of arena clothes and into something more night out appropriate. When Sarah walked out of our room with an outfit that molded to her curves, I had to open the freezer to cool off and the sound of her laughter made my reaction to her even worse. I was told what she's wearing is a jumpsuit. It covers her more than a dress, but again, with the way the fabric molds to her body, I'm entirely too grateful that I'm the only one who knows what's underneath. She must've taken into account the weather as the outfit covers her legs. The front of her outfit exposes an ample amount of cleavage and the back dips down to right above the curve of her ass. And don't get me started on her shoes. Silver glittering red bottoms that give her just the right height to where I don't have to curve my body to take her lips in mine.

I nip at the spot below her ear and stand up. Keeping her body flush against mine and making sure that she doesn't fall with the new position. "Let's dance." I say and drag her with me.

I haven't been to a club since our hookup almost a year ago. That night is a blur but I do remember when I saw her and my gaze zeroed in on her after her second trip to the bar. I watched in amazement as she ignored the guys who approached her and her give no-fucks attitude. I watched as she let the music take away her worries and she danced like she was alone at home. When I slid up behind her, I prepared for her to push me away. But she must have deemed me safe when she tangled her fingers with mine and pulled me closer. My subconscious must have played tricks on me because I knew I wouldn't let her go.

Moving our way onto the dance floor, I twirl Sarah in front of me and pull her flush to me, back to front, as the crowd continues to dance around us. The bass from the music almost puts a spell on us. It's heavy and sensual. It's the perfect song to make you ignore the outside world if only for a few minutes. Our bodies move together and my hands roam freely up and down her body. My cock grows harder with every brush of Sarah's ass against my jeans. I slide my hand down to the front of her body and hold her in place as I swivel my hips. Her moan is only audible to me and I place a kiss on her neck.

I watch as her chest heaves with each circle of my hips. Grabbing her hand, I lift it and hook it around my neck. Both of my hands fall to her hips and I watch as a bead of sweat trails down Sarah's chest.

We stay like this. Bodies moving as one song bleeds into the next until the DJ announces the final song of the night. Sweaty and out of breath, I drag Sarah off the dance floor and to our mostly empty table save for Jax.

"Where's Trent?" Sarah asks when we sit back down.

"I don't know," Jax tells her.

"Have you been sitting here the whole time?" I don't know her that well but I ask anyway.

"Yeah. But it's fine. I'm not much of a dancer." The tightness in her jaw says otherwise. And I know if I were her and I saw my sister and friends dancing with their significant others, I'd be a little hurt as well.

Sarah glances at me before scooting next to Jax. Whatever she says to her has Jax blinking fast to keep from crying. I like seeing Sarah like this; in problem-solver mode, in caretaker mode. She'd be a great mom one day if given the chance. And it startles me how natural saying that about her is.

More from our group joins us back at the table.

"What's wrong?" Kamryn asks when she sees her sister upset and Sarah talking with her.

"I guess her boyfriend left her alone," I say assuming that's what happened.

If humans had the possibility to breathe fire, Kamryn would do it. "That fucking asshole. I'm gonna end him."

"Easy firecracker," Mason cajoles.

"No. I've been telling her for months to dump him. He doesn't care about her. He's only with her because of her proximity to you."

Mason rubs his hands up and down her arms as if that'll soothe her. "Jax has to see it first, honey. I know you want to go all big-sister mode, but when it comes to love, or whatever it is between them, you have to let her make the hard decisions on her own."

Kamryn looks toward her sister and if I'm not mistaken she wants to cry on her behalf. "He's already breaking her heart."

"Then you just have to trust that she'll break his more when it comes time."

I don't know what it's like to have siblings. I have teammates who I consider family. But we're obligated to get along with each other. It keeps the chemistry of the team peaceful.

"Do you have siblings?" I ask when Kamryn goes over to her sister and Mason takes a seat next to me. I'm still pinching myself that the invisible strings have been able to put me in this legends vicinity.

He nods. "Yeah. Two brothers and a sister. They're still in college so it's a bit of an age gap between us. What about you?"

"Just me," I say. "Which I guess is why Sarah and I get along so well."

"Gotta say, I did not see you two coming."

"Why is that?" I ask but don't take offense to it.

"She's a lion. She's loud in a good way, protective, and loyal. She stands up for those she loves. It's one of the reasons Kam and I asked her to officiate our wedding."

I turn to Mason. "You did?"

"She didn't tell you?"

I shake my head. Was she asked before or after we said to hell with fake dating? Maybe with her migraine she forgot. It's possible so I try not to let it get to me.

Mason and I talk while the girls console Jax. Emily and Adam left as soon as they could. And who knows where the guys went. The girls stand up with Kamryn's arm around her sister's shoulders. Shielding her in the way I can only assume a big sister would.

Sarah walks over to me and stands between my spread legs. I loop my arm around her waist and look up at her. "Is she okay?"

"I think so," she tells me as I stand up and we all walk towards the entrance.

We garner a lot of looks. What with Mason being as tall as he is and me fresh off a game. We nod to some people, too impatient to say hi but not too rude to ignore them.

When we're outside, I pull out my phone to order a car and I see Mason doing the same. Sarah burrows into my body when the wind swoops down between the buildings. Thankfully we don't have to wait long before the cars are pulling up. The girls do their goodbyes and Mason and I do our man shake before we file into our respective vehicles.

"Is everything okay with Jax?" I ask as the driver pulls into the road.

"I don't know," Sarah says. "I think she's so used to his behavior that she doesn't know anything else."

"How long have they been together?"

"About three years."

"And he treats her like that?"

"He's her first true boyfriend," Sarah states. "I think she's always been a little self-conscious and guarded. But he was weirdly the first guy to say all the right words."

"Well, you're my first true girlfriend and you don't see me acting like him."

"That's because Momma would spank you into next year if she found out you acted like him towards any woman."

I snort. "True."

When the car pulls up to my complex a few minutes later, I drag a sleepy Sarah out and towards the elevator bank.

"Can I tell you a secret?" I whisper when the elevator whisks us up to my floor.

"Yeah," she speaks into my chest.

I wrap my arms tighter around her and kiss the top of her head. "I like you a lot."

She wraps her arms tighter around me. "I like you a lot too, baby."

The elevator opens on my floor and when we're inside, I push Sarah to the bedroom as I go to feed the girls a small snack before turning the lights off and closing the door to our room. It's funny how now I think of my place as our place. Are we going fast? Maybe? But I have no other relationship to compare us to. Which, as I think about it, is a good thing. This relationship is ours and ours alone.

And as I crawl into bed after my shower, and Sarah wraps herself around me, I can't think of anything better than this.

21

SARAH

My phone rings for the third time this morning. And for the third time this morning, I press the red dot on the screen with more force than necessary, effectively ending the incoming call. My mom is probably freaking out, realizing I'm not in Charleston for Thanksgiving. It's been about three months since I last talked to my parents and it's the longest time between our phone calls in existence. Until my mom learns to put me first, I have nothing to say to her.

My phone rings again. "Ugh! Give up already!"

"Blue, shouldn't you answer that?"

I turn my furrowed brow to Riley who's spread out on the couch. "No."

"Okay," he relents and turns his attention back to the parade that's on the TV.

We woke up this morning and decided a walk around his neighborhood would be a good idea before we consume copious amounts of food. While this isn't my first Thanksgiving with a significant other, this is the first one that I'm excited to celebrate. I finish drafting up my end of the year reports when my phone buzzes again. Looking at who's calling, I ignore and then turn my phone on airplane mode.

Once Riley met my friends, Kamryn took it upon herself to give him everyone's numbers in "case of an emergency" was the reasoning she told me.

My mind is no longer on work after those attempted calls, so I close my laptop and shuffle over to Riley on the couch. He taps his chest and I gracefully crawl onto the couch and lay on his body. He places a kiss on the top of my head before settling back down.

The steady rise and fall of his chest mixed with his classic leather scent makes me feel more at home than my current home does. And that's a scary feeling because I made a vow to myself to never feel that again. But Riley has made himself out to be the exception.

"Would you ever visit back home?" Riley asks. The vibration of his question soothes me.

"Not if I had a choice," I say and trace one of the tattoos on his arm. "Now that I'm here, I realize how tiny that place was. I felt almost suffocated. Being here gives me the chance to breathe...to explore. Like I can finally see what's beyond the horizon."

"I'm glad you're here."

"Me too."

We watch the rest of the parade in silence. Riley runs his hands up and down my back in a comforting gesture. When the parade is done, he switches it to a Charlie Brown special.

I snort. "You're such a child."

"Just wait until Christmas time when that's the only thing on the TV."

"Is that your favorite holiday?" I ask and pop up, resting my chin on my hand still on his chest.

"Yeah. Now that I think about it," Riley says. "What's yours?"

"Probably New Year's Eve."

"Why probably?"

"I think because most are afraid of the future. You know, the what's to come. But I like it because everything I did in the past is just that. It's in the past. We get 365 new days to begin again. We get 365 new days to start a new hobby. I think I just love the end of the year in general."

"So you won't be mad if I get us matching Christmas pajamas."

"As long as you're okay with all the gold and sparkly attire on New Year's Eve."

He holds his hand out. "Deal."

"Deal," I say and shake his offered hand. "What time do we have to be at your parents house?"

Riley holds his arm up and looks at the time. "Not for a few more hours."

"Okay. I'll just take a nap right here." I tell him and slide my hands under his torso to get more comfortable.

He kisses me on the top of my head again and pulls one of the many throw blankets over me. The rise and fall of his chest lulls me into a quick nap.

"Wake up sleepyhead." The light strokes on my arm are meant to wake me up but just put me further to sleep. "Would you wake up for an orgasm?"

"I thought you said we were going slow?" I ask through my still-sleepy state.

Riley nips at my neck. "Slow is overrated."

"Don't tease me," I mumble, finally coming out of my nap caused by Riley's warm body.

His chest shakes with laughter. "Who said anything about teasing? Besides, I need to eat my appetizer before the main course."

I lift my head and narrow my eyes. "Are you comparing me to a turkey?"

"Not at all," he says teasingly. "Now get up here so I can kiss you."

My legs fall to either side of Riley's body and I slide up until I stop on his hardening cock. His drawstring pants do nothing to hide him and I feel every ridge of him. I can't help my body's reaction as I roll my hips over him. The flex in his jaw tells me he's about to chastise me. But I stop his words when I press my lips to his. Soft and sure at first until Riley's tongue licks at my bottom lip begging for entrance.

Kissing him feels like the first kiss every time. My breath catches and my heart skips a beat.

My hips grind down, causing Riley's breath to stutter and our tongues to tangle. We're all teeth and tongue as we battle to get closer. Riley shocks me by sitting up from the couch and moving us to his room. The sound of his door closing is not enough to break our focus. He climbs onto the bed and lays me in the middle. His cock rubs against my center and it takes my breath away.

Riley breaks the kiss and trails down my body. He pulls my sweatshirt off and places open-mouth kisses on my stomach. My sweats are yanked off my body and Riley settles between my spread legs.

"Watch me enjoy my appetizer." He tells me before running his tongue up my slit. Riley closes his eyes and groans, almost as if he's savoring me. "Delicious." He holds my thighs down and spreads me open with his thumbs. My hips try to lift as he blows cool air on my exposed center but his arms lock me down. Riley is focused and determined as he eats me out. His thumb rubs at my clit as his tongue pushes inside my opening. He pulls back and watches my face as he slides two fingers into me and pumps slowly. Riley strokes my inner walls and rubs at that spot that takes my breath away. His thumb goes back to rubbing my clit and I gasp.

"Oh, f–fuck, Riley," I whine out as he continues rubbing in tandem. My hands fist the sheets as I feel my orgasm getting closer and closer. Riley's mouth replaces his fingers and my orgasm crashes over me as he suctions onto my clit and flutters his tongue over the nub. His fingers rub me through the shockwaves of what feels never-ending.

When my breathing returns to normal, Riley rips my sweatshirt off. His clothes soon follow and then he's kissing his way up my body. He takes me with him as he falls to his back and I'm splayed across his body.

His tattooed body is a stark contrast against the bright white of his sheets. My eyes meet a sparkling sky blue and his lips curve up.

"I had my snack and now it's time for the show. Ride me, Blue."

Leaning down, I take his cock in my hand and rub it through my wetness. I tense when the head rubs over my clit. I rise up on my knees and line him up at my entrance. Slowly, I lower onto his length. I sigh out Riley's name when I bottom out and I hold still to let myself adjust to him in this position. Tentatively, I rise up on my knees and fall back down. I know Riley is doing everything he can to hold back from taking over. My hands fall to the sides of his head and my hips lift and swivel over his cock. Our eyes lock when I hold my hips in place and clench around him.

"Fuck." Riley whispers before taking my lips in a bruising kiss. Our position changes when he sits up, keeping me in his lap. We slowly rock into each other while keeping our lips fused together. My fingers glide through his hair and his hands roam down my back. In this position, it's intimate. It's no longer a quick fuck to get off. It's more. It's terrifying. Because somehow this blond hockey player I met almost a year ago, wormed his way into my heart. He knocked down every brick I layed and stacked to keep him and any guy out.

I break the kiss when I feel my orgasm building up and ready to release. Riley and I hold our stare and see the same thing mirrored back at me.

"I know, baby. But I need you to come." Riley says and takes control, laying us back down as he strokes my orgasm out of me. I come and feel Riley's pulsing cock and the warmth of his cum branding my pussy. He works us both through our high until the aftershocks are no more. With a kiss to the tip of my nose, Riley pulls out and falls to the side next to me.

It's now that I know. With my chest heaving, skin sticky with sweat, and the realization that I've fallen in love with Riley Theodore Jones. That there's no going back. But I can only hope that he's at the bottom to catch me if he's not already there.

22

SARAH

The smell of dessert hits us as we walk into Riley's parents place. We had to go through the front door as Pops has a deep fryer in the garage and the temperature change would've thrown off the heat of the oil. At least that's what he's been telling Riley since he was a kid.

"Momma?" Riley calls out as we place our jackets on the hooks.

"Kitchen, honey."

Riley hangs on me as we walk through the house. My arms twist back as if I plan on carrying him on my back. It's fun being able to experience life and love through him. More importantly, it's fun having fun in this relationship. He's made every day we've been together a new adventure.

"Hi, Pop," Riley and I greet in unison.

"Hey, you two."

"It smells really good in here, Cassie." I say when I untangle Riley's arms from around me and walk over to her.

She kisses me on the cheek. "Thank you, sweetheart. Are you ready to get your hands dirty?"

"Yes. Put me to work," I tell her. I pull my hair back and

head to the sink to wash my hands. Riley kisses her on the cheek and pats me on the butt before joining his dad on the couch to watch football.

We get to work on rolling out the pie crust for the chocolate chess pie along with mixing up dough for chocolate chip cookies. Those will sit in the fridge until they're ready to be baked. Cassie then shows me how to make Riley's favorite macaroni and cheese dish.

"It's a lot of steps," I confess.

She looks over at me, stirring the roux. "It is. But after a while this can be done in under two hours and without a recipe."

I look over at her with a deer-in-the-headlights look. "No recipe?" I squeak out.

Cassie's smile is that of familiarity. "I promise it can be done. When I made my first dish with Dean's mom, I felt like I was under a microscope. Even with her very watchful eye, I still felt like the noodles were overcooked or the sauce was too salty or there wasn't enough cheese."

"So what happened?"

"Oh, that all still happened. But I practiced, unbeknownst to Dean. And that next Thanksgiving, I wow'ed him, his Mom, and the rest of his family."

"Do you both come from big families?" I ask because I'm curious about Riley's parents.

"Dean does. He has three sisters and two brothers. He's firmly in the middle of the bunch. Me on the other hand, I grew up with a half-sister that I lost contact with after our Dad passed away."

"I'm so sorry," I say and try not to come off as pity.

"Thank you, sweetheart. What about you?"

"I'm an only child. Which is a blessing and a curse I suppose."

She motions that the roux is done and to add the noodles to start the process of assembling everything. "Go on."

"My parents were great when I was in high school and college. It was after college that I realized they expected me to do things the way they wanted. Get a degree, but don't plan to use it as your husband will be the one to take care of you. Stay with this guy even though he steps out on you." I get to mixing the noodles and sauce. We top the dish with the leftover cheese and pop it in the oven.

"Okay. Everything looks like it's about done."

"Really?"

"Mm hmm. Now what we do is grab a glass of wine and head out to the fire pit to talk more."

I wring my hands in front of me. "Okay."

Cassie pours us each a hefty glass of wine and leads the way to the backyard. "Riley, keep an eye on the food."

He looks over from the TV. "You got it Momma." His brow furrows at the two of us and his baby blue eyes meet mine with a silent question. I nod him off and follow her outside. Cassie presses the button for the fire pit and two minutes later the fire has warmed our chilled bodies up.

"Has Riley told you what I do for work?"

I take a sip of wine and then shake my head. "I can't say he has."

"I work as a part-time sex therapist," Cassie states.

I choke on the wine that's still traveling down my throat.

Cassie's laugh is of amusement to my shock. "Riley acts the same way. You both are adults so it shouldn't come as a surprise that part of growing up is realizing that sex is not something to be embarrassed over."

"Definitely not embarrassed. Is this where you tell me to be careful?"

"I have a feeling I don't need to tell you that," she surveys me the way only a caring mother should. "Tell me more about the relationship with your parents."

"I don't know if you can classify it as a relationship." I take a sip of wine and Cassie waits for me to gather my thoughts. "I think my mom resents me a little. I rebelled against what she wanted for me. And when I pushed back she pushed harder."

"I think most parents just want what's best for their children, even if at the time we're clouded by the hypotheticals," Cassie notes.

"This was different. This was her encouraging me to ignore my morals by taking someone back who got someone else pregnant. That's not what was best for me."

I take a healthy swallow of wine to choke down the emotion. The more I think of and talk about my crumbled relationship with my parents, the more resentful I feel towards them.

"Do you think there's a chance for reconciliation?"

"I've thought about it. But it would take my mom some big wake-up calls to realize that the longer I stay away and the longer we go without talking for that to happen." I say off-handedly.

"What was your first thought when you found out your ex got someone pregnant?"

"Betrayal was the first word. He and I agreed that while we were working our way up the corporate ladder that kids weren't our priority. And I agreed. Also at the time I didn't even know if I wanted kids in general or I just unconsciously decided I didn't want kids with him."

"And now if you had to choose, where do you stand on the idea of having kids?"

"Are you asking me this as Riley's mom or as a therapist?" I raise my eyebrow at her and try to bring some lightness into this conversation.

Cassie chuckles into her wine glass. "Maybe a bit of both. You two are–I've never seen my son happier than he is now. When his parents passed away, it was like watching one of those commercials of someone wearing the happy mask to the world but coming home and taking that mask off, revealing all of that sadness." She blinks fast to stave off the tears and I find my eyes getting watery as well. "Dean and I did, and still do, what we can by keeping his parents' memory alive without making it seem too braggy that we knew them longer. Happiness is all I've wanted for him."

"He brings me happiness too and that scared me at first because I put all of my eggs in one basket before. But he lets me feel things in a way that's healthy. And as far as kids? I don't know. If I chose to have kids and if my body allowed me to carry to term, I wouldn't be opposed. And if I had kids with Riley, I also wouldn't oppose to it," I finish with a smile.

"I was right about you." Cassie notes and I tilt my head in a silent question. "You're good for him and he's good for you."

Conversation between us flows effortlessly. I talk to her like I would to any mom. We eat dinner as a family. Laughing and joking. Breaking out into out of the blue TV monologues. It's the most fun and stress free Thanksgiving I've ever been part of.

And as Riley and I crawl back into bed later that night, I promise to myself to tell him how I feel by the end of the year.

~

Kisses dot my face the next morning. I feel as if we just fell asleep and now a new day has begun. Kisses continue to run over my face and down my body.

"Wake up sleepyhead," Riley's husky voice beckons.

"I can't. Too much tryptophan."

Riley laughs into my neck and drops his body weight onto me. I can't complain because I get a free heater so I wrap my arms around his neck and hope this brings him back to bed.

"No way. We have a lot to do today."

"Is it too late to mold you into someone who sleeps in?" I joke through my still-sleepy state.

"Momma and Pops asked the same thing." He kisses me on the neck and unwinds my arms from around his neck. "We're decorating today."

I peek and eye open and see him already decked out in a holiday-themed sweatshirt. "Oh no. You really do love the holidays."

"Don't think you're getting out of this without matching. And on the thirty-first of December, you'll get this chance too. Now get your cute butt up and ready."

Riley hops up off the bed effortlessly and strolls into the living room full of chatter. I can't help but laugh at his joy. While I love Christmas, I clearly don't love it as much as Riley does. Doing as he says, I get out of bed and head to the bathroom to do my business and shower. When I'm dressed for the day, I head out to the living room with Sasha on my feet and halt when I see what greets me.

"Baby, we really need to talk about this," I tell Riley as it looks like the entirety of Home Emporium threw up in his living room.

Plates being set on the counter being my attention to the

man in the kitchen. "It's a lot now but I promise once everything is in its place it'll look good."

I eye the decorations warily and make my way to the bar. My mouth waters at the omelet in my spot along with an iced chai with just the right amount of milk. Riley takes a seat next to me and I lean over to kiss him on the cheek. "Thank you for breakfast."

He sneaks a kiss on my lips as I'm pulling away. "Feeding you is one of my favorite things to do."

"What else is your favorite thing to do?" I ask and shovel food into my mouth.

"I like watching you sleep," he says in that low *Edward Cullen* voice.

I drop my fork onto my plate and cover my face with my hands, laughing into them. "I can't believe you said that."

"I also just love being with you. That's my most favorite thing," Riley says and my breath hitches at the word 'love'.

I look over at him with slightly pink cheeks from that one word. Not wanting to poke the bear, I finish my food with a lightness I can't describe. It's different than anything I've felt before. This feels like more.

Riley and I put up the decorations with very little bickering. Once I found out the way he used to decorate, I straightened his order up. The balcony is the last to get decorated. We work as a team to wind and connect the garland to the railing.

"Baby, why don't we sit out here more often?" I ask after placing the outdoor pillows on the couches. Because yes, this balcony is big enough for two love seats, a two-seater cafe table, and a fire pit.

"Because I'd much rather cuddle with you inside." He says while tying the last bow on the garland.

"Fair point."

The rest of the day is filled with so much holiday joy I almost get a toothache. But Riley makes the day memorable with laughter, hot chocolate, and a Home Alone marathon of one through three.

With every second spent with him, those three words that aren't so little anymore, threaten to break free with every breath.

23

RILEY

I toss my bag on the floor and flop on the hotel bed. Travel clothes and never-washed duvet. Gross? Most definitely. But this stretch of away games is tiring. Good news is that this is the last away game for the week.

I miss my bed.

I miss Sarah.

I miss being in my bed with Sarah.

"You were supposed to wait for me," Logan whines when he finally makes it to our room. We've been roommates since last season and decided that messing with the flow wouldn't work for either of us.

"I told you I was coming to the room. You're the one who wouldn't stop flirting."

Logan shucks off his suit jacket and places it on the other bed. "Not all of us have someone waiting for us at home. I need to find a bed to keep warm."

"Well, you better go now."

He and everyone else knows what time curfew is. And with traveling all day, I just want to get some food and Face-Time with my girl. Logan grumbles his way into the bathroom to shower off the airplane. While he's in there, I call down to room service to place an order for dinner of a turkey burger and sweet potato fries.

Me: Hi, baby.

Blue: Hi, handsome. How was your flight?

Me: Noisy. Logan talked my ear off.

Here's what people don't know about Logan. He likes to talk. A lot. Especially when you're one of his best friends. Sure, he may be shy when you first meet him. But the all-star goalie has untapped information to tell you whether you want to hear it or not.

Speak of the chatterbox. Logan walks out of the bathroom sans towel.

"Dude!" I exclaim and look away.

"What? I'm comfortable in my nudity. You know this," he points out. Rooming with him has shown me more of him than I care to see. He may hide away in the locker room, but that modesty ends there.

I throw a pillow over my face and listen to the telltale signs of him getting dressed.

"Okay, Theodore you can take the pillow off your face," Logan says at the same time as a knock on the door sounds.

The door opens and I hear "Food order?"

I pop up from the bed. "That's me. Thank you." I tell the food runner and tip them a five dollar bill.

"You got food without me?"

"Yeah, you're going out. Remember?"

Logan huffs and I can't help but laugh at his dramatics. "Fine. I'll see you later."

I take the lid off my food and bring my phone to the small table.

Blue: Uh oh. What fact did he spout this time?

Laughter spills out. More times that I can count, Logan has waltzed into my condo with the key that's for emergencies only. Sarah gave him a pass at first since she suggested he might be lonely. But he took that upon himself to come over when things would get hot and heavy between us. Meaning one of us, mainly Sarah, was topless when the intrusion would happen. To say I almost punched my best friend in the face for seeing something he's not privileged to see would be putting it lightly.

Me: Did you know that a blue whale's heart weighs almost 400 pounds and can be heard up to two miles away?

Blue: Can't say that's something I ever knew.

Me: I didn't know it either until today.

Blue: You poor baby.

Me: I know.

Me: You should make it up to me.

I finish up my food and head to the bathroom to wash my hands.

Blue: Oh, yeah? How do you suggest I do that?

I pull up her contact and hit the button for FaceTime. She answers right away.

"You're a sight for sore eyes," she greets and all of the unacknowledged tension melts from my body.

"God, you're fucking beautiful."

"My bed isn't the same without you," she tells me.

I groan and throw my head back. "I can't wait to hold onto you and never let go."

"That sounds like a plan I can get behind. What time do you guys get in?"

"Monday morning and we go right to light skate." I say and put a hand behind my head as I lay on the bed.

"Well, I'll be at your place Monday evening."

"I can't wait." We look at each other through tiny screens and to say I miss her is an understatement. "You know what I want to try?"

"What's that?"

"What are you wearing?"

Sarah laughs nervously. Something I've noticed about her is that sex sometimes makes her uncomfortable. And I mean sometimes. Like when we're apart because of my road games. So I like to push her just a little.

"Tell me it's the black silk set," I guess.

Sarah pulls the covers back and pans the camera down her body. My cock hardens at the sight of her lush body. "Do you like it?"

"So much." I say, voice gravelly. "Prop your phone up and let me watch you take it off."

I take my dress shirt off and the camera jostles when Sarah gets off the bed and props her phone up against the base of light on her nightstand that's illuminating the otherwise darkened room. She's bathed in shadows, a temptress on the other end with the black silk set a stark contrast against her milky skin. An angel in the devil's clothing. Because that's what she is to me. An angel.

Sarah slips the straps off her shoulder agonizingly slowly. Her hair falls in auburn waves over her shoulder and the look she gives me is one of pure sin. The air must've turned on because I watch in real time as her perfect rosy nipples point to hardened tips.

I've already taken my cock out of my pants and have been slowly stroking myself as each inch of her was bared to me. "Get on the bed and turn the camera to you." Sarah does what I say with no rebuttal and it gives me a thrill that she's turning desperate for what's next. "Good girl. Spread your legs and let me see my pussy." Glistening the way I knew she would be. "Fuck, baby. That's a fucking beautiful sight." Pre-cum beads on the tip of my cock and I use that to ease my strokes. "Rub your clit for me, baby. The way I would."

I watch her hands trail down her body tantalizingly slow. I have to grit my teeth when she teases around the area I need her to touch most, but then I almost swear when I hear Sarah's gasp at the first touch of her clit. "Riley."

"I know, Blue. You're already drenched. I can see. Dip two fingers inside of you and pull them out. I want to see how wet you are."

Sarah does as instructed. Going even further to rub her clit. The sounds that are coming from her cunt is how I know she'll come at any second.

"That's enough," I bark and she mewls. "Pull your fingers out. Let me see how wet you are." I almost weep when I see her essence all over her fingers. "Damn. Baby, I can't wait anymore. I need you to make yourself come. I need to see you come."

I watch this beautiful woman take control of her pleasure and I get a sick amount of satisfaction watching her.

"Oh god, Riley," Sarah moans. I watch as her fingers

tunnel in and out of her pussy and the other hand plays with her clit. Her toes curl into the sheets on the bed as I continue to murmur filthy words through the phone. A moment later, her body stiffens and a gasp of my name spills from her lips as her orgasm hits her. Her fingers pause on their assault before she's working herself through her orgasm. Fingers in her pussy and the other playing with her clit.

Mine hits moments later as I watch her orgasm spill down to her asshole. "Fuck, fuck, fuck." I moan as I come all over my stomach. My chest heaves from the orgasm and I look at my phone to see Sarah laying in the same spot from moments ago. She must realize the vulnerable position she's in as she sits up and looks at me through the camera.

"I am counting down the minutes until you're back in my arms." She says, face flushed and pupils blown.

"Ditto, baby girl. Get some sleep and I'll see you soon."

"Bye," she blows a kiss to the camera then hangs up.

I look down at the mess now dried on my stomach and decide to shower and then head to bed. This last game in our away stretch can't get here and done sooner. Something changed with Sarah these past couple of weeks. Like she's been holding herself back from saying something huge. If we're on the same ride like I know we are, then it's the same words that have been threatening to spill from my lips as well. But it's too soon. It is, right? The times I've wanted to say it have been after sex and that could be blamed on the orgasm high. But what I feel for her is still there when we're doing normal things.

I don't want to scare her though. Sarah has a past that is beyond what I could imagine. Granted, I have a past as well. But her past scared her away from love while I made sure to grasp onto every ounce of it. Maybe this is something I talk to my coach with, he always gives good advice. What's another life lesson he can't teach me?

Our home crowd cheers as we head to the locker room for a quick intermission. Washington has matched us move for move. With a score of one to zero in the second period, we have the chance to win the first home game back after being away for so long.

"Hey," I say to one of the athletic training assistants. "Will you do me a favor?"

He looks at me doe-eyed. "Yeah."

We get to my locker and I pull out a twenty dollar bill. "I need you to buy some fries and send them up to the friends and family box. They're for Sarah. She'll probably be with my parents so just call her name out. And keep the change if there's any leftover."

"I can do that," he turns to leave but stops abruptly. "Any sauce?"

"Ranch with a little bit of buffalo sauce if they have any."

"Done."

"Thanks, Grant."

Noah chuckles next to me. "You've got it so bad."

"You have no idea."

Coach runs through the small mistakes we made and how we need to tighten up if we expect to win. With ten minutes left to spare, we head back out to the ice. The crowd's cheers get louder and little kids pound on the plexiglass hoping for a picture or a puck. I watch as Noah points to a little kid with his jersey and tosses the puck over.

"He'll officially have the coolest story to tell his friends tomorrow." I say to Noah as we do a final lap around the rink.

He smirks and taps me on the head before heading to center ice for the face off. Washington is one of the toughest teams we've faced so for us to hold our own says something about our teamwork. Noah wins the drop and quickly passes it back to Max who swerves a defender and flips it back to Noah. Two of Washington's players flank Noah stride for stride and I hightail as fast as possible to get in his line of sight. My stick taps on the ice and he passes it to me. I turn to get in position but am blocked against the boards. My possession on the puck is sloppy, but I manage to push it free back to Noah.

When I'm finally released from the block, I find Noah and Max on the offense as they find an opening at the net. I skate around and block the path of Washington's top scorer. Noah rears back and slaps his stick against the puck. I watch from my spot as the puck slips through the goalies glove and a small part of the net. The roar from the crowd is deafening and I can't be prouder of my forward.

I skate over to Noah and pat him on the head a few times before skating over to Logan. While a lot of work hasn't been done on this end, he's still put in work when the action did make it over here.

With five minutes left to play, my line switches out. I grab for a water bottle as I sit on the bench. My helmet comes off and I watch the second line battle it out. Washington crosses center-ice on a three-man drive.

"Fuck," Max says from next to me. We both stand up and hug the wall, chanting at our defense to hold strong and to not let them pass. Logan's eyes never leave the puck. He expertly defends the net, but a scuffle causes him to lose the puck.

"Right, right, right," I yell to no avail. When Logan spots the puck the buzzer is going off. I hear Logan's *fuck* yelled across the ice as Washington celebrates back to their half of the ice.

Max, Noah, and I give each other a look before we're switching out to hopefully come out of this game with a win.

"CAN'T WIN EM ALL GUYS." Coach says in the middle of the locker room with his clipboard tucked under his arm and a furrow firmly on his brow. We went into overtime and it was like Washington had fresh legs on them. "Defensive skate tomorrow at ten and mandatory conditioning at two. I don't care if it's here or at a studio. Now, hit the showers."

I beeline to my locker to my phone and open it up to text Mischa.

> Me: Any openings for after two?

> Mischa: At this moment, no. But I'll let you know before your practice is done.

> Me: Thank you.

I exit out of the conversation and to the one with Sarah.

> Me: Showering and then headed up.

> Blue: I'll meet you at the locker room

> Me: 🤍

I get undressed and to the showers with one goal in mind: getting home to my girls. Once I'm showered, I throw on a gray hoodie, some worn jeans that Sarah loves, and my black Timberland boots. I decide to stop at Anderson's office before heading out because his advice is the one that I desperately need.

"You have a second?"

"Just a few. Kylie pouted and stomped her foot, said we were watching a Christmas movie tonight so I need to get home."

I move and sit down in front of his desk. "She learns that from Mischa."

Jared throws a pen at me. "Get on with it or get out."

"How did you know you loved Mischa?" I ask out-right. I never got the chance to ask him after our stretch of away games and now seems as good of a time as any other. Those three little words are closer and closer to being freed.

"Wow," Jared says and leans back in his chair. I know he wants to tease me, but he must see the desperation on my face. He sobers up and leans forward and places his elbows on the desk. "We were dating for a little while by this point. Still casual because of football and volleyball. And it was after one of her games where she dominated at the net. I couldn't take my eyes off her more than what was normal. Later that night we were at the student center, playing a game of pool. She beat me and I told her I loved her. I love her competitiveness, her fierce loyalty to those in her life, her hunger for more. I told her that night I was going to marry her because I wanted her competitiveness, loyalty, and hunger in my life for the rest of my days."

"Sounds like she settled, then," I joke because that was the most sentimental thing I've ever heard coach say. He throws another pen at me and I rise with my bag on my shoulder. "But in all seriousness, thank you. That helped a lot."

"No problem. I'm proud of you, Riley. You've really

turned it around this season, so I guess I should be thanking Sarah."

I toss my hair back with an exaggerated flip. "Whatever, I'm the catch. Get home before Kylie screams your ear off."

Jared checks his phone and smiles. "Yeah. I'll see you tomorrow."

I walk back into the locker room and dodge a towel from Max before pushing out into the hallway. Sarah is tapping away on her phone, unaware of her surroundings. I shake my head on an exhale and creep over to her. With the sounds echoing throughout the hallway, it's easy to do undetected. I gently wrap my hand around her neck and mash our lips together. I feel her moan against my hand and my tongue tangles with hers. Sarah slides a hand into the back pocket of my jeans and pulls me against her.

Outside of the locker room at the arena isn't the place to do this. But when she rises on her toes to get closer, I realize I don't care.

A shrill whistle causes Sarah to jump away from me. I look down at her puffy lips from my assault and her rosy hued cheeks and realize that what I feel for her is real. That it's not a result from lust or endorphins. But this is real. I love her.

Only now I need to figure out when the best time to tell her would be.

And if she feels the same way.

24

SARAH

"I know it's late, but I have a surprise waiting for us," my voice is giddy as I tell Riley and I'm barely able to hold in my excitement.

His face is lit up from the glow of the dashboard and I see a smile lift his cheeks. "Well it's clearly not you sitting on my bed wrapped with a bow."

I lightly hit his thigh. "Perv."

"What? It's Christmas time. The time to unwrap all of the presents." He states his case as he pulls into the parking garage and whips into his spot.

"Play your cards right and that might be a present for you." I unbuckle my seatbelt and hop out before Riley can stop me.

With Riley no longer my client, I've never felt more balanced in all areas of my life. Mason officially announced his retirement, Nate is visiting family in Virginia, and the soccer player I was working with decided he no longer liked my direct approach with his image so we parted ways. It was no skin off my back as I managed to sign on two more football players and one of Nate's teammates. I meet with them before the end of the year to discuss their goals and what they want their personal brand to reflect.

"Oh are we making lists?" Riley asks when he finally steps out of the car. He snags his bag from the backseat and we head over to the elevator bank.

"No," I draw out and push the button to go up. We have no wait and head straight into the elevator car. "Besides, I wouldn't even know what to ask for. I buy all of my own things."

"Hmm," Riley starts and I rest my body on his and look up at him. His eyes are darker in the elevator, but that's what I love about them. "I'll have to do some serious re-con."

I narrow my eyes at him and push off when the elevator opens. Riley's "re-con" involves texting my best friends and getting their input. Jokes on all of them because none of them will have a clue as to what to get me. Although, I'll never turn down a pair of shoes.

Riley moves around me to open the door and swats me on the butt as I pass. I go right to the bedroom because the surprise is in here.

The sound of Riley's bag hitting the floor with a thud signals he's saying hi to the girls. Pixie is still coming around to me being around while Sasha usually hangs off my body anytime I'm here.

"Blue, I know it's late, but–what is this?" He asks when he gets to the threshold.

I'm standing by the bed with my arms pointing to the bed.

"You got us matching jammies?"

"Mm hmm. Baby, you're freakishly tall and muscular, so I had a tough time tracking down a matching set."

Riley wastes no time and pulls off his sweatshirt while I eye his tattooed and rippling torso appreciatively. His sweatshirt hits me in the face and his chuckle is muffled. I'll never stop appreciating his physique for as long as we're together.

Our matching pajama set in question is a navy blue color with gingerbread houses, candy canes, presents, snowmen, and basically everything Christmas print all over. Riley pulls on the solid blue henley, which I've come to find that he favors over any other type of shirt so his excitement is palpable when he puts the shirt on.

I'm not shy about changing in front of Riley. But anytime I take something off my body, he takes everything else off and we end up in bed.

"Are you going to change?" Riley asks as he slides his jeans down his legs.

"Yep. When you leave the bedroom."

"I can control myself." He states as he also slips his boxers off and I meet his eyes. The devilish grin is telling.

I cross my arms and pop my hip to the side. He's so full of shit and he knows it. His pants slide up his legs and they fit perfectly.

"Okay, princess, I'm going to the living room." Riley holds his hands up in surrender and walks backwards to the living room.

I wait until I hear his shit talking to Pixie about how it's me who can't control themselves. Shaking my head, I peel off my arena layers and decide to rinse off before heading back out there. I'm brushing my hair out when I hear Riley complain that I'm taking too long.

"Do you know how hard it is to see you skating across the ice and then having to wait for you to finish your post-game talks and then shower?" I point out to him and I look into the bedroom to see him spread eagle on the bed.

With my Christmas pajamas on, I turn the bathroom light off and crawl over him on the bed. His hands land heavy on my hips and his eyes land on my face. It's definitely love I see reflected back at me. And I realize that it no longer scares me. Love with Riley is an adventure that I'm not afraid to take.

His position shifts suddenly when he stands up and carries me to the living room. My legs wrap around his waist and his hands lock under my butt. I place a kiss on the side of his head before he's dropping down onto the couch with *The Santa Clause* already cued up.

"Now, we only have time for the first movie since someone took so long getting dressed," he explains and I pinch him in the side resulting in a yelp. "But, we can watch the second one tomorrow night."

"If I'm back in time," I tell him and press the play button on the remote.

"What do you mean?"

I cover us with one of the many throw blankets, this time a festive throw blanket, which is more like the size of a large tent, and turn to Riley. "Kamryn and Mason are wedding planning. Well, mainly Mason since Kam is busy with the holiday season."

"Did they set a date?"

Scott Calvin's holiday work Christmas party fades onto the screen. If the 90's had a vision for what it looked like, they nailed it.

"Yes. They chose April."

"That soon?" Riley's surprised.

"Trust me. These two talked about marriage when we were in college. So this speed is no different. Plus, I think they want to start a family sooner rather than later." At the time, I wasn't going to ask him since we were temporary, but now I can. "Would you want to be my date to their wedding?

I mean, we can't sit together during the ceremony since I'm officiating it. But there's always the reception."

"I would love to."

I turn back to the movie with an uncontrolled smile on my face but I feel Riley burning a hole in the side of it with a question ready to fly off his tongue.

"Do you want a family?"

There it is. I lean forward and press the pause on the remote. Turning, I slide my leg over his and give him my full attention. "I thought you wanted to watch a movie?"

"I do. But I think–no, I am curious about what you want for your future. You're much further ahead than I am in life and I wasn't sure if that's something you thought of." In this moment, he looks much older than his twenty-three years and it shocks me that he could even be thinking about a family this soon into our relationship.

"Momma and I had this talk at Thanksgiving," I tell him and his eyebrows fly to his hairline and I nod with a closed smile. "When I was with my ex, we were of the mutual understanding that work came first. We were both so–I don't want to call it power hungry, but that's what we were. Our jobs were our top priorities, or so I thought. Maybe I was so hellbent on succeeding that I brushed off his little comments about how our friends' kids were cute or how this couple just announced their pregnancy." I smooth out the furrow in the middle of Riley's forehead. "That may have been why when he told me the girl he cheated on me with was pregnant, I was in shock. Mostly angry that he did that behind my back. So that day, I pushed away any thought of ever having a family or loving someone. But then you came along and threw everything I thought I didn't want out of the window. Kids were never in the cards with anyone from my past. Neither was a future. And maybe that was a good thing. Because with you now I think I can see it all."

Riley lunges forward and takes my mouth in a burning kiss. He effortlessly pulls me over so I'm straddling his hips. My explanation was more of a silent love declaration and if this kiss means anything it's that this is it. His tongue teases at my lips and I open. My breath is stolen as he licks into my mouth and Riley's hands wrap around my waist, holding me in place. This isn't just a kiss. It's a declaration that we might finally be on the same page in the same chapter and on the same sentence. Not that we were ever on different pages. But this feels like our story may finally be written and completed at the same time.

I slide my hands through his now almost shoulder-length hair and break the kiss. His eyes are wild and his lips are red from our kiss. "I love you, Riley. I had this big speech planned–"

"I love you too. I remember telling you to let it be me when you decided to love again. I've been wanting to say those words to you for weeks. But I didn't want to scare you away."

"The only thing that would've scared me was you not feeling the same way."

He leans forward and shakes his head. The tips of our noses brush together and my heart sings. "No, Blue. You wouldn't have scared me away. But I think I was just waiting for you to catch up." With a kiss to the tip of my nose, he slides me off his lap but keeps me tucked close as he presses play on the movie.

Is it possible to want to burst from so much joy? This has to be what Kam and Emily felt when they declared their love to Mason and Adam. Because I never felt this with Paul. In fact, he was less of the touchy-feely type.

Maybe I'm finally realizing it wasn't love with him. Just...contentment.

THE ALARM BLARING causes me to jolt and cover my head with a pillow. "Turn it off," I groan.

While we finished the movie, we went to bed later than either of us was used to. Riley told me that he had an alarm set for 06:30 but it felt like we just closed our eyes. The sound stops and he slides over me, staying under the covers, and laying his head on my stomach with his arms wrapped around me.

"I snoozed it, so we have ten minutes of extra sleep before I have to head to practice," he tells me groggily.

His body weight on me is like having a personal weighted blanket that's also heated. I pull the pillow off my face and tuck it back under my bed. Lifting the covers, I see Riley's back rising and falling in a deep sleep. How he manages to fall asleep so fast is a surprise to me. Soon sleep pulls me back under. If only for a little while.

It's only when I'm back to sleep that the alarm goes off again. I reach under Riley's pillow and turn it off. His breathing has changed so I know he's waking up.

"Time to get up, baby."

He holds me tighter and presses his face into my stomach. Rumor has it, is that when couples enter the dating stage, they put on what's called 'love weight' and while I was never overly toned, being with Riley has ensured that I never skip meals. He's also a health freak during the season so we fit in daily walks as part of his light exercise training. I remember complaining about my extra curves because the fit of my clothes was different and he made me stand in front of the mirror and point out every flaw while I watched as he loved on every inch of my body.

His lips trailing over my stomach pull me out of that memory. If it's one thing Riley loves is our mornings in bed. He's especially needy when he knows I have to go back to Cincinnati for the day. My breathing changes when his hands cradle high at my rib cage and I sling my leg over his waist.

"What do you want, Riley?" I ask as he trails up my body and leaves no spot untouched with his kisses.

"To slide my cock so deep inside of your pussy it's all you think about for the rest of the day." He tells me and gently pulls a pointed nipple between his teeth.

I whimper when he teases the other with a light touch. "So do it."

Riley kisses up my torso and hooks my other leg over his arm. He slides into me with no resistance and groans into the pillow behind my head. "Fuck, baby. How does this get better every time?"

I ask myself that every day. If I love sex, then Riley loves sex with me in general. I've come to learn that hockey players have an exceptionally high sex drive. No spot in Riley's condo has gone un-Christened. No sexual position has gone untested. But this–sleepy morning sex has to be my favorite.

My hand fists his hair and I lick a trail up from his neck to the spot behind his ear that I know drives him wild. His thrusts stutter before he's sliding back into me. I feel the early sign of my orgasm and Riley's swear tells me he can feel it too.

"I want to try something," I manage to squeak out.

Riley pulls back and I can see the sweat glistening on his

inked chest. His thrusts never stop and I bite my lip when his pubic hair rubs against my clit. "What's that?"

"Are you close?"

"Yeah, baby. Just waiting on you."

I moan through the pleasure. "Okay, stop moving."

Riley stops his thrusts with confusion. "Did I hurt you?"

I shake my head and move my hand between us. His eyebrow quirks as I rub my clit in fast circles with him still inside of me. The eye contact and the zing of pleasure that shoots up my toes and to my spine causes my orgasm to pulsate out of me.

"Fuck, fuck, fuck. What are you doing to me?" Riley asks as I feel his cock swell and his release spill inside of me. He falls down into the crook of my neck and I squeeze around him while still rubbing my clit as I milk him for all he's worth. That causes another tiny orgasm to rack through me. "God damn, you're fucking perfect," Riley says and kisses the side of my neck and my shoulder.

When the last of my orgasm fades, my body sinks into the bed and I wait for my heart to stop trying to pound out of my chest. A few moments later, Riley pulls out of me and places a kiss on the center of my chest before rolling off the bed and into the bathroom. The toilet flushes and the shower starts up seconds later. I roll off the bed as gracefully as possible and lightly jog to the toilet to pee. I look up and see Riley cheesing at me from behind the glass and I roll my eyes. Living with Riley, I got acclimated that there is essentially no privacy. He likes to remind me that he's had his tongue in my pussy so why shouldn't he see me pee.

I join him in the shower after flushing and wrap my arms around his waist. He switches our spots to get my hair wet even though I didn't plan to wash my hair.

"Do you have to go to Cincy?" He asks and grabs the shampoo.

"Yeah," I sigh. My eyes close when he rubs the soap into my scalp and my head droops back. "I'm also meeting with my new clients."

"Lean back," Riley whispers. "Who are you working with this time?"

"A couple of Mason's former teammates and one of Nate's teammates."

Riley wrings my hair out and applies the conditioner to the middle to ends of my hair. "What happened to the soccer player?"

I feel the soft tug on my hair as he brushes the conditioner through my tresses. "He didn't like the way I made him walk the straight and narrow path. So we parted ways right before Thanksgiving."

"Blue, that was three weeks ago," Riley says and gently tips my head back to rinse the conditioner out. He grabs the bar of soap and loofa deciding he'd rather wash me than himself.

"There was no skin off my back. Plus, he was already giving me trouble and a lot of pushback at the beginning of the year."

He steps away to wash the front of my body and his forehead crinkles in concern. "Does Jeff know?"

Shaking my head, I place my hands on his shoulders to keep steady. "No. I'm a big girl, Riley. I can take care of myself when it comes to pompous, rebellious athletes."

"I know you can." He stands up and turns me to face the water. "Is the soap all gone?"

I look down my body. "Yep."

"Okay. Get outta here ya goof."

I slide past Riley and grab a towel from the warmer rack.

I watch him as much as I can before I brush my teeth and wash my face. After last night, I thought we'd have a bit of awkwardness hanging around. But no, everything is all the same between us.

When Paul and I said those words to each other, I felt like I had ants crawling over me. Was that a bad sign and I just ignored it for that contentment? Because with Riley I feel like I can say it a million times and he'll show me just how much instead. And maybe that's where I should scold myself by thinking our age would be the biggest obstacle to overcome. Riley has debunked everything I thought I knew about him, about love, and about life. And as we stand in domestic bliss getting ready at the bathroom vanity I think, maybe, just maybe, I've finally found my true pair.

25

SARAH

"So we're going to start from top to bottom. Starting with your socials. No one likes to see party picture after party picture on an athlete's feed. I know you both are young, but the fans want some form of para-social connection. And partying every night is not the way to do that." I run through the rest of my plans with Deon, Michael, and Bryce. How I hope to find them both brand deals that align with their personal interests and if a press release needs to be made I need to be aware of it.

It's as if time flew by and an hour later they're both looking at me like I started spouting French.

"I know it's a lot. Especially on the social media end. I can run them for now until you both hire reputable people to do that. Same with your websites. And when it comes to your brand deals, I'll be by your side every step of the way."

They both look at each other and I have to bite my lips closed to keep from laughing. It's a look that Mason and Nate gave me when I gave them a rundown of my plan and how I operate my business. Deon and Michael look at each other before he looks at me and is the first to speak up. "Mason's right. You're good."

"Thank you." I preen because I can't help it, I love praise for my work. "So you two are playing Sunday at one and I'll be there. Are either of your families going to be there? I know some publicists don't like to mix business and personal lives, but me working with you two is as much personal as it is business."

"Yeah, they'll both be there," Michael speaks up.

"Okay, perfect. You two have everything from me and I'll see you on Sunday." I stand up and walk them to the door of my office.

The three of them say their goodbyes and I head back to my desk. It felt weird walking into the office after working remotely for the better part of two months. My jeans and sweater combo made me feel out of place in a place where I felt like I belonged prior to meeting Riley. And I'd be lying if I said I missed it around here. But something feels off about being here. I know I would never work for someone else because I know that no other PR agency would make me feel as seen as this one does. Does that mean I've let my priorities change? Does that mean I love being a publicist any less than I did a year ago? Maybe it's me who's changed and I'm finally accepting that.

> Kamryn: What time are you headed over here?

> Me: Wrapping things up now. So say thirty minutes?

> Kamryn: Okay! See you soon.

I knock out a couple of more emails that need my attention before closing up and peeking my head into Jeff's office before I leave. "Hey, stranger."

"Me? You're the one no longer in the office."

"You know I love you like a brother I never had. But I love working from my boyfriend's couch even more," I brag as I come to sit in the chair in front of his desk.

"So I take it things are going good with Riley?"

"Try fantastic. And thank you for letting me change up my work schedule."

He waves me away like it's nothing. But him allowing me to work in Columbus, even though it's just over an hour away, has helped mine and Riley's relationship strengthen in a way normal long-distance relationships would have crumbled.

"So what's new with you? One of the downsides of not being here as much is not being able to bother you." I chuckle and swat at a pen that Jeff jokingly tosses at me.

"I started seeing someone," he tells me casually.

"Who?"

"Olivia. She works with your friend, Kamryn."

"She's so cute. And you're robbing the cradle a bit with her," I tease.

"Shut up before I fire you."

"Just remind me again how old you are and how old she is."

If looks could kill, I'd be dead. "I'm forty as you very well know." I wave my hand out for him to continue. "And Olivia is twenty-five."

"You know," I start and hold my hand up to stop him from interjecting. "My best friend and her boyfriend have an age gap. Jeff, I like to tease you. But if what's happening between you two makes you happy, then you deserve it more than anyone."

Jeff's widow status is not something we discuss a lot. Like Kamryn and Emily losing people they loved, it's not something we need to talk about. And while I know Jeff's loss was bigger than theirs it was still a loss.

"How do your kids feel about you dating?"

He sighs and leans back in his chair. "Zoey is hesitant of course. All she knows is her Mom and I together. Thomas on the other hand is too young to understand what my dating someone who isn't his Mom means. I mean, it makes sense since he wasn't even walking."

"Dating is terrifying," I admit.

Jeff turns his grey gaze, which shines with unshed emotion, to me. "Yeah, but being lonely is even more terrifying. For the record, me dating Olivia isn't me filling some sort of void."

"So what is it between you two?" I ask and sit back in the chair and get comfortable.

"It's like watching the first snow fall of the season. So peaceful, but also fun." Jeff says it all with a smile and I can't help but bask in his happiness.

"Her age doesn't bother you? Wait, how did you two meet? No offense, but you two don't look like you'd run in the same kind of crowd."

He swats at my hand that's on the arm of the chair. "I take offense to that. And happy hour at Breakers of all places."

My eyes widened at the name of the bar we used to frequent. "You went to happy hour?"

"I get out on occasion when I can get a babysitter. But, yes. She was there for a birthday and was dared to kiss a stranger of her friends' choosing."

"Scandalous," I feign shock. "But also those are the kind

of games I'd expect the younger crowd to play. Let me guess, the kiss was love at first sight?"

"Not at first. And no her age doesn't bother me," he admits with a faraway look on his face.

"If anyone deserves happiness, it's you."

He looks at me and smiles. "So do you."

"Thanks. Have you introduced her to the kids?"

"I want to. But until Zoey is comfortable with me dating someone else, I'm going to wait. Olivia is also understanding."

We tease each other about our love lives and he loops me in on what's happening around the office before I say goodbye to him a little while later to head to my car to make the short drive to Kamryn's house. Or should I say Mason and Kamryn's house. To say I'm still shocked that she agreed to move if he found them a place to live that was spacious for all of them is an understatement. While I'll miss her cozy little house, it was just that. Little. And not the best place for her huge quarterback boyfriend and her two pets.

I pull into the long driveway and park off to the side. I don't pay any mind to the extra cars in the driveway as it's probably a crew they hired to start planning the remodels. These two have been in full go-go mode for the last two months to make this house a permanent home and Kamryn is picky. On the walk to the front door, my phone buzzes with a text from my favorite guy.

> Riley: T minus how many hours until you're back home?

> Me: Someone's needy.

> Riley: Yes. Yes, I am.

> Me: You can survive a few hours without me.
>
> Me: I'm about to walk into Kamryn's and then I'll be home.

I knock on the front door and open up without waiting for an answer. Should I wait? Definitely. I've found my friends in too many compromising positions to count and have seen way more than I ever wanted to see. I keep my eyes to the floor as I make my way to the kitchen.

"Happy birthday!" Cheers greet me when I walk by the living room and my phone slips from my hands, clattering to the floor.

I look around the room at my friends and the athletes I've worked with who've become friends. And in the center of the group is Riley holding up a banner. Kamryn is the first to break from the group and tackle me in a hug.

"Did we pull it off?"

"Did you see my face?" I ask rhetorically. "How..?"

She pulls back but leaves her hands on my shoulders. "It was all Riley's idea. He texted me a couple of weeks ago about setting up a surprise party for you."

"He did?" I ask and my gaze moves over to him as he talks animatedly with Mason.

"Yeah. He's a good one. And maybe a little hurt that you didn't tell him when your birthday was."

I nod wordlessly in agreement before Kamryn moves around the room being the gracious hostess.

"You're tough to surprise, you know that?" Emily asks when she comes over with Dylan on her back.

"It's because I hate surprises," I tell her and stick my tongue out at her.

"Why do you hate surprises, Ms. Sarah?" Dylan asks with his chin popped on her shoulder.

"Because sometimes they're scary. Do I not get a hug? It is my birthday after all." I ask, popping my fist on my hip.

Emily shuffles around and Dylan slides into my waiting arms. I know he's a bit too old to carry, but he is on the shorter side for his age. Plus he still somehow has the baby smell. I dramatically squeeze him tighter and blow raspberries on his neck before setting him down.

"Emily, can I have cake?"

Her hand falls firmly on top of his chestnut brown head and gently shakes. Emily looks at me to make sure it's okay that he gets cake before me and I nod my head. "Sure. But only one slice."

He runs off and she turns to me. "You look happy, Little Bird," I tell her.

"I am. I could say the same for you," she observes.

Her and Adam finally got back together a couple of months ago after we had a small intervention. Watching him run out of his restaurant to kiss her for their reunion was like watching a romantic comedy.

"God, I feel like you and Kamryn," I tell her unabashedly.

"And how's that?"

"Nauseatingly happy."

Emily snorts into her fresh glass of champagne. "Coming from Ms. Doom and Gloom, I take that as a compliment that you're actually a girl underneath all that snark."

"Thank goodness for that." I jump a little when Riley comes up and wraps his arms around my waist. He places a kiss on my cheek that has Emily smiling at us in her *I know a secret* look.

"I'm going to go find my boyfriend." Emily says and leaves us as fast as she can.

I lean my head back against Riley's shoulder and then move out of his arms as I turn to face him. "How did you keep this from me?"

"Do you know how easy it is to plan things during road games?" Riley wraps his arms back around my waist and holds me to him. "Also, we're going to have a little talk about you not telling me when your birthday was."

I wince. "It just wasn't something that came up. I'm sorry."

"Don't worry about it. But do you know what this means?"

"No." I say skeptically and a little nervous.

"That we're both fire signs. Which now makes sense as our sex life burns hotter than the fucking sun," he finishes with a smile that has me leaning forward and laughing into his chest. "Happy birthday, baby."

I tilt my head back and look up into the eyes that have become my favorite to look into these past couple of months. "Thank you."

What I thought would be a day of going through and helping Kam and Mason plan their wedding, turned out to be one of the best days of my life. The man I love has effortlessly woven his way into my world. The man I love has made me fall deeper and deeper in love with him than I ever thought possible.

Is the happiness I once thought to be an illusion something tangible? What Riley's parents gave him, an everyday adventure in the form of love and living in the moment, he's somehow given me. Something I never had when I was growing up. Something I wish to never lose.

And as I blow the candles out on the second cake that

Kamryn had provided for me, I look straight into the eyes of the one my heart sings for and wish on every candle, eyelash, and shooting star that he's in my life for as long as possible.

26

RILEY

I place kisses up Sarah's sleeping body. It's Christmas Eve Eve and I'm excited to have off for the next few days. But we need to get in a light skate before I know the majority of us don't leave our couches–or beds for that time. She throws her arms around me and tries with all her might to drag me back to bed.

"Blue, I can't. I have to get to practice." I say and press kisses to her cheek and neck.

She unwinds her arms and relaxes back into the bed with her eyes still closed. "Fine."

I kiss her on the forehead and eyelids, then leave the door cracked. God bless our schedule for not having a game these next two days. And when I pull up to the practice arena, we all look equal bits upset that we had to leave our beds and the women in them.

Weirdly, we all walk to the locker room at the same time. One of the vets pulls the handle to the room, but it doesn't give.

"Are you guys sure we have practice today?" Noah asks us.

"Yeah. Coach told us after the game and texted us." Carter, the vet, says.

A whistle from the opposite end of the hallway causes an almost comical sight from us. "This way boys."

We all look at each other suspiciously before doing what Anderson says. All twenty-three pairs of feet shuffle the opposite direction of the locker room and ice, trailing after coach and the film room.

"I know you all were expecting to practice today. But my wife very sternly told me that you all deserved something less strenuous."

"So we're not practicing today?"

"Nope!" Coach says and stands up in the front of the film room.

"No offense coach, but I left a smoking hot girl in my bed for team bonding?" Max asks.

"Oh, great, we have our first volunteer. Gharety, up here."

Logan snickers next to me and I have to bite my cheek to keep from laughing. Max drops his duffle where he's at and walks up to the front.

"Since we're not practicing," we all grumble, groan, and suck our teeth. "I know I'm the worst. The front office has requested team holiday photos that they'll post on socials today. After we're done you all can head home and enjoy these next three days with your loved ones."

One of the interns pulls out bins of overflowing holiday attire.

Anderson claps his hands together loud enough to make us jump. "Let's get a move on, boys. I have two daughters and a wife ready to watch holiday movies and drink hot chocolate with."

We all get into gear and find what we want. A red photo

backdrop is set up on the far wall and one by one, we take our pictures. Several of them until the photographer says they have what they need.

"So, hot girl in your bed, huh?" Logan jokingly asks Max.

"Yes, and no you can't join."

Noah and I stop in our tracks and slowly turn to face them both. Not that we're against sharing but this is the first time either of us have heard about them sharing.

"It was one time!" Max claims.

"Twice," Logan corrects him.

"It's always the quiet ones," Noah says, referring to Logan.

"Well, happy holidays to you both," I say appreciatively. "And may your balls get jingled."

I turn and start my walk to my car with Noah falling in step. Logan's groan is laughable but he and Max soon follow. We say our goodbyes and I peel out of the lot once my car is warmed up for more than ten seconds.

When I get back to the condo, I realize I've only been gone for about an hour and hopefully Sarah is awake and ready to eat. The girls circle my feet when I walk back in and it's clear that my girl is in fact still in bed. After feeding them, I head back to our room and strip out of my street clothes and down to my boxers before climbing back under the covers to cuddle with my girl.

I WAKE BACK UP with a human-size weight resting on top of me. Since we were set to have practice at an ungodly early hour, I glance over at the clock and see it's not even noon so it's the perfect time to start brunch.

Sarah's fingers are teasing the tattoos on my side and I wrap my arms around her.

"Max and Logan have shared before," I say and her tracing halts its repeated pattern.

"Hello to you too," Sarah teases. "And when you say *share*, you mean..."

I snort and run my fingers through her hair. "Oh, yeah. That's not what I expected to learn today."

"Huh."

"'Huh' what?" I ask and lightly pinch her side.

"It's just weird that it's the quiet ones who are always the freakiest." Sarah trails off and I think she's about to move on from the conversation when she surprises me. "You've never wanted to share with anyone?"

"If you're asking if I want to share you, then the answer would be a 'Fuck no'."

"Easy, macho man. I wasn't asking with me. I was asking more before like in college?"

My heartbeat slows back down. "Um, no. I was very hesitant in college. Like, I was a virgin until my second year. And then I just stuck to the occasional party hookup because it was easier. Once I made it to Columbus I tried to actually date, but that...dating as a pro athlete had its challenges."

"The money," Sarah voices what we've already talked about when we originally started fake dating.

"Yeah. What about you?" I ask and twirl a lock of hair around my finger.

She adjusts her position and turns her head the other way, kissing me on the chest as she does. "No. I lost my virginity in high school so I wasn't as reserved as apparently you were. But my first week I met Kamryn, I was out of our dorm more than I was in it. I had a thing for athletes, still do apparently. Plus, I really liked sex. I ignored the labels the other girls would give me because I refused to ignore my own pleasure."

"So is that where you learned that one trick?"

Her arms slide under my shoulders and anchors herself to me. "Nope. That was a spur of the moment thing. Sex requires a lot of trust and I trust you more than anyone I've ever met or been with. But I do have other tricks up my sleeve. So I promise this relationship will never be boring."

"That night we first hooked up, is that why you were okay with us foregoing protection?"

"Yeah," she breathes out as if remembering that night all too well. "I couldn't explain it even if I wanted to. Or maybe I can. It was the surety in your eyes and your voice when you told me you were just tested and had the results on your phone."

"I'm glad you trusted me enough for that."

"Me too," she kisses me on the chest and then her stomach grumbles breaking up the moment.

I pat her on the butt and slide her off my body with a chuckle. Rolling out of bed, I pickup my discarded pajama pants and step into them.

"I love you," she sings from the bed.

"I love you too, angel." I call out as I walk out to the living room. To my surprise snow flurries backdrop my balcony. I always get a childlike feel when snow falls around Christmas. The quiet, the smell, and the peace from that first flake.

"So where are we going?" Sarah's muffled question comes from the closet.

While she hasn't technically moved in, I have made

space for her. She has a section that she's slowly filling up in the closet and a couple of drawers in the dresser. Spots on the bathroom vanity hold all of the things she doesn't need to make her beautiful and her soap, shampoo, and conditioner take up room in the shower. We're here more than at her place only because of hockey, but once the season is over I'll be at her place more. Hopefully I'll convince her to allow Sasha and Pixie to come with me. It wouldn't be fair to leave them for my mom to take care of. I also remembered I have to cancel the lease on the abandoned apartment that I rented as I'm just throwing money down the drain which gives me hives thinking about it.

"Just the town square. They have light shows, games, hot chocolate stands scattered around, and a few more festive things. I figured this would be a fun thing to do before we lock ourselves away in here tomorrow."

"What's wrong with that?" She asks and her voice is crystal clear when she pops out in a thick dark green sweater and black leggings with thick Christmas tree printed socks bunched around her ankles.

"Absolutely nothing," I say as I picture us doing nothing but eating and getting tangled under the sheets for the better part of the day. "Are you about ready?"

"Mm hmm." Her vanilla scent floats behind her as she walks past me.

Out in the living room, Sasha and Pixie are decked out in Christmas sweaters that Sarah managed to find that fit. Her dressing them up won more points in my eyes. And Pixie actually let Sarah hold her, which is a big step. We give them an exaggerated goodbye before heading out.

Since the town square is a block away, we decide to use this as our daily walk. We haven't done much in terms of exploring the city together and I feel like I dropped the ball on that. But chancing an outing during the season is just asking for a crowd and when I take Sarah on a self-guided tour, I want as little distractions as possible.

We walk through the square hand-in-hand. Or should I say glove-in-glove due to it being freezing and we both would love to keep our fingers. The town usually splurges on a snow making machine, but it's been snowing on and off all week with snow starting back up this morning. The past years you've been able to hear conversations from everyone blending together. But with the snow that's started falling steadily in the last hour, everything is silent. Sounds are muffled due to the fluff falling from the sky and with the smell of the falling snow mixed with the scent of hot chocolate and popcorn coming from different booths, it's what Christmas in the city should smell like.

Sarah and I hit every booth. Her joy when she feeds the reindeer is palpable and I make sure to capture the moment in pictures and video. I realize that while she's a few years older than me, we have lived completely different lives as she hasn't lived the way I have. So as we continue through the Christmas festivities, I make another promise to give her a life full of adventure. And seeing this activity through her eyes is like experiencing my childhood all over again.

"Well look who it is," a voice to the right bellows.

After feeding the reindeer, we moved off to the side for some more hot chocolate and to watch the family's ice skate.

"Mischa, hey. Other Anderson's," I joke and Sarah swats me on the thigh.

"Good to know you don't change off the ice," Jared drawls.

Mischa looks at me as she bends, holding the sleeping

baby on her chest closer to her, to whisper not so quietly in Sarah's ear. "You can still leave him. Move on with someone more mature."

"I'm quite fond of him," Sarah says with a wink.

"Kylie, don't you have a Christmas movie to make your dad watch?" I ask, because I know Jared hates Christmas movies with a passion. I mean, the guy thinks *Die Hard* is a Christmas movie.

The curly-haired girl with a toothless smile and caramel brown skin, a perfect mixture of Jared and Mischa's, bounces on her toes and swings Jared's arm back and forth. "Daddy said after we feed the reindeer."

Jared narrows his eyes at me with a silent threat to make me skate until I puke. Luckily I'm used to his empty threats and just sip on my rich hot chocolate.

"I fed them for the first time and they seemed like they could eat more than the handful I gave them." Sarah announces.

"Really?" Kylie's eyes light up. "Daddy let's go." His arm stretches as she tries to pull him away.

"Okay, babe. Let's go let her feed the reindeer and then get out of here," Mischa cajoles.

Jared's eyes soften as he looks at his wife. It's easy to see that she's his number one. Apart from Kylie and little Benny, Jared has never softened like that.

"Have fun," Sarah tells the family as they head towards the feeding pens. "She's so cute."

I boop her on the nose as she turns to face me. "So you do want kids."

"Not at this moment. But definitely in the next few years."

"Noted. What do you say we go back home and practice making said baby?"

Her cheeks pinken deeper from my suggestion. "Okay."

And that's exactly what we do. Late into the night with the Christmas lights from the balcony twinkling in the back and early into the morning as the sky turns from a midnight blue to a dusky pink. Sarah and I practice until we pass out curled into each other.

27

SARAH

The clanking of hangers hitting each other as I slide pieces I don't like fills the dead space. Since Riley had a game on New Year's Eve, which I'm not complaining about as they won, we didn't get to celebrate the way we intended. But now he has two weeks off from the ice and it's Valentine's week so we get to celebrate at my house.

I know the holiday is top tier cheese-fest. But this is what Riley turns me into. Since he has these two weeks off, we've been staying at my house. It's a good change of scenery and the cats have seemed to adjusted fairly well to the new space. Plus, hearing them run up and down the stairs has been free entertainment.

"Did you need me to start a dressing room for you?" The sales associate asks as she comes up next to me.

I look down at my weighed down arms. "No, actually. I have a few of these sets at home, I just need more." I don't tell her it's because my boyfriend goes full caveman when I wear these sets and he's been ripping them off my body since we made us official.

"I can take these to the register for you." She offers kindly and holds her hands out for the items I've chosen.

"Thank you." I tell her and hand them over.

I sift through the rack of lace bodysuits with distinct caging on the ribs and demi cups. I wasn't wrong when I said I had a few at home. But since I've been in Rileyland, I've missed out on the newer drops and have to get some new colors. Same with the sets. If shoes are my number one weakness then lingerie is a close second. I add a few casual bodysuits to my stack along with some matching sets before I cut myself off from buying anymore.

An hour later, I'm walking out of the store with two bags filled to the brim when my phone rings.

"Hey, baby," I greet Riley on the phone.

I hear his car starting up in the background. "Hi, Blue. How did shopping go?"

"You'll find out as soon as I get home."

"I like the sound of that. I'm gonna run to the store and pick up something for lunch and dinner, then I'll be home."

"Okay. I love you."

"I love you too, baby."

See? I'm a sap. I place my bags in the trunk of my car and navigate my way out of the parking garage. With football season done and baseball season getting ready to start back up, my schedule of what I need to do for my clients is in the in-between. I'm still busy but not as busy as I was last year.

Pulling up to my house, I see a few cars parked on the street and think they must be guests of my neighbors. The girls greet me when I shut the front door and I'm not sure if they're more excited for my return or if it's that my return means a snack. They follow me to the kitchen where I do in fact feed them. I'm reaching for a glass for water when the doorbell rings. Thinking it must be Riley but his hands are full I open the door without checking the peephole.

"You have that many...bags." The words die on my tongue as I see who's at my door.

"Did you miss us?"

The ghosts of my Christmas past have made their presence known in February. My mom, dad, and Paul fill the space in front of the door. My being fills with emotions I'm unable to grasp. But anger and disbelief that they can show up without warning takes over.

"What are you doing here?"

I haven't talked to my parents in over six months. I ignored every phone call from them because it wasn't worth my getting upset to hear her out. I hear Sasha and Pixie scramble past us at the door and barrel upstairs.

"You got cats?" My mom asks, completely ignoring my questions. Granted I didn't answer her first question.

"Can we come inside? It's cold out here," Paul snipes. His pea coat has the collar popped up to shield his neck from the winter wind. And I cringe at the man I thought was the one.

I do everything I can to school my facial features at the three unwanted guests on my front step. But I open the door wider and motion them to the sitting room off to the side. I don't want them here any longer than need be. And having them here already soils the happy bubble I was living in.

I close the door, but leave it unlocked because I know Riley will be home any minute. I lean against the frame to the sitting room and watch them take in what little decorations I have in this space.

"What are you doing here?" I ask again and curl my fingers into fists, probably leaving crescent indents.

"We came to see you. We missed you at Thanksgiving and Christmas," my mom says like it's not obvious.

"Why are you with them?" I ask my question to Paul.

He looks at my parents and they nod. "The baby wasn't mine. And when I found out I moved out and I've been living with your parents for the last year. We were hoping you would visit last year so I could explain things to you. But you never answered any of our phone calls."

The last year. "Do you know what I do for work? Do any of you know what I do for work?"

My mom waves me off. "Honey, you shouldn't have to worry about working if you were still with Paul."

"That right there is why we have gone so long without talking." I say as I hold my hands out. "I want to work. Hell, I love to work. And you may think that it's fine to be unfaithful to the person you pledged faithfulness to, but that doesn't work in my eyes." I hold my mom's stare. Because while I have no doubt my dad has been faithful, I can't say the same about my mom. Her personal training sessions at the country club went beyond the country club. It's something I kept a secret and with a look, she knows.

"Oh, and you're so happy up here. Away from your family and with your cats." Paul spits and breaks up the stare down between my mom and I.

I feel a gust of cold air hit my legs and I know that Riley is finally here as evidenced by the three sets intruder's eyes looking behind me.

"As a matter of fact, I am. Because despite the betrayal I felt when you told me you got someone pregnant, I found love. I let someone in who didn't find it hard to love me. In fact, I learned I wasn't hard to love at all like you said. I just needed the right person to love." I take in Paul's clenched jaw and the clenched fists at being outed in front of my parents. He probably told them his version of a story and they took his side. I then turn my focus to my parents. "The first day of college, I remembered wanting that version of you two forever. You were a perfect blend of my parents and friends. But as soon as I came home it's like I didn't know who you two were anymore. You weren't the parents who let me cry on their shoulder when I found out my friend died. Dad, I don't even know where you disappeared to, you let Mom control everything, including me. Mom, one day you're going to wake up and wonder why you no longer have access to certain parts of my life. Because living the way that you live sounds more like a prison sentence than anything." Riley comes up behind me and rests his arm over my front. Securing me. Anchoring me to him. I ignore their puzzled expression at this obvious form of trust between me and Riley. "Anytime you would call, it would never be to check up on me. It would be to see what my friend and her rich football player boyfriend were up to. But I'm your daughter. Not Kamryn, or Jax, or even Emily. Me. And you became so blind to this version of your life you wanted me to have. Maybe it was a product of how you were raised. But that's not how I want to live."

Riley wraps his other arm around me and kisses the side of my head. The three uninvited guests stand off to the far side of the room unsure of what to say or what to do. To be frank, I don't know what to do either. Because the relationship I thought I had with all of them has been soiled by their own behavior. Maybe one day I could have been brave and made the first step to reconciliation. But finding out that Paul has been living with them ruined any chance of that. That type of betrayal doesn't just mend with a few words and an unexpected visit.

"We just wanted a good life for you." My dad speaks up and my mom turns her eyes to him.

"I have an incredible life here, Dad. Maybe my life was fine in Charleston but now that I'm here I realize that wasn't my life. I don't even remember that life that you wanted for me."

My mom sets her stony gaze onto me. And I realize that I'm looking at a stranger. In all my time growing up, I don't think I ever heard my mom own up to her faults. Siding with my ex who did cheat on me and then had him live with them is a fault I know she'll never own up to. And for that she's lost me.

They leave after more awkward seconds of silence and my chest finally deflates from the breath I was holding in. I think I'm more in shock and that's why the emotions haven't hit. But I feel empty. Maybe that feeling of freedom is floating around just waiting for me to catch it.

"So that was them, huh?" Riley asks after he shuts and locks the door.

"Yeah. Can Momma and Pops adopt me too?" My voice cracks on the last words and Riley rushes over to me and pulls me into his embrace.

"Shh. They don't deserve your tears, baby. None of them do. You handled them with such poise that it amazed me."

"Seeing them here just threw everything off. I thought I was prepared for if and when I saw them." The horrifying realization that my relationship with my parents is now unfixable brings a wave of tears to my eyes. But through it all Riley holds me together as I fall apart. His reassuring words slowly put me back together because being the one to keep myself together is exhausting.

"Paul was really your type?" Riley asks with a sneer after a few moments.

I watery laugh leaves me as he leads us to the kitchen. "I had a thing for the button up guys."

"Huh," he starts and grabs a pan out of the cabinet. "You're saying I should change my style?"

"Absolutely not. I love what you wear and if you get rid of those jeans that mold to your thighs I'm withholding sex for a week." I threaten and jump up on the counter beside him.

"I was just joking about the style change. But good to know where your head is at."

I pull Riley between my spread thighs and rest my hands on his shoulders. "Thank you for letting me handle them." I say getting serious, my eyes stinging from the tears that are now threatening to fall again.

"I was never going to step in unless I absolutely needed to. But you didn't need me. Because you are stronger than any of us give you credit for." His hands lightly cradle my face and I feel his gaze move everywhere.

"I love you. In case I haven't said that enough."

He looks up to the ceiling and moves his head side to side as if in thought. "You have. But I'll never stop loving the sound of those words coming from your lips. I love you too, angel."

I slide my hands up and wrap them around his neck, pulling him towards me and pressing my lips to his. It's a kiss that's full of gratitude that he lets me fight battles on my own. I've never been so thankful to have someone in my corner who's not silently trying to tear me down day by day. Riley champions for all of my successes and I were a better woman, I would let him go and let someone other girl experience his joy. But I'm selfish in my need for him, in my need for him to lift me up when I wake up feeling low, and in my need for him to make everyday feel like an adventure I've yet to take.

$\sim$

"No."

"Sarah, please!"

"Kamryn, I'm not letting you design the dress I wear to marry you two in. That's not happening," I say to the grumpy future bride from across the table. "If you don't want wrinkles before you're thirty, I'd stop frowning." She sticks her tongue out at me and I dish it right back.

Riley and I decided at the last minute to have a double date with Kam and Mason at my place. I think it's cute the way Riley likes hanging out with him as he's like an older brother that he never had.

We're two months out from their big day and planning has been relatively smooth. Do I have a dress yet? No. Has my best friend made it her mission to convince me to allow her to design and make it for me? Yes it has been.

"But, I need something to keep me busy," she's outright begging at this point.

"Don't you have your actual job to be doing?"

"Yes!" Mason shouts from the living room.

I give Kamryn a look and get up from the table to head to the living room, leaving her sputtering at my retreating form. Riley opens his arms to me and I fall into the space next to him and throw my legs over his lap. No sooner than I'm settled does Kamryn join us.

"Where are your plans to honeymoon?" Riley asks.

"I want somewhere hot, like a beach. Or anywhere tropical at the moment," Kamryn says when she sits next to

Mason. "But, I'd have to make sure I haven't committed to any shows."

"How do you not know?" I ask with a laugh.

"They all just blur into each other year after year. I have no clue what I have or have not committed to yet."

Mason looks at her with the most content smile on his face. Since they got engaged the man has not stopped smiling. It's a bit creepy. I feel like I'm back in college watching these two.

"What about you Mason? What do you want?"

"I want what Kamryn wants."

She snorts and turns to him. "You know you have a say in where we go."

"I know."

Riley looks at me with a bemused look on his face. "Are they always like this?" he whispers.

"Sometimes," I tell him. "And what about after the honeymoon?"

"We won't prevent anything from happening if that's what you're asking. And my brand is at the point where, when it comes time for kids, I could always pull back to part-time."

I watch Mason and Kamryn's interaction with an unbiased view. I know they both want kids. The question is how many and when. Because Kamryn is a planner. She has a five-year and ten-year plan for her brand. But with kids you can't plan. And I'm not entirely sure she left space in her work plans to involve kids.

"Enough about us," Kamryn says, done with the conversation revolving around kids and their wedding. "What about you two?"

"Did Sarah tell you we had uninvited guests?" Riley asks.

I snake my hand under Riley's sweatshirt and pinch his side. The only sign he gives away is the clench in his jaw.

"No. She didn't. Care to tell me something?"

"No. Because there's nothing to tell," I say through clenched teeth.

"Your boyfriend seems to differ," Mason interjects.

I drop my head back and huff out a groan before facing my two friends. "My parents and Paul unexpectedly showed up this afternoon."

"Fuckers," Kamryn spits. "What did they want?" she asks.

Kamryn has always liked my parents. But she doesn't like that they swayed me away from my first choice of fashion design and she really only tolerated them because of me. And if that's not a true, ride or die bestie, then I don't know what is.

"The baby wasn't Paul's," I say and the gasp she lets out is subtle. "And he's been living with them for almost a year."

"What?!"

"I'm sure they thought strength in numbers and all of that. So he was befuddled when I all but refused his offer to reconcile and pick our relationship back up where we left it."

Riley tenses under me and I weave my fingers through his hand that's resting on my legs.

"Is your mom still of the opinion that you don't need to work?" Mason asks.

"Yeah, she'll never let that go."

"So where does your relationship with your parents stand now?"

"Irreparable," I whisper and distract myself by tracing the lines on Riley's palm. I can feel their eyes on me. But admitting that I want something that I don't think I can have makes me feel hopeless.

"Well, Emily fixed her relationship with her parents," Kamryn tentatively says.

"That's different," I tell Kamryn and the look she gives me sees everything I'm not saying.

While Emily's parents ignored her to further their careers, mine sided with an ex who cheated on me. And even though the baby wasn't his, he still cheated. That's not something a person can redeem themselves so easily from.

Throughout the night, we try our best to move on from my doomed relationship with my parents to lighter topics like if we think Adam will propose to Emily soon or if Jax will finally break up with her loser boyfriend. Even though I still have a rain cloud hanging over my head, this is good. Eating with the boy I love and two of the most important people sitting across from me. If they're all I have, I'll forever be the luckiest girl in the world.

28

SARAH

We are gathered here today. I scowl at the screen and delete those five words. Kamryn and Mason's wedding is in a month and I've yet to start on my speech. Plus, I still have yet to figure out what to get Riley for his birthday.

The blinking cursor terrorizes me. What can I write that I haven't already said to them?

A key turning in the door gives me an extra form of distraction as Riley comes home from practice. Pixie trots to him as the door closes and seeing him melt for the ball of fur warm my heart. Plus, men who like cats are sexy as hell.

I tap my finger on the edge of my laptop and swing my legs back and forth sitting at the bar while I eavesdrop on Riley's conversation with Pixie. Even though I call him a distraction, I'm hoping he'll be able to spark some sort of motivation in me to write this speech.

His arms wrap around me and he places a kiss on my neck. "Huh," he starts and I drop my head back against his shoulder. "It's um, an inspiring speech you've got written."

I close my eyes and a mix of a laugh with a groan comes

from my throat. "Don't start. I've written the same five words and deleted them every time thinking they'd spark something else."

"Blue, how long have you been sitting here?"

"Since you left for practice."

Riley moves around me and closes my laptop. "Nope. This won't help you."

"Riley, their wedding is in less than two months. I need to get this written. Not to mention, I still have to get ordained."

"Sarah Jane, sitting here and staring at this blank page and hoping that the words will write themselves is not productive. What you need to do is get outside." He pulls me off the barstool and waits for me to get shoes and a jacket on. "Actually, put your other boots on. We're gonna go for a drive."

"Really?" I ask, barely able to contain my excitement.

"Yes," Riley starts and leads us both to the bedroom where our stuff is. Since he was under strict orders to not ride his motorcycle at the start of the season, with it winding down I'm guessing Riley got the okay to ride. Or he doesn't care and is doing this for me because working remotely has given me less reason to get outside. But once that cool air hits my face, it's like I can breathe again.

I follow Riley to where his bike is parked behind his Range Rover.

"You had this planned the entire time. Didn't you?"

"I was hopeful." He says with a grin.

We get our helmets on, taking care to make sure they're secure before he pulls the bike away from his spot and starts it up. Holding his hand out to me, I take hold of it and swing my leg over, settling behind him. The purr of the engine sparks an untamed feeling that's indescribable.

I lean forward and wrap my arms around Riley's waist before he's pulling out of the parking garage and headed towards the interstate. I have no clue where he's going and I don't care. Getting out of the apartment is exactly what I needed. My brain is finally free from the blank page that had been taunting me for the last four hours.

The further we get away from the city, the less muddled my mind is. It's like now I can picture what I want to say at Kamryn and Mason's wedding. We head west for hours but it only feels like a few minutes. Riley taps my leg and lets me know we're planning to stop soon. The exit he takes looks like it leads to nowhere. But I trust him.

He pulls off on a secluded stretch of road and stops when we get to a lookout point. Ahead of us is miles of green and the sun shining down on us. Riley stops and cuts the engine leaving us in an eerie amount of silence save for the birds tweeting and cawing in the distance. He holds his hand out for me and I grab it to hop off the bike. Once he's off, I place my helmet on the seat and walk towards the edge.

I'm murmuring my speech when Riley hands me his phone to type it out. He doesn't have to say anything more. My fingers fly over the screen as I type my speech into the Notes app. I stop right before I get to the vows and the repeat after me section of my speech. Walking over to Riley, I slip his phone into his back pocket and wrap my arm around his waist.

"All done?"

"I am. Thank you, baby."

"Of course."

"How do you know about this place?" I ask after a while when I still hear no sounds of other cars.

He places a kiss on the top of my head and moves me to

stand in front of him. His arms wrap around my chest and I feel treasured when his arms are around me. "I found it my senior year in high school and I'd come here once a month just to get out of the house. You're the first person I've brought here."

"I'll keep it a secret."

Riley's hand drops from around me and he comes back with his phone in front of us. I see him scrolling through his music app and pulls up Ed Sheeran.

"Dance with me, baby."

I turn in his arms and link mine around his neck. We sway to the music about how he can still fall as hard in love at twenty-three. That line makes me smile and I see the same expression reflected back at me from Riley. We sway and turn to the music with the forest and wildlife our only audience. Our moves are in sync and I follow his lead as the song bleeds into the next.

"What are you thinking?" I ask as I gaze up into his eyes that match the sky.

His own eyes roam over my face and a smile teases the corner of his lips. "How much I love you. And how happy I am that we met all those months ago."

"It was definitely fate that you waltzed into my office."

Riley dips me suddenly and the laughter that spills free brings a dazzling smile to his face. "I'm more of a destiny fan, baby."

"Just so it's clear—I think about how much I love you as well."

"Do you love me enough to do something different?"

"Will it get me arrested?" I ask in a joking matter.

"Not if a cop doesn't come back here."

I laugh but then stop at the wicked gleam in his eyes.

"Here?" I ask as the excitement running through my body has already been decided.

Riley encroaches on my space and I take a step back. He matches me step for step until I'm pressed against a tree with the leaves overhead as shade and cover. His hand circles around my neck and tips my head back. Our faces are a breath apart and I'm sure he can feel my pulse at the thought of nature being our place. "Yes here." He says and his lips brush against mine as he says it.

I've already made up my mind and I close the little space between us. My breath stutters and my heart skips a beat like it does every time we kiss. The hand around my neck squeezes just enough to make my heart rate spike. Riley's tongue licks at my bottom lip and his other hand grabs my legs and wraps it around his hip. I slide my hands up under his shirt and pull him closer to me. Our tongues tangle. I drop my leg and my hands make quick work of unbuttoning and unzipping his jeans. My hands slide around his hips and past the waistband of his briefs. I shimmy them down his hockey butt and free his cock. Encircling my hand around his length, I give him a firm tug and circle my thumb around his tip.

Removing my hand, I flip our positions and push him up against the tree, refusing my mouth to his. My hands roam and Riley's fingers weave through my auburn strands. Breaking the kiss, I pull his shirt up and off his body exposing all of his tattoos in the light of day. I kiss each of my favorite tattoos then trail my lips down his body until I'm on my knees and fisting his cock. I lap up the pre-cum and hold eye contact as I slide onto his length. Bobbing up and down and sliding forward until he hits the back of my throat.

Riley's hand lands on the top of my head, fisting the

strands and holding me there. "That's it. Swallow around my cock and take me deeper like the dirty girl you are."

His voice is gravelly and it sends a wave of arousal to my pussy. With a whimper, I look up at him and swallow around his length and that small movement sends him down my throat, cutting off my air supply. I hold him there until black spots dance at the corner of my eyes and I pull back. A trail of saliva mixed with his cum connects us and I lick it up before I'm swallowing him whole again.

"Your mouth is pure fucking heaven, Blue," Riley's praise is everything I need. I bring my other hand up and massage his balls as I gorge myself on his length. "Holy hell. Either I come down your throat or in your pussy."

I look at him with a look full of innocence mixed with sin and make him choose.

Riley pulls me off his cock and pushes his tongue into my mouth on a kiss that has me unbuttoning my jeans and pulling them down my legs. "Atta girl."

Our positions are switched and Riley hefts me up in his arms. My legs wrap around his waist and his cock teases my soaked entrance.

"Is this all for me?" Riley asks as he slides in with ease. "You sucking me off gets your pussy wet?"

His thrusts are slow and steady as he hits my clit on each movement. "God, yes," I respond with a whimper.

The sun beats down on us as Riley moves in and out of me. His hands hold me up and I wrap mine around his neck, pulling him closer and taking his lips in a searing kiss. His tongue mimics his cock. Plunging in and curling around me. I bite and suck on his lower lip and revel in the groan it brings from him. His thrusts get wilder as I continue to tease him.

"Play with your clit. I need you to come and I'm right there." Riley demands after he breaks the kiss.

I move my hand between us and bring my fingers to my clit. Rubbing the sensitive spot as he thrusts in and out of me sends me higher. Riley pulls my shirt up and ducks his head under, pulling a nipple between his teeth. Light tugs and licks along the beaded tip combined with my rubbing my clit and his thrusts is just enough.

"Riley," I gasp as my orgasm rolls over me. My head flies back on a moan as he doesn't let up. My orgasm continues to roll through me until I feel Riley swell and the warmth of his cum paints my walls. His thrusts slow down as he milks every last drop. He holds me to him and wraps my legs tighter around his waist. I kiss up and down the side of his neck and his temple that's covered in a light layer of sweat.

"Outside is much better than inside." Riley says, still holding me.

I laugh a little and don't miss the grunt from him still being buried inside of me. "You're right. We should do this more often."

"Do you have a bit of an exhibitionist side to you?"

I pull back and run my fingers through the hair that never stays pushed back. "Only with you."

I've experienced more than just mind blowing sex with Riley. The adventure that he always talked about, whether it was a drive out of the city or experiencing things through his eyes, I'm discovering that the adventure with Riley, is life.

29

RILEY

I s what I open my phone to after practice. We have our last game of the season tomorrow, which happens to be my birthday, and then Mason and Kamryn's wedding is next week. As upset as I am about us not making the play-offs, I am excited for a vacation with my girl.

I put my phone in my duffle and head to the showers. The energy is mixed with the team. Naturally, the veterans are upset that we didn't make it to the play-offs. As we only have two veterans on the verge of retiring, I can see the upset as I'd want to play one play-off game before retiring my skates. But us younger kids have a lot of game left in us. So for me, I'm not too upset about the season ending tomorrow. Would I like for us to end the season on a win? Of course. A birthday and a win. Who wouldn't want that?

Walking out of the shower stalls with a towel around my waist, it's eerily quiet as half the team has left. Only me and a couple other players linger in the room. It saves me extra distractions from getting home. When I'm dressed I tap on coaches door in my exit.

"Later, Riley."

Me: I'll be home in 10.

Sarah: See you soon.

To say I love presents is an understatement. So I'm not proud that I maybe, sort of, most definitely sped home. Whipping into my parking spot next to Sarah's white Mercedes, I grab my bag out of the back and quicken my steps to the elevator. I tap my thumb on my thigh the entire ride up and attempt to Hulk the doors open when they stop on my floor.

"Sarah?" I call out when I push through the door to my condo. I drop my bag by the table with the keys and head towards our bedroom which is closed. Maybe for good reason?

I do a quick walkthrough and see nothing else out of sorts. The girls are passed out on the couch and don't acknowledge my presence. Walking back towards our bedroom, I open the door and stop at the threshold with my hand on the doorknob.

"Holy fuck."

Standing at the foot of our bed wrapped in a blue bow, one of the many shades of her eyes, is the woman of my dreams. With a matching silk G-string and her hair curled in waves down her back. Her hands are behind her back as if she's nervous but also wanting to present herself to me like the present she is.

"I know your rule about no sex before your game, but tomorrow is about to be insane and then this next week will be all wedding stuff."

I close the door and take the five steps to stand in front of her. My hands fall to her bare waist and goosebumps sprout over her skin. Her head tips back and we stare into each other's eyes. Words unspoken pass with the look.

"I can make a pre-game exception," I say before crushing my lips to hers. My hands travel up her back and into her hair. I fist the handful of hair that I have and tip her head back, deepening the kiss. Her tongue tangles with mine and her hands roam over my body, pulling me closer so no inch of space is left between us.

Sarah abruptly breaks the kiss and backs away from me.

I furrow my brow. "What are you doing?"

"What are you doing? You're supposed to unwrap your present."

I invade her space again and my hands go to the ends of the bow she's in. Slowly, I pull until the bow loops are just strands hanging to the floor. I pull the rest of the fabric loose and watch as she's bared to me. Her chest heaves and nipples harden to pointed tips. From the cold or my hungry gaze, I'm not sure.

"This is by far the best present I've ever had," I tell her as my hands gravitate back towards her waist. My thumbs brush the underside of her breasts and her ribs expand on an inhale. I cup and push her breasts together and watch her reaction as I lightly circle her nipples. Her chest heaves from the light movement and dip my head to take one into my mouth.

"Riley," Sarah whimpers when I scrape one with my teeth and tease the other to a pointed tip.

I continue giving her breasts the much needed attention, moving from one to the other until Sarah's hands fly to my head and pulls on my strands. My hands slide down to the back of her thighs and I pick her up effortlessly. Walking over to the bed, I place her down and crawl up her body. Kissing her thighs and stomach before resting between her legs and returning my attention to her breasts. Her moans, gasps, and stuttered breaths is one of my favorite sounds. Sarah's legs wrap over mine as I continue to bring her higher and higher.

"Are you gonna come for me, baby? Just like this?" I ask and look up at her head thrown back in pleasure.

"Please," she sighs out.

"Please what?" I ask and tease her with a twist and tug on her nipple.

"I nee–I need to come."

"So do it." I order.

I suck a nipple into my mouth and tug on the other. Not letting up the pressure as I bring her closer and closer to the edge. With a gentle bite, I feel her shuddering beneath me. Looking up, I see her bottom lip tugged between her teeth as she comes. Letting up, I kiss up her body and trail a hand down her body to the scrap of blue covering her. Moving the fabric to the side I'm met with zero resistance as I push a finger into her center. Sarah's hands lead me up to her mouth and our lips meet in a breathless kiss. My tongue mimics my finger as I move it in and out of her soaked pussy. I add a second finger and Sarah moans into my mouth as I fill her up with my digits.

Breaking the kiss, I pull back and pull her underwear off and toss them over my shoulder. I slide back down her body and settle between her legs. The smell of her hits me and it's unlike anything else. Keeping my eyes on her, I duck down and swipe my tongue through her slit, groaning when the taste of her invades my senses.

"Keep your eyes on me the whole time. I want my present to watch what I do." I demand before lowering my head back to her and sliding my tongue through her opening. Her pupils dilate and watching them go to a midnight blue the more she gets turned on is a new shade I'm determined to memorize. I pull her closer to me when she tries to back away. My arms wrap around her thighs and I suddenly flip our positions.

"Oh my god," Sarah cries as I keep the lower half of her body on my face. My tongue spears her pussy and her hips start moving instinctively.

"That's it. Ride my face baby," I say and look up as she grabs her breasts forcefully.

Her body sways over my tongue back and forth, chasing her pleasure. When I hit a particularly sensitive spot, she tries to pull away. But I lock her down and flick my tongue over her clit and into her opening.

"Riley," Sarah gasps as I continue my assault. "I'm close."

Without answering, my thumb moves to her clit and rubs in circles and my tongue slides into her. I feel her coming before she's yelling my name and flooding my mouth with her release. I keep up with licking her through her release, her body spasming with the aftershocks and she tries to pull away, but I refuse to let up. She falls forward and cries out as another orgasm hits her.

I slide out from under her and shed my clothes. I gently flip Sarah onto her back and make her watch as I pump my cock that's harder than steel. Her chest heaves the longer I pleasure myself and her legs close to possibly stave off the pulsing between her legs. Kneeling back on the bed, Sarah slides back to accommodate me and her legs fall open, landing on either side of me. With my hand still fisting my cock, I rub the head through her opening and push in a little, watching as my cock disappears inside of her. I tease the both of us as I pull in and out, over and over before Sarah's hand covers mine. Our eyes meet and hold as I push and she pulls me inside of her. We both watch as my cock sinks in inch by glorious inch. When I'm full seated, I pull out and slide back in.

I fall forward and my arms fall on either side of Sarah. Her hand comes up and weaves her fingers through my hair. In a breath, our lips meet. This, us, we take it slow. My thrusts and our movements slow down until it's just us. Falling into each other over and over. I hook one of her legs over my arm and slide deeper until I hear her gasp.

Sarah's eyes bore into mine and they say everything I'm not. The love and friendship that's so potent between us bleeds into this very moment.

"I know, baby."

Her eyes take on a layer of tears as I feel her orgasm crash over her and takes me too. We fall over the edge together in a tangle of limbs, hands in hair, and breathless sighs. I work us both until our orgasms fade. Pulling out, I fall on my side and take her with me. Not wanting to lose this, I keep our mouths fused. Kissing her until she pulls away and places a final kiss on my lips.

"Happy birthday, honey." She tucks herself under my chin and wraps her arm around my waist.

I kiss her on top of her head and pull her closer. "Thank you, Blue."

～

SWEAT DRIPS into my eyes and the roar of the crowd is like static from a radio when you're finally out of range. The puck hits my stick on our drive and I push myself past the defenders blocking me. Noah shouts that he's open and I find my moment to pass it to him. The defenders quickly change direction and beeline towards Noah who's in the groove with only the net in his sight.

With the final game of the season being a home game, the fans came out in handfuls. We feed off of their energy as the clock winds down. We're up by one with thirty seconds left on the play clock. Max comes to Noah's aid and helps him get a clear path to the net who takes the shot. A collective hush momentarily falls over the stadium as they wait for the buzzer to sound.

You know those moments where every scene is like a stop-motion? No noise, noise. Over and over until the stop-motion is done and it's just motion. That's this moment. The crowd goes bonkers in the stands and our celebration isn't over the top as we still have twenty seconds left to play.

We line up for the final drop, the crowd's energy is infectious and when the puck drops, the volume in the arena is deafening. Noah gains possession and passes it to one of our enforcers who passes it to Max who drives past a defender and passes the puck to Noah. I flank him as we move down the ice. I look over at Noah and see if he wants to try and score one last goal and he subtly shakes his head. I think Toronto is under the same impression. While they're playing hard, they're not playing all out. Some of the defense starts to head to their bench and the locker room. I look up and see the play clock winding down. When it hits zero, the buzzer goes off and the crowd goes mad. Throwing stuffed animals and whatever else they have in their possession onto the ice.

I slap hands with those from Toronto still on the ice and do a victory lap around the ice with Max and Bear on my tail, hyping up the crowd. Final game of the season and while it's bittersweet, I'm more than ready for a break. We gather on the ice in front of our family, friends, and dedicated fans and sing the fight song that was started decades ago. When the song ends, one of the guys at the entrance opens the door and our family members file onto the ice.

A rush of auburn hair catches my attention and eyes as blue as the sweatshirt she's wearing. "I'm so proud of you," Sarah claims before jumping into my waiting arms.

"Thank you, Blue. Nail biting enough for you?"

"I ordered two things of fries, I was so nervous."

My smile takes over my face as she recounts how the game was from the family box and how she and Mischa squeezed each other's hands so tight they were afraid the circulation would cut off.

"Good game, Riley," Pops says off to the side. I didn't even notice them join us on the ice, I was so wrapped in Sarah.

I set Sarah down on the ice and accept Pops's hug. "Thanks, Pops." I hug Momma next and slide my arms over her much to her protest.

"Riley Theodore, I love you, but you stink." Momma emphasizes her point by pushing me off of her.

Sarah and Pops are off to the side and snort. I bring my hand to my chest in mock hurt. "Momma, you wound me."

"I'm sure your ego will be just fine."

A sharp whistle sounds from Anderson and pulls our attention that way. "Gotta go." I turn my attention to Sarah.

"I'll wait for you by the locker room," she tells me with a smile.

"And we'll see you tomorrow," Pops confirms as we head towards the door.

"Yep. We'll both be there." I confirm as we get off the ice. They wave me off and I file with the rest of the team to the locker room where music blasting greets us.

Anderson stands in the center of the room and the music turns off. "Well, this season didn't end how we all expected. But you all played more as a team this season than last. I'd say practice tomorrow but now you all have four months to be normal people." He nods towards our captain who huddles in the center.

"This season was a good one. Again, not the way we all hoped it would end. But I'm proud of us." He finishes his short speech and puts his hand in the middle. We all move forward and place our hand on his. "Blue Jays on three. One, two, Blue Jays."

"See you tomorrow, Riley," the guys call out as I sling my bag over my shoulder and head to the hallway.

I send them a wave over my shoulder and push out of the door. Sarah's smiling face greets me when I'm in the hallway and it's funny how I look at her and have my entire future with her laid out at my feet. She bounds over to me and wraps her arms around my waist and my arm falls around her shoulders. Together we walk down the hallway and towards the parking lot.

"So what now?" Sarah asks with humor in her voice.

I wave to a couple of the security guards as we step outside. "Food and then sleep."

"I meant with hockey, ya goofball."

"I know." I tell her and kiss the top of her head. "I have a meeting next week with Derek to go over my contract and Tyler to discuss brand promos."

"I love Tyler. He's exactly who I would have picked for your publicist."

When Sarah and I parted ways in terms of our working relationship, I had her and Jeff help me out with finding a new publicist and agent. Tyler was the top recommended publicist and my agent, Clay, is more on top of the ins and outs for my career than I ever thought anyone could be. It's different from my last team. These guys have my back and don't try to use me for monetary gain. Plus, Clay is married with two kids and Tyler just moved in with his boyfriend of three years.

"Yeah, him and Clay are great for me." I tell her and open up the passenger door for her.

Sarah hops up and turns, sitting on the edge of the seat. "I'm proud of you, you know that?"

"I do," I say and roam my eyes over her heart shaped face. "But it's nice to hear every once in a while."

Her smile is soft and she shocks me by pulling me to her by the pocket of my hoodie. Our lips meet in a kiss that's full of passion and longing. I crowd her on the seat and angle her head to deepen the kiss. Her tongue licks at my bottom lip before I open and her tongue tangles with mine. I slow the kiss down when she whimpers and it's a reminder that we're in the parking lot. Although I know she doesn't mind, judging by our outdoor escapades, but not here.

"Let's go home and finish what you started," I say, and peck her on the lips one final time for maneuvering her legs in the truck and shutting the door. Rounding the back, I toss my bag inside and hop in the front seat. Barely waiting for my car to warm up, I peel out of the parking lot with only Sarah and our bedroom on my mind.

30

RILEY

I lean against the bathroom door frame and watch Sarah apply her makeup. It's finally Kamryn and Mason's wedding day. And all week I've watched my girl run around Cincinnati like a chicken with her head cut off. Making sure her dress is altered to perfection, her speech makes sense, and that our timing from her house to the football field where they're having the ceremony hits no snags. I've reassured her that we can't avoid snags or bumps in the road to get to our destination. But her perfection tendency knows no bounds.

Her hair is in rollers and she's wearing a navy blue robe that Kamryn gifted her with it saying *Team Bride* on the back in gold, despite her marrying them. I watch as she expertly applies color to her eyelids and pink to her cheeks before running a brush coated in black that somehow makes her eyes look bigger.

"Hey, baby," she says, finally noticing my presence.

"Hi, beautiful," I greet and walk over to her. "You look stunning." I say and smile bigger when she snorts, noticing my eyes taking in the rollers in her hair. "Rollers and all," I send my point home by lightly kissing her on the cheek and then moving off to the side to finish watching her get ready. Damn, I really love this woman.

She looks over at me and down to what I'm wearing. "Is your stuff ironed?"

"Blue, relax. Yes, it is. It's in a garment bag in the closet."

Sarah blows out a breath and turns back to the mirror. "Okay. I'm almost done and then we can head out."

I don't respond to her, because she doesn't need my words. Sarah is an action type of woman and that's what has made our relationship as strong as ever. It came from realizing that her last relationship was full of empty words. Slowly, without her knowing it, I undid everything she thought she knew about relationships by showing up in the way that she needed.

I take her free hand and kiss her on the back, leaving her with a wink before heading back out to her bedroom. My phone is just going dim from a text and I pick it up to see a text from Momma.

Momma: 1 image attached

Momma: See? They don't even miss you.

Me: Traitors.

Momma: Have fun tonight.

Me: We will. Love you.

Momma: Love you too, Riley.

"I'm ready to get dressed," Sarah announces from the bathroom.

I set my phone down on the bed again and turn to face her, ready to say something smart. "Holy hell."

"That good?" She asks, voice shaky from nerves.

"I think you're the hottest minister I've ever seen," I tell her, feeling like a cartoon character with my eyes falling out of my face, my jaw slack, and my tongue lolling out.

"I'm not even dressed yet," she points out with her familiar sass in place.

"Doesn't matter."

Sarah pads over to me with a sultry sway to her hips that I love to grip when I'm inside of her. Her perfectly mani-cured nails trail up my torso and the sensation is like a bat signal to my cock that's thickening against my thigh. Her hand curves around my jaw and I have no clue if I'm breathing because I'm already so turned on.

"We don't have time to take care of your issue," she says and I know she sees the bulge in my sweats. "Unless..."

"Unless what?" I ask desperately.

She turns me and backs me up to the chair that's in the corner of her room. "Take off your pants and sit."

Just call me *Bruce Almighty* because my pants have never come off my body so fast. I sit on the chair with my legs spread, cock resting against my stomach, and wait for what's next. And what's next turns my mouth dry. Sarah unties her robe and shrugs it off her body. The material pooling at her feet, followed by the lacy material she calls underwear.

"In order for this to work, your hands need to stay completely still. I did not spend all of this time on my hair and makeup just for it to be ruined before the night is over. And this needs to be quick. Got it?" She asks and prowls closer to me, stopping in between my legs.

The urge to place my hands on her hips is strong. So I curl them into fists and bite down on my back teeth as she straddles my lap.

"Got it?" She asks again.

I look up into her eyes and nod hard. "Got it."

Sarah rises on her knees and takes my cock in her hand. I swallow hard as she swipes the head through her slick opening and my head falls back on the chair as she slowly slides my cock inside of her.

"Your cock feels amazing, baby," she breathes out as she rises on her knees and drops down, swiveling her hips as she does.

The natural instinct to grab hold of her waist is strong, so I move my hands behind my back which pushes me up as she moves down.

"Riley," she whines, with her eyes closed and her face a picture of pure lust.

I watch my cock disappear as she slides down on me and groan as she lifts back up. "Blue, I thought you said this needs to be quick?"

Her head lols down until our eyes lock and it's like she's remembering where we need to be. She lifts up halfway and clenches around me. "We do. Now use my pussy and make us both come."

"Done. Hold still, baby."

I watch as she steels herself and stiffens her legs before I'm topping from the bottom. My hips start their movement tentatively before I'm pistoning in and out of her. The sound of her arousal mixed with the sound of our skin slapping together is one of dreams. I hear the hitch in her breath when I hit a sensitive spot.

"Right there, right there," she coaches.

I do the movement over and over until she's yelling out my name. Her pussy sucks my cock in ever further as she comes which starts my orgasm. My strokes get sloppy as I chase my release and still as I come. Painting her walls with my release. Our panting breaths mix as we come down from our joint high. Her hips lightly swivel over me and my hands gently rest on her hips.

"Better every time."

She kisses me on my sweat-dampened temple and gingerly climbs off. My limp cock falls against my thigh, but I pay it no mind as I watch her peach shaped ass walk towards the bathroom so she can clean herself up.

"Damn, Blue." I groan when she walks down the stairs.

When she picked out her dress, she made it seem like she was the one getting married and refused to let me see her dress. And now for good reason. The dark teal silk halter dress cascades down her body leaving her back completely exposed, but the front of the dress completely covers her. It's an absolutely stunning color on her that she paired with subtle gold jewelry. While I thought she would wear her hair down, she pulled it back to a high ponytail, with the ends softly curled. She's an absolute vision.

"You don't look half bad yourself, handsome." She ogles me without shame and she's about to cause another problem that we definitely don't have time to fix.

With a spritz of her perfume that I've stocked her up on, we're finally heading out the door. We have a car waiting for us to take us to the stadium and it's good because I can ogle Sarah without having to pay attention to the road. I play with the rings and bracelets that adorn her hands, not so secretly trying to memorize the size of the one on her important finger.

The car pulls up to a stop outside of the entrance twenty minutes later. The driver opens my door and I hold my hand out for Sarah. Other guests are filing in and I realize I'm going to be surrounded by current and former football players. That thought makes me shiver and it catches Sarah's attention.

"Nervous?" She jokingly asks.

"About being around all of these football players? Absolutely."

"They're just boys who play with balls," she says in an attempt to calm me down.

That gets a laugh out of me and I finally relax. We walk down the tunnel to the field where the ceremony is taking place. My eyes widen when I take in the space. I knew Kamryn and Mason knew a lot of people, but this blows my mind.

There looks to be about two hundred brown oak chairs setup, starting at the end zone. Leading the way up the aisle is white roses with the green petals still attached, with what looks like battery-powered candles on both sides, creating a romantic path. The altar is on a raised dais with an archway in the middle draped with gauzy light pink drapery and more of the white roses framing the arch.

"Wow," I finally breathe out.

Sarah's hand squeezes my hand. "Yeah. And to think they sized the wedding down."

I shake my head because this is a lot and will probably be the biggest wedding I'll have ever attended.

"Come on. They planned for the guests to meet upstairs for cocktail hour."

I'm still befuddled as we make our way back through the tunnel and towards the elevator bank.

"It's a lot, I know."

I usher Sarah into the elevator and she presses the button to take us up. "Is this the type of wedding you would want?"

"Are you asking me what I think you're asking?"

I hold my hands out and pull her to me, still careful not

to wrinkle her dress or mess up her hair and makeup. "No. Besides, you'll know when I ask you."

The blush that peaks through her makeup and brings forth a timid smile turns me all gooey inside.

"To answer your question, no. I would rather have a courthouse wedding, still with the white dress and two witnesses. Then a big party."

"Noted," I say, taking in every little thing about her facial features.

We stay like this as the elevator continues its ascent. Blue eyes to blue eyes. Heart to heart. I've filed everything she would want for a wedding in my mind. And what she described is exactly what I one day pictured. It sounds weird when a guy says they imagined their wedding. But growing up around so much love ensured that I would have what they have. And it is a heady feeling knowing that the person you're with wants that too.

The elevator stops and pings before whooshing open. Noise from those already in the room filter down the hallway and we step off just before the doors close to go back down. The clack of Sarah's shoes and her fingers entwined in mine, really makes me feel like I'm headed to prom.

Animated chatter and laughter, high and low, greet us when we step across the threshold.

"Geez," I voice aloud.

"You can officially cross 'attend a fashion designers' wedding off your bucket list," Sarah exaggerates and waves her hand in front of her.

We're greeted by Dylan, Sarah's friend Emily's boyfriend's son. "Hi, Ms. Sarah. You look really pretty."

"Thank you buddy. You look handsome yourself."

Adam walks over to us sans Emily. "Hey, you two."

Sarah greets him with a kiss on the cheek and steps back to my side. "Are you finally ready to watch these two get hitched?"

"Yeah. Em has been stressing over the musical choices since they asked her to help them choose the playlist."

The love in his voice when he talks about Emily is what I imagine I look like.

"I'm sure the playlist is perfect," I tell him.

We mingle with some of the guests before Sarah lets me know she has to head to the makeshift bridal suite. She excuses us from some of Mason's former teammates and I walk her to the elevator bay.

"I'll see you in a few. Go have fun," Sarah says and kisses me before disappearing into the elevator.

With her, being around new people has made being around them easier. Especially since most of these are athletes. I shake out my hands and head back into the room.

I SLIDE my sunglasses on my face as the late afternoon sun shines in the stadium. I'm sitting in the second row with Adam next to me. Dylan is the ring bearer and Nina's daughter, Kamryn's friend from college and co-designer, is the flower girl.

Sarah steps onto the altar first, followed by Mason and his groomsmen. Our eyes clash and she sends me a wink and an air kiss. An instrumental version of an Ed Sheeran song starts playing and the first bridesmaid walks down the aisle. One by one until the kids come down the aisle and then the song switches to *Can't Help Falling in Love*. Sarah signals us guests to rise from our seats as Kamryn makes her grand entrance.

A vision in white with lace and beads covering her dress. Thin straps hold her dress in place and a white veil trails behind her as her Dad walks her down the aisle. Her joy is evident based on the smile that hasn't left her face since she took her first step. And when she gets to Mason, their combined joy is enough to make any doubter believe that they're meant to be.

"Who gives this woman away?" Sarah asks, her question amplified based on the tiny microphone that's clipped onto her dress.

"Her mother and I." Kamryn's Dad responds and kisses his daughter's cheek before placing her hand in Mason's.

Kamryn hands her bouquet to Emily and then steps up onto the altar with Mason.

"Please be seated," Sarah instructs us.

The music ends and we settle in our seats. The energy in this stadium is unlike one I've ever experienced. And it all comes back to love.

Sarah's hands are clasped in front of her, a microphone placed in front of her, but her position is as poised as ever. "Dearly beloved, we are gathered here today to witness the union of Kamryn Rawlins and Mason Brooks. And as their closest and dearest friend, finally!" The crowd laughs and some even nod their heads. "When you two asked me to be the one to marry you, I thought 'why me?' because I'm sure there was a better option. Like an actual minister." Kamryn and Mason both roll their eyes and laugh. "But then when I snapped out of that daze, I found it an honor that you two would allow me to be a part of this special day and in this way. Eleven years ago you two met and I knew it then, that you two were meant to be. Mason, your calm and quiet presence made you a force to be reckoned with on the field. Which then helped you balance out your other half.

Kamryn, your wild and chaotic aura made everyone marvel at your energy. You two together were a couple that most were envious of. You loved with a love that was bigger than most at that young age experienced. You both hurt in the way that no one should have to. Most of us know your story, but for those who don't; these two are proof that second chances can work when the one you love is willing to work just as hard." The three of them look at each other with fond expressions. "These two have written their own vows. So, ladies first. Sorry, Mason."

Sarah steps back and hands Kamryn the microphone. "You swept me off my feet when I was eighteen, we hit a big pause a couple of years later, and when I least expected it you showed back up and would not leave me alone." Sarah, Mason, Emily, and Jax bark out laughter as do the rest of us in attendance. "You see me, the way no one ever has. You challenge me, the way no one ever has. You love me, the way no one ever has. I can't wait to spend the rest of my life with you. Laughing with you. Fighting with you. Making up with you. Having babies with you. I love you." She ends with a watery laugh.

She passes the microphone to Mason who blows out a breath. "Thank you, baby. I'm not sure how I'm going to top that. The first day I saw you, I knew then that I would give up everything to spend the rest of my life with you. While we faced a major obstacle that forced me to lose you, I thank fate and even destiny, that we landed in the same city after all those years. Kamryn, I promise to be your biggest fan, your number one motivator, and the one you always lean on when the going gets tough. I can't wait to spend the rest of my life with you, and that includes babies. Lots and lots of babies. I love you." He ends with a smile that takes up his whole face.

Sarah steps back up to the center. "Well, by the power vested in me, and the state of Ohio, I now pronounce you husband and wife. Mason, you may kiss your beautiful bride."

He steps forward and cradles Kamryn's face in his hands like she's the most delicate flower. They share whispered words and a smile before he's claiming her in front of all of us. Cheers, hoots, and whistles from us are loud enough to be heard from outside of the stadium. Love is a powerful thing. And when it's between two people who would do anything for each other, nothing can break what they have.

31

SARAH

Riley finds me in the tunnel after the last of the guests leave the ceremony. "You did great, Blue."

"Not too nervous?" I ask and wrap my arms around his waist and look up into his eyes. The ones I honed in on when I felt myself get a little nervous speaking in front of so many people. The eyes that never left me the entire time I was giving the minister's speech. The eyes I love waking up to every morning.

"Not at all." He says and dips down to take my lips with his. I lift up on my toes and try to deepen the kiss but he lightly brings me back down.

"We'll have all night for me to bury myself in you."

"Don't make promises you can't keep," I tell him and raise my eyebrows jokingly.

He shakes his head and I love the way he looks at me. Noise from the end of the tunnel signals that people are headed over to the reception. I love that Kam and Mason chose a place where we could walk to. If I know these two it's that they spared no expense and everything from the drapery to the flowers and what we'll eat is picked with care.

"Let's go, pretty girl."

We run into some of the wedding party on our way to the reception and I see Adam and Emily at the curb saying bye to Dylan for the night. When they turn around and see Riley and I slowing down, they join us on the stroll over.

"You'll see him tomorrow." I tell Emily as I loop my arm through hers. "Think of this as one of the many kid-free date nights."

"She's right, Em. Plus you know my parents will fill him up with all the sugar..." Adam trails off as he says it and swears under his breath before pulling his phone out of his suit jacket to presumably call his parents.

Emily shakes her head and laughs under her breath. "You're right. I am super excited to spend the night dancing away until my feet fall off."

"Atta girl," I champion and the guys hold the doors open for us as we get closer.

Servers with flutes of champagne are positioned at the entrance and we each take a glass before clinking them together and head towards the reception hall. Twinkling string lights create a path towards where the reception is held and music floats towards the entrance. We all step into the room and stop at the threshold in awe of what we're seeing. They continued with the twinkling light theme and brought them into the room along with white sheer curtains draped from the ceiling as string lights swoop and curtain to the floor.

The bride and groom table is at the front of the room on a lift. It's a simple two-seater table with a white tablecloth and gold chairs. For us guests, circular tables with the white tablecloths cover the surface and big glass candle holders sit in the middle of the tables with eye-catching flowers as the centerpiece. The center of the room is strategically left empty for the dancing that is guaranteed to take place.

Kamryn and Mason decided to forego a seating chart, so every seat is a free-for-all. We find a table that's empty and wait for the rest of the guests to filter in.

"Have you seen Jax?" I ask Emily softly when we settle into our seats.

She looks around the room for her. "Not since the ceremony."

I tap on the stem of my champagne flute and contemplate what to do. It's her sister's wedding reception and she should be here. I lean over to Riley. "I'm gonna go try to find Jax."

"Do you want me to come with you?" He asks, and I could kiss him all over his face for asking.

"No." I say and stand up from my seat. "But if I'm not back in ten minutes, come find me."

I swiftly walk back out of the reception hall and decide to go the opposite way we came in. Checking a few of the doors, but not budging from being locked, I keep trying until I hear a raised voice coming from the last door.

Trent's voice is raised as he berates Jax for something that most likely isn't her fault.

"Hey!" I yell sharply when I push my way into the room. "Who do you think you're yelling at?"

"Back off bitch," he spits and the mask that he's always worn around Kamryn and Mason is finally off.

"Hey!" A voice booms from behind me. A flash of blond whirls past me as a fist is sent into Trent's face.

"Riley!" I gasp at a loss for words of what else to say.

"Is this how you treat women? Tearing them down until you feel a fraction bigger than them?" His anger is like a live wire as he stands over Trent's crumpled body.

The tiniest man I've ever encountered cradles his possibly broken nose if evidenced by the blood pouring from it. I look over at Jax with her face devoid of all emotion and tears silently trailing down her face. I've never seen her so defeated and I realize I have no idea how to approach this other than affection.

"Jax?" I tread carefully. I step in front of her and wait for her gaze to meet mine. And when it does my heart cracks in two for her.

"I don't–I can't..."

I shake my head and pull her into my arms. Her body shakes with sobs and fear. I look over and see security escorting Trent out of the room we're in and hopefully making sure he leaves altogether. Riley stands off to the side with a furrow in his brow and his fist clenched.

"How long has this been going on?"

Jax pulls away from me and wipes under her eyes. "Longer than anyone knows."

"Jaclyn Marie Rawlins, tell me that you didn't hide this from your sister. From your parents."

"And say what, Sarah? That my boyfriend was verbally abusing me for the past year? Using me to get closer to Mason for fame? That every remark he made about me and how I didn't look like the Instagram models he followed tore at me day after day until I started to take matters into my own hands. Is that what I should have said?"

My mouth is agape and I look at her. Really look at her. And I swallow hard at everything she lays at my feet. Everything she went through at the hands of him. The man she loved. My therapist gave me tools for when I needed them for me. But now I feel completely useless because none of those tools are good enough for her.

"Jax–" I start, but she holds her hand up to stop me.

"I'm not like you, or Emily, or even my sister. So it was easy for me to stay with someone for the fear of being alone forever. But this is my life and what I've chosen." Jax says and turns out of the room.

I bite the inside of my lips as my eyes well with tears. Riley rushes over and holds me to him. "How can she just shake it off? That's not love."

"That's her version of love, Blue. No matter how sick and twisted it is. That's unfortunately her version. Mason told Kamryn that she needs to be the one to end it with him. And hopefully this will be the driving force for her to end it with him."

We stay like this in the middle of the empty room and I let what happened wash over me. Did Jax leave too? Did she rush after that waste of space? It's her sister's wedding for crying out loud. And if she's not here then I won't know what to say to Kamryn.

I pull back and wipe under my eyes. "Okay. Let's go back."

"Are you sure?" Riley asks and ducks down a little so he's eye-level with me.

"Yeah." I nod.

He takes my hand and together we walk back to the reception hall. I hope we didn't miss Kam and Mason's entrance. I don't think she'd forgive us for that. But would she forgive me for keeping this important piece of information from her?

"Ladies and gentleman, please direct your attention to the

dance floor for the bride and groom's first dance," the DJ announces.

Riley moves me to stand in front of him as Mason pulls Kamryn onto the dance floor with him. His arms wrap around me and I'm completely immersed in him as we sway to the song while the couple dances their first dance.

Jax returned to the reception and managed to sneak Trent in with her. I've swiftly avoided both of them. Not because I'm mad at Jax, but I'm disappointed. I know those in abusive relationships can't just leave. But I at least hoped that with all of the examples of love around her, she would see that she deserves more.

"I love you," Riley says in my ear. "I love your heart, I love your devotion, and most of all I love that you never give up on the people who matter the most to you."

I lean into him and pull his arms tighter around me. "I love you, too."

Aside from the tension within our group, the rest of the night goes on without any issues. The bouquet toss ends with Emily winning the bouquet, while Adam wins the garter toss. If my senses are as accurate as I claim them to be, then Adam has something up his sleeve.

Riley and I stay wrapped in each other's arms for the rest of the night. Dancing to all of the songs and swaying to the slow songs. Declaring our love to each over and over.

When the announcement is made that the bride and groom are preparing to take off, those of us still left head outside for their farewell. Jax and I end up standing across from each other and I've never felt like more of a trash human. She doesn't return my smile and does everything she can to focus her attention on Trent. Sparklers are passed out and lit right before the bride and groom make their exit. While our cheering is genuine, it's subdued for how exhausted we all are. And when the car pulls off, we all put our sparklers out and start to collect the things we brought with us.

"Jax," I say and try to start a conversation with her. But she pulls on Trent's hand and they disappear into the night.

"Try again next week, baby." Riley says and wraps his arm around my shoulder.

I sigh in defeat and follow him to get the rest of my things. We say goodbye to Emily and Adam with promises to double-date soon. Our car is waiting to take us back to my place and tiredly, we climb into the backseat. Riley holds my hand in his and reassures me that I did nothing wrong.

The problem with wanting to fix things, is that you want to try to fix people too. No matter your profession, put a problem in front of someone and they'll try to fix it. I don't want to fix Jax, but I do want to help and show her that she's worth so much more than some guy who constantly compares her to other women and tears her down just so he can feel better about himself. But did I go about it the wrong way? At the time, I saw nothing wrong with easing into her life. Maybe she would confide in me and tell me she wants an out. But maybe, just maybe, this is a problem for Kamryn to fix.

Our car stops at my house and Riley tells the driver he'll get the door. He loops his fingers in mine and pulls me up to the front door. We set our loose belongings in the front room and lock up before heading upstairs.

I grab a makeup wipe when in the bathroom and start taking all of my makeup off. I'm exhausted, but going to bed with markeup on is shown to age you faster. And, no thank you. I toss the cotton round in the trash and turn to Riley, "Will you unhook me?"

He pushes my hair to the side and my dress loosens as the two buttons keeping my dress in place separate.

Silently, I step inside the shower and wait for him to join me.

"What can I do, Blue?" He asks and holds me to him.

The water from the shower mixes well with my tears that I finally let free. "If I had the answer, I would tell you. But I feel...helpless."

"You saying something could possibly be one of the things Jax needed to hear."

"I hope so. My ex was not verbally abusive like Trent, but I still had no one tell me I had an out."

"And you're scared that if you didn't say anything, something irreparable would have happened?"

"Yeah."

You read about it, you hear about it, but until you're experiencing it with someone in your life, you'll never know how to go about getting someone out of a bad situation. Riley washes my hair and body, shooing me once I'm done so he can wash himself.

I dry off and do my skincare before taking care of my hair and then crawling into bed. Riley joins me a few minutes later and shuts off the light.

I'M WOKEN up with a jolt. My heart rate is through the roof and my breathing is shaky.

"Hey," Riley whispers carefully. "You're okay. I'm not going anywhere."

"I don't know what's happening," I cry, my body trembles as sobs wrack my body.

He pulls me until I'm laying on top of him and rubs my

back. "I'm no expert, but I think everything with Jax is bringing your painful time back."

I inhale a shaky breath and keep breathing until the tears dry up.

"Do you think maybe you should take a trip to Charleston?"

A protest is on the tip of my tongue because I have no reason to set foot there. But maybe it wouldn't be such a bad idea. Everything is still up in the air with my parents, especially after their surprise visit, so maybe a trip won't hurt.

"Will you come with me?" I ask even though I already know the answer.

"You couldn't stop me." He says and I nod against his chest as sleep comes back to claim me. "Go back to sleep baby."

I fall asleep to Riley's reassurances and wake up later in the morning on my side with him wrapped around me. I look at the time and see it's almost noon. Which is odd because I swear we just fell asleep.

"Morning, baby," Riley says and kisses the back of my head.

"Morning." I say and grab one of his hands and kiss it. I link our hands together and relish in this silent moment. Where the sun has risen but the life of a new day has yet to invade this space.

"How are you?"

I turn on my back and set my focus on the ceiling fan. "Tired, still."

"That's to be expected. What about your feelings over Jax?"

A whoosh of air escapes me when I think about how to talk to Kamryn about this. "I feel stuck and like the tools my therapist gave me are completely useless. What good are those tools if I can't loan them to other people?"

"And your feelings about going back to Charleston?"

"I feel like I've accepted that I need to go back there one final time. Not for them, but for me. I need to confront them, my parents especially, and find a way to put them in the past. Because until they learn to accept my need for independence then we'll never have a relationship." I swallow tightly at the possibility of cutting off all contact with my parents. It's been over two months since they bombarded me with a visit. But maybe if I'm on their turf they'll find a way to see things from my viewpoint. "The sooner we get there the better. Otherwise, I'll keep finding reasons to not go there."

"Let's fly down on Monday and if things don't go the way you hope, we'll make a vacation out of it. We'll turn the sour into sweet."

"You really are the best boyfriend ever," I tell him and turn to look at him. His blond hair is tousled, unfortunately not from my hands, and his eyes are still holding onto that sleepy gaze.

"You bring it out of me."

Riley slides out of bed after he kisses me on the forehead and I hear as he takes care of business in the bathroom. I grab my phone off the nightstand and open it to texts and emails. But I forgo those and start a new chat with Kamryn and Emily.

> Me: Riley and I are headed to Charleston on Monday. But when I get back, we need to have a chat.

> Emily: Sounds serious.

Kam: Yeah, what's wrong?

Kam: And why isn't Jax in this thread?

Me: I wouldn't keep her out if it wasn't important.

Me: I am begging you to not say anything to her until we all talk.

Kam: Okay…well, I'll do my best to ignore that you texted me at all.

Me: I'm sure Mason will have no problem getting you to forget.

Kam: He does do that thing with his tongue that I love.

Emily: EW!

Me: Party foul!

I exit our thread to check hotels in Charleston. Wanting a bit more of an escape, I find one with vacancies in Charleston Village and book it for five days. That should be enough time. Plus we'll be close to all of the touristy spots that I've always found to be romantic.

"I booked our hotel!" I shout so he hears through the bathroom door.

Said door opens and steam billows out. My mouth dries at the sight of Riley with a towel wrapped around his waist and his chest still damp from the shower.

He snorts and my attention trails up to his smirking face. "That was fast."

"If I didn't do it now, I'd never do it. We just need to book our flight."

"I'll take care of that," he tells me.

We settle into domestic bliss for the rest of the after-noon. With him I've never felt so at peace or at ease in the little things. Some moments I pinch myself or psych myself out and think that what he and I have is too good to be true. That I'm held hostage somewhere, drugged up, and at any moment whoever is holding me hostage will let up on the drugs and I'll wake up in my life before Riley. So I don't take any moment with him for granted.

32

RILEY

We touchdown in Charleston and immediately fight through the cluster of other passengers to grab our bags and to get a good rental car. The sliding doors open and humidity slaps us both in the face.

"Welcome to South Carolina, Riley," Sarah presents the outside to me like she's Vanna White.

"Is it always so wet?"

"Not all the time," she says and holds her hand out, tipping it back and forth. "But we are coming up on the hotter months, which means the humidity will be at an all time high."

"You're lucky I love you. I wouldn't brave this weather for anyone."

"I'm honored," she jokes as we get the key for our car.

The instructions for how to find our car is easy enough and we argue over who's set to drive. But Sarah being the native, wins that she already knows where to go and that I should just enjoy the drive. While driving there, Sarah's hand wraps around mine and I take in the view. Palmetto trees occupy almost every empty space and it's just so beautiful down here. Thirty minutes later, she pulls into the entrance of our hotel.

I turn to Sarah with my eyes wide.

"I don't want to hear a thing about how expensive this might be." She says and holds a finger to my lip to stop me from doing just that when she parks.

If I'm careful with where my money goes, Sarah is even more careful. We both obscenely track our expenses and save every receipt for our monthly purchases. Which aren't a lot as we're both homebodies. But when we do spend our money, we keep track of where it goes.

After we're checked in and parked, we make our way to our room. It's a simple one bed with an incredible view of downtown. I don't expect us to spend much time here so I don't pay too much attention to the details.

"Let's go get some food. What are you in the mood for?" Sarah asks and puts her things in her small Chanel clutch.

"Something light. Seafood, maybe?"

She nods her head with a smile. "Now, that I can do. There's one within walking distance."

Hand in hand, we walk to the restaurant. Sarah plays tour guide on our walk and her joy while here is something I don't even think she notices. But I won't be the one to point it out to her.

We get to the restaurant right before the dinner rush is set to begin and decide to just share our food. She finally gets me to try boiled peanuts and they're not that bad. Same with oysters and I see why they're considered an aphrodisiac food. The mood in the restaurant is light and fun. Bricks cover one side of the wall and wooden planks cover the other. It's a very mom and pop space and I can see why it's so popular.

Towards the end of dinner, I can sense Sarah getting

antsy, so I pay for our meal and take her back to the room where I make her forget her name until she passes out.

I WAKE up to the sound of feet shuffling across the floor. Feeling across the bed and there being a cold space means that it's Sarah.

She's murmuring to herself and hasn't noticed me awake.

"Hey," I say, groggily.

Sarah jumps at my voice interrupting her thoughts. "Hi."

Today is the day that we go to her parents house. We figured that the earlier in our trip that we go to see them, the better.

"How long have you been awake?" I ask and pull my discarded pajama pants on, moving to sit at the foot of the bed.

"Not long," she tells me quickly, but backtracks when I raise an eyebrow at her. "About thirty minutes."

I hold my hand out and wait for her to grab onto it. "You can do this. You are stronger today than you were last week, last month, hell even last year. Sarah Jane, I am in awe of you. Let's get this day started and then we can come back here and I'll wipe away anything bad that happens."

She leans forward, dropping her forehead against mine. "Okay."

I sneak a kiss on the tip of her nose and head to the bathroom to get ready for what lies ahead.

I do my best to distract her through the lead up to seeing her parents. But when we pull up to their house a little while later, I even find myself nervous. Sarah's hands are white-knuckled on the steering when I look over.

I drop my hand on her headrest and carefully run my fingers through her hair. "You can do this."

She takes a deep breath and releases the hold on the wheel. The car turning off is next and I match her motion when she opens the car door and steps out. I look straight ahead to the house that raised her. It sits on a main street with white siding and light brown brick making the home look inviting. Sarah and I walk hand-in-hand up the steps in tandem and she rings the doorbell when we've reached the top.

Her hand squeezes mine and I give her a reassuring rub of my thumb against the top of her hand. The door opens to her Dad who's scowling. But his face smoothes when he sees it's his daughter.

"Sarah," he breathes out and takes off his glasses.

"Hi, Dad."

He looks like he's seen a ghost. Probably thinking he'd never see his daughter again. "Please, come in." He says, and opens the door wider, stepping aside to let us in.

Stepping in the foyer, I see where Sarah gets her taste for the fancy things. What might look like an affordable entryway table is actually more than some make in a month. I should know as my interior designer tried to get me to purchase one.

We follow him into the living room in the back of the house and he excuses himself to get his wife. Huge windows take up the two walls letting in all of the natural light. Sarah and I drop onto one of the loveseats and I bring my arm around her waist, pulling her to me. Whispering words of praise and love as I do my best to naturally bring her heart rate and breathing down to normal. Her hand falls to my thigh and wraps around when her parents walk into the room.

Sarah's body stiffens when her Mom surveys her. Probably judging her for her clothing choice or her hair in its natural wavy style. I love Sarah in every state of done and undone, so i have trouble accepting that her Mom expects her to be polished all of the time.

"Sarah." Her Mom coldly says as she takes a seat in a chair across from us.

"Mom."

"To what do we owe this visit?" Her Dad asks with more excitement as he sits in a chair next to his wife.

Sarah looks to me and I give her a small nod. "A few things happened this week and it brought on my first nightmare in over a year."

"Oh, not this again," her Mom scoffs.

"Mrs. Callahan, I urge you to listen to your daughter before you lose her for good." My voice holds no room for argument.

"Erica," Sarah's dad scolds his wife who looks put off by being put in her place again. "I'm listening," he tells his daughter.

"Kamryn's sister is being verbally abused by her boyfriend. She's changed herself to fit what he looks at. She's no longer the girl I met when Kam introduced us. And it reminded me of my relationship with Paul."

Her Mom's expression brightens. "Oh, he'll be so happy to know you're back in town."

"Are you high mom? Because how you're correlating that with thinking I would *ever* want him back is beyond me." Sarah holds onto me tighter.

"He still loves you."

"I don't give a shit if he becomes President. He cheated on me and that's not something I would ever excuse. Never mind the fact that he constantly shielded me from the negative side of living in this bubble, when the best thing would have been for me to see it first hand. Because if it's one thing I learned it's that I deserve to be cherished. I deserve to be loved and treated like I matter. I deserve to see everything, the good and the bad."

"Paul, did all of that," her Mom says, still holding onto hope that a relationship between them will restart. Biting my tongue while she dismisses me sitting next to her daughter is hard.

"No he didn't. He just made *you* see what you wanted to see. Don't you get it Mom? The longer you keep thinking he's this perfect guy, the easier my decision is to cut you out of my life."

"You can't possibly be serious."

"Would you rather have your daughter or some guy whose only claim to fame is his last name?" I ask because I can no longer take her dismissiveness towards Sarah. Towards me.

Her face relaxes as much as the botox will allow and I see something I said making it through to her. But it's hard to undo years of behavior in a day. And Sarah's Mom is that.

"I would love to be part of your life," Sarah's Dad tells his daughter and leans forward.

I feel Sarah's body trembling at this first step. "I would love that Dad."

His gaze turns to me. "We haven't been formally introduced. I'm David."

I take his offered hand and shake it. "It's nice to officially meet you. I'm Riley."

"I have to thank you for loving my daughter in the way I've failed. I was so focused on other things that I let other people take the reins on her. For that, sweetheart, I'm so sorry. I'm glad she has you in her life. She hasn't been happy in a long time and I could never pinpoint what that was. Until you came along and her happiness, her spirit lifted higher than I ever thought possible."

"Sarah has brought a joy into my life that I didn't know I needed." I wrap my arm tighter around her and kiss her on the forehead. "Loving her has been one of the easiest things I've ever done. I know all too well how easy it is to lose the people you love."

"What can you give her that Paul can't?" Sarah's mom, Erica, asks in a dismissive tone.

"A piece of mind that I'll love her and provide for her, build her up and not tear her down, support her when she needs it, and laughter. So much laughter that she'll never know what her life is like without it. And I'll do all of that the way my parents did because I have had two of the best examples of how to be an amazing partner."

We sit in silence as what I said hangs in the air. I've told Sarah I love her multiple times. But I don't think she knows how far and how deep that love runs. She leans into me as she waits for her mom to meet her on her side. When she turns her nose up at us, Sarah accepts defeat and taps my leg to signal it's time to leave.

"Well, Dad, we're going to head out. I would love for you to come and visit us. We can catch a baseball game and you can maybe meet Riley's parents?"

"I would love that, sweetheart." He says and we stand up from our seats. Her mom stays seated and ignores us as we walk to the door. The goodbyes are still slightly filled with tension but Sarah's spirits are much higher than when we got here.

We spend the rest of the week doing everything the hotel suggests. Rainbow Road and The Battery are the top two places that were at the top of our list. We eat more in that week than we usually do and walk more than normal. And by the end of the trip, with a final visit from David, Sarah is excited for what's to come and how her relationship with him will develop now that she's older.

Multiple times this week, I told her how proud I am of her, how much I love her, and how much I can't wait for more of this; enjoying this life that we've begun to create.

33

SARAH

"Ready for this?" Riley asks before we walk into Kamryn's house.

"As ready as I'll ever be," I tell him, because how ready is anyone when you have a planned intervention for someone you care about?

The plan was for a girls night and that hopefully Jax comes alone. We get to the stairs and Riley kisses me on the cheek before heading upstairs to join Mason and Adam in the man cave. I take a seat next to Emily at the kitchen island and Kam passes me a margarita that smells suspiciously like more tequila than margarita mix.

"Jax should be here soon. She had to finish editing a video for a brand." Kamryn says and pours herself a glass of water. She's in a Cincinnati sweatshirt that looks like it belonged to Mason and ratty grey sweatpants.

I raise my eyebrow at her choice of drink.

"If this is about my sister, then I need a clear head." She tells me and sets her glass down when we hear the front door open.

"Hey guys," Jax greets when she sees us in the kitchen.

Her face is devoid of makeup and her hair is pulled in an effortless messy bun on top of her head.

"Hi, sister. How did the video go?" Kam asks and holds up a glass as a silent ask for a drink.

"Just a small one. Pretty easy. They wanted three thirty second videos in a specific way that ended up being more time consuming for me to film and edit."

Emily and I look at each other out of the corner of our eyes and I feel like I'm going to be sick when Kam speaks up.

"Jax, are you okay?"

Fuck.

"Yeah. I've never been better."

"Are you sure?" Kamryn asks and I know she's trying to use what small therapy tools she also has.

"What did you tell her?" Jax asks, this time pointing her question at me.

"Nothing," I firmly say.

"So why are you three here, sitting like someone died."

"The way you could if you stay with Trent?" I ask and don't miss Kamryn's gasp.

She turns her gaze on Jax. "What is she talking about?"

"Nothing."

"Jaclyn Marie. Wha–what is she talking about? And I won't ask you again." Kamryn sounds as if she's either on the verge of yelling at her sister or crying because of what her sister is going through. Chances are it could be both.

"She was eavesdropping on a conversation between Trent and I at your wedding reception..." Jax says and tries to blow our concerns off.

"If you mean, him yelling at you and berating you a "conversation" then I should rethink how Riley speaks to me."

"He what!?" Emily and Kamryn ask at the same time.

Jax and I hold each other's glare and I will her to tell them what she told me. Movement from behind Jax signals that the guys have made their way to the landing on the stairs and have equal looks of fury and the need to find Trent and beat his face in.

"So he yells at me from time to time. It's no big deal," she waves off.

"No." Emily says at the same time I say, "It is a big deal."

"How long has he been verbally abusive towards you?" Kamryn asks. And I think she wants to beat herself up for not pushing her sister further.

"He's not–" she starts but I cut her off.

"If this were one of us, what would you do?" I ask her, my throat thick with emotion after her constant brush-off. "Because I would hope that you all would ask me if I was okay and then help me to find a way out. I would hope that the people in my life cared about my well-being enough to show me how a healthy relationship should be."

Jax's jaw is clenched incredibly hard and her eyes have welled up with tears. "You guys don't understand."

Kamryn walks to her sister and holds her hands. "Then help us understand, please."

"I'm not like you three. Guys don't want me for me anymore when they find out who I'm related to."

"So you settle for less than what you deserve?" Kamryn asks and I hear the tears and the pain in her voice. I look up and see Mason ready to burn down the world for Jax, for Kamryn. "Do what we have, with the men who treat us like gold, prove that you deserve everything good? Because I can't think of any reason why you would stay with him."

"Because I love him," she says and I feel her conviction lessen.

"I loved Paul and I thought he loved me, but that didn't

stop him from cheating on me," I tell her and I don't miss all three of their heads whipping towards me. Riley looks to the ground as he already knows this story and how hard it was for me to come to accept that it was never my fault. "And that didn't stop my mom from trying to get us back together. I realized my worth, that it wasn't my fault, and I found someone who treats me like I matter. Don't you want that? Don't you want someone to treat you like you matter?" I ask her and the tears for my friend becoming smaller for someone else trail down my face.

Jax's head falls back and then falls forward. I don't miss her own tears or her sobs that wrack her body. "I'm in so deep that I don't know how to get out. He made me feel so big and then so little that I'm scared I'll never find someone good."

"You will find someone who is worthy of you. You will find someone who will make you feel like the stars are so close you can touch them. You will find someone who loves you for you and not who you can introduce them to," Kamryn says and pulls her sister into her arms. "It might not be tomorrow or next week, but when you find someone who makes you forget all of the bad, then you'll realize why it never worked with anyone else."

Jax and Kamryn stay wrapped in each other's arms and they need this. If anything, Jax has probably felt Kamryn slip away as she moved into her life with Mason. And I don't blame her. But latching onto whoever will give you attention when you're in a vulnerable state, can set you up for an unhealthy relationship.

I just hope with everything that this night will be the sign that Jax needs to end things with Trent.

"How come you didn't tell us about Paul?" Kamryn asks later on when we're all seated on the oversized couches in her living room. The guys headed back up to the man cave after we gave them all reassuring smiles.

I lean forward and rest my arms in my lap. "I was embarrassed. And telling you guys at that time...I couldn't dump that on you when you both already had bigger things going on." I tell them and look into my glass because I'd rather look at the contents in the glass than look at their faces and see judgment.

"What could have possibly been so embarrassing about that? Yeah, no one likes when their partner cheats. But you could have told us and we would have been there for you."

"I know that now. But burying myself in work and focusing on your three was just what I needed at the time."

"Can we make a promise here?" Emily asks and looks around at the three of us. "That no matter where we're at in our relationships, we tell each other everything."

"Promise." Jax, Kamryn, and I say.

"So how was your trip?" Kam asks me once we've all slightly settled.

"It was good." I say and fall back into the cushions. "I've finally got my dad back. But I don't see any hope with my mom."

"I'm sorry, sweetie. I know all too well how hard it is to lose a relationship with a parent." Emily says and places her hand on my leg.

"Yeah, but you have your parents back."

"I do. But that doesn't mean that everyday I didn't miss them or didn't instinctively want to pick up the phone to call them. We just weren't in that space."

Emily's relationship with her parents was one of neglect. But not in the way that she was neglected physically. It was more of an emotional neglect. They left her alone while they were chasing their career dreams. But that also opened the door for her to fall for the boy next door.

We spend the rest of the night catching up and dumping on each other. It turns out the more we fall into who we become, the easier it is to neglect the part of you that just needs your girlfriends to talk with.

34

RILEY

TWO MONTHS LATER

The Italian sausage sizzling in the pan mixes with my parents animatedly talking with David, Sarah's Dad, and they all catch up like old friends. It's still blowing my mind that he's here and when Sarah invited him up here for the week, I knew I wanted to step my plan into overdrive. So I offered to pick him up from the airport while she attended a meeting with Nate, her baseball client.

My heart is pounding and I've gone up against some of the toughest opponents while playing hockey. But, this. Asking a very important question to the woman I want to spend the rest of my life with? Yeah, I'm terrified. Not that I think she'll say no. We've talked about marriage and babies several times. Is it too soon to propose to Sarah? Maybe. But when you know, you know. And I know that I want to spend the rest of my life with her.

I add the noodles to the boiling water and chop up the peppers and onions that will pair well mixed into the pasta and the champagne I have tucked away in the back of the fridge. When everything is assembled, I shake my hands out and begin.

"Hey, Blue?" I ask as I add some more seasoning to the pasta, if only to keep my hands occupied as reason for needing her assistance.

"Yeah?"

"Will you go in that drawer and hand me a pot holder?" I ask and nod to the drawer in front of where the bowl-plates are located.

"Sure." She gets up and I look over my shoulder and my parents and David, who all nod and try to hide their smiles.

My heart is pounding louder again and it's like the thumping is in my ears now. The sound of the drawer sliding open is like a baseball crashing into a window. I look over at Sarah and her eyes are fixed on the sole ring box in the drawer. Turning the burners off, I walk the two steps to where she's standing.

In her ripped jeans and black tank top with her hair falling in wavy auburn strands down her back, she's perfect. I grab the ring box out of the drawer and flip it between my fingers before dropping down on one knee.

"What are you doing?" She whispers.

"I remember months ago, I told you if you ever allowed yourself to fall in love again, to let it be me. I love you. More than I thought I could ever love someone. You challenge me to step out of my comfort zone, you challenge me to be a better son and teammate, and you challenge me to be a better partner. I know this is soon, but why do we need to follow a timeline before deciding that we want to spend the rest of our life with one person? You are that person for me. You are who I want to spend the rest of my life with." I open the ring box and her eyes go to the 2-carat elongated diamond nestled in the blue velvet box. Taking the ring out, I ask her the only question that matters. "Sarah Jane Callahan, will you marry me? And challenge me for the rest of my life?"

She's nodding her head before I finish and instead of looking at the ring, she's looking at me. "Yes. A million times yes."

I slide the ring onto her delicate finger and catch her falling body as she wraps her arms around my neck. Our parents clapping in the background is like white noise as all I can focus on is her. I stand up with her in my arms and revel in the feel of her body against mine and knowing that she is mine for the rest of my life.

She pulls back and kisses me quickly before fully admiring the ring I just slid on her finger. "You really know how to surprise a girl."

I gently cradle her face in my hands and wipe away the stray tears. "Consider this my motto."

"For the rest of our life."

WE CRASH into our bedroom later that night. My parent's left an hour ago and David went to the hotel he booked for this week despite Sarah saying he could stay here. Selfishly I'm glad he's staying at a hotel because then we wouldn't be able to celebrate the way we want to.

Our clothes go flying and our lips reattach after each item is removed until we're both completely naked. I pull Sarah against me, her skin smooth as silk and nipples pointed tips against my chest sends a shiver down my spine. We walk backwards until Sarah tips back on the bed. I stay standing and kiss my way down her body. Our eyes lock as I place open-mouthed kisses on her thighs, teasing the place where she wants me most if evident by her huff of frustration.

"Stop teasing me," she whines and I raise an eyebrow at her demand. "Or I'll take care of the job myself."

"While I'd love to see that." My cock agrees and twitches against my leg. "I'd rather be the one to make my fiancé come."

"God, I love the sound of that word coming from your mouth..." her words trail off with a moan as I take a swipe through her pussy with my tongue.

"What was that?" I ask, my face hovering near her sensitive area.

"Oh, God," she cries out as I lick into her. "Be a good fiancée and make me come."

"With pleasure." I tell her before spreading her open and spearing her with my tongue. Her moans and gasps of pleasure as she gives into the sensation is strong. My hands wrap around her thighs and I pull her closer, holding her in place as I shove my tongue further inside of her. Sarah's thighs clamp down around my head as I continue to eat at her like it's my first time with her.

I slide two fingers inside of her and curl, thrusting while I flick at her clit with my tongue. Adding another finger until she's stuffed, I work her fast and quick to the edge of one orgasm, but slow down when I feel her tighten around my fingers. I do that over and over until I finally let her have what she wants.

"Riley," she moans when I finally let her come. I work her through her orgasm and kiss a trail up her body. I love that Sarah doesn't care if I taste like her. In fact she thrives off of it if her rubbing against my cock is any sign.

I crawl up on the bed with her and fall on my back, taking her with me. My hands fall on her legs as she straddles me and she continues to kiss me like she'll never get the chance to again.

"What do you say my fiancé puts my cock in her pussy?" I say in her ear and I push her hips down, grinding her over my dick.

She whimpers and it's the hottest thing I've heard. With a kiss on my lips, she sits up and fists my cock in her hand, pumping it a few times before sitting up on her knees and swiping the head through her opening. I'll never get over the sight of us joining, of my cock impaling her as she slowly sinks down on me, and of my cock tucked tight inside of her.

"I wish you could see this view, baby." I tell her as she lifts and lowers on my cock.

"Maybe we should get a mirror," she jokes as she falls forward and places her hands on the headboard. Sarah braces herself as she uses me to come. Bouncing up and down on my dick, the sounds of our arousal and skin slapping is a sound unlike any other. Her movement stutters as she rolls her hips over me and I feel that movement to my balls.

I place my hands on her hips and help her move. Sweat trails between her breasts and I lick it up, and move to her swaying breasts. I pull a nipple between my teeth and tease a tip with my tongue.

"Riley, Riley, Riley," she chants and I know she's getting closer to coming.

"Do you need to come baby?"

"Yes."

"Then hold on." I tell her before I'm rutting up into her. My hips lift in fast succession and my thumb plays with her clit that's a hard nub. Over and over until I feel her walls fluttering and she throws her head back. I continue my thrusts as I finally fall over the edge and spill into her with a shout of her name.

Sarah collapses onto my body, breathless and boneless, with me still buried inside of her. "Holy shit engaged sex is so much better." She says and kisses a trail across my chest before taking my lips in hers.

I turn, flipping our positions and laying her on her back. "Blue, I just emptied my brain into you. I need at least ten minutes to recover."

"Fine," she says and looks at the ring on her finger. I pull out and stretch my body alongside hers. "I still can't believe we're engaged. How? When?"

"I get a lot done when you have meetings in-office," I tell her and laugh a bit as she faux punches me on the arm. "I already had the ring, but I asked your dad for your hand when I picked him up from the airport."

She smiles a watery smile and looks at her ring again. I know she's thinking about her Mom. But it turns out her Dad filed for divorce right before he came up here. He said her treatment of Sarah, plus the infidelity that he was never okay with, were two things they couldn't come back from. David is using this week as time to decompress and possibly look for a house. He hasn't told Sarah that part yet. But get a man alone and he'll spill all his deepest secrets. He doesn't want to be away from his daughter anymore and this is just one step of many that he's doing to repair their relationship.

"I love you." She tells me.

"I love you, too, Blue."

EPILOGUE

Sarah - 10 Years Later

I shut the refrigerator with my hip just as a gaggle of kids run past me. "No running in the kitchen, please! And take it outside."

It's a very busy week in the Jones household. My husband played his final game last week and is set to announce his retirement this weekend. Along with that we're celebrating our oldest, Jagger, as he turns six today. So our house is overrun with kids, pets, parents from his hockey team, and Riley's teammates along with their partners.

I pinch myself when I wake up and realize that this is the life I live now.

My husband, who's only gotten more attractive with age, strolls into the kitchen with our daughter Avery perched on his shoulders. My eyes track him like a sniper and he's my only target.

"Down girl," Emily says in my ear, noticing where my attention has landed.

At thirty-nine, I feel like I've lived a fuller life than most. After Riley and I got engaged all those years ago, we put off wedding planning as he was about to head into training for his third season with Columbus. And I was working with more athletes as their publicist. A year went by and we still had yet to hire a wedding planner.

"Do you have a white dress?" Riley asked one night after dinner as we're sitting on the couch. I was perfectly content sitting next to him with my legs in his lap, but my touchy-feely boy couldn't stand not having me closer. So he dragged me onto his lap where I've been for the last ten minutes fiddling with the strings from his hoodie.

"Have you seen my closet?"

"Right. Silly me. Well, how about tomorrow we go down to the courthouse and just get married."

"Really?" I asked hopefully.

He holds me steady as he leans back on the couch. "Yes. Neither of us really want a big wedding. And I've been ready to call you 'my wife' since I put a ring on your finger. Let's stop avoiding the inevitable."

"Yes, yes, yes," I cheer and throw my arms around him.

"Damn. And I thought that word was only reserved for when my tongue is in your pussy."

I pinch him on his side and his laughter is one that's rare, but freely let loose around me, sets free a swarm of butterflies in my stomach. "Stop that."

True to his word, we got married on a Wednesday at the courthouse in Columbus. Momma, Pops, and my Dad were our witnesses as we committed to and tied our lives to each other. Of course, the girls were livid when they saw we got married, so they took it upon themselves to throw us a kick-ass reception. Which is what we always wanted.

"There's my girl," Riley announces when he sees me in

the kitchen. He picks Avery up off his shoulders and places her on the floor. As soon as she's on her feet, she's off to find Kamryn's kids.

"Hi, baby." I greet him when he joins me at the kitchen island.

Despite us living in this gigantic house since before Jagger was born, I'm still getting used to all of this space. Sometimes I miss my townhouse and his condo where everything was steps away. Riley takes my hand and pulls me into the open walk-in pantry and pushes me up against the wall, devouring my mouth while our kids, and friends and family are just outside.

"I missed you." He tells me when we come up for air. His lips have taken on my lipgloss and I wipe them off on my jeans.

My hands slide around to rest in the back pockets of his jeans. "You just saw me this morning. Matter of fact, you saw a whole lot of me this morning."

Having two kids hasn't lessened the drive between us. Nope. It's only forced us to get more creative about where we have sex. Having Jagger walk in on us when he was three was enough for us.

"You act like that was enough for me." Riley says and presses his body to mine. His eyes roam over my body before landing back on my eyes. He has that look that I know means something.

"What...why are you looking at me like that?" I ask him and twine my fingers through his, swinging them side to side.

"I found a breeder," he tells me and looks like the boy I met a decade ago.

"You did?"

It's something we talked about and I know we should

head to the shelter to adopt. But since losing Sasha and Pixie due to age, my husband has been lost. Losing them was hard for me, but Riley took it harder. We agreed to wait until he retired to look into breeders. But we weren't exactly sure when he would announce his retirement.

"Yeah," his excitement makes *me* want to jump up and down. "They have a cat that's about to give birth any day now. I thought after next week, we could go and look?"

"You know I can't say no to you when you get all little boy, sad face."

He steps forward, backing me up to the shelves. "Oh, yeah? Well I'll–"

A knock on the pantry door has us jumping. "Jagger is ready for cake!" Kamryn yells and Riley drops his head on my shoulder.

"He is so your son." I tell Riley and kiss him on the neck before pushing him back from me. He swats me on the butt as I pass him and head to the refrigerator again to get our little boy's cake.

Riley helps me place the candles and light them and we look up to see Jagger sitting, rather impatiently, at the table. His feet are swinging beneath him and he hasn't stopped smiling since he woke up.

"Happy birthday to you..." we all begin as Riley brings the cake around and sits it in front of him. My husband and I stand on either side of Jagger while the singing is loud and out of tune, but it's oh, so perfect.

Jagger blows out his candles when the song finishes and Riley and I can't resist kissing him on the cheeks. He looks so much like Riley, just with my hair color. He has my attitude, God help us all, but his kindness is what makes him the best son anyone could ask for.

A long time ago, I stopped wishing for something like

this to happen for me. But I had a boy knock down every single wall I built and instead he rebuilt those walls with him inside. Ten years with the love of my life has gone by in the blink of an eye and I wouldn't change this life we built for anything else.

$$\sim$$

Riley

"Are you ready for this?" Clay my agent asks before we step onto the makeshift stage.

I look over at my family and smile at all that I'm gaining by stepping away from the game. At thirty-four, my body is done. And with two kids, I want to enjoy them without hurting all of the time.

"Yeah. I'm ready for this."

I step onto the stage alone, my teammates stand off to one side and my family stands off to the other side. I look at Sarah and see the woman I fell in love with ten years ago, giving me the same reassuring smile that she gave me at that hotel bar before I schmoozed the big wigs.

We've come a long way. From the boy who loved freely and the girl who refused to love at all, we have created a life that I always dreamed about.

"Hi, little skater," I coo to my wife's swollen belly as I lay on the bed. He picks the right moment to move and kick at my lips resting against Sarah's belly. "You want out, huh?"

"Don't rush him. We still have two months," my beautiful wife says.

We celebrate four years being married soon and it's kind of a race to see which comes first: our son's arrival or celebrating another year of marriage. These last years with Sarah have been nothing short of adventurous. During the off-season we've traveled while still keeping up with her job. And when it's hockey season, we go back and forth from Columbus and Cincinnati like a well-oiled machine. One day we'll settle down in one city, but for now, we're enjoying life where we can.

"How're you feeling, Blue?" I ask and move up the bed to sit next to her. Sasha is curled on the other side of Sarah with Pixie on one of the beds by the window.

She runs her hands over her stomach and sighs contentedly. "The normal aches. He moves a lot when he hears your voice."

I place my hand on top of hers and link our fingers together. Leaning over, I place a kiss on Sarah's lips. I was unprepared for how having a baby would change us—change her. With me being in season, it's been hard to miss the milestones she's had and I've kicked myself for missing appointments that couldn't be moved due to road games. But she's been a rock through this journey.

"What's on your mind, honey?" Sarah asks and runs her hand through my hair.

I sneak a kiss on her wrist and sit back against the headboard. "I'm thinking about a lot of things. Mainly us and how long I want to play."

"You and I are forever, so that's settled," she chuckles with me. "Are you thinking about retiring? Because you have a handful of years left, babe. And you are in your prime."

"Maybe I'm just tired and full of guilt for missing things when it comes to you and the baby."

"Riley Theodore Jones do not beat yourself up for this. We knew this was a possibility when you knocked me up on your birthday," she teases.

I smirk and look at the product of my birthday growing. "And I'd do it again."

"Okay, caveman. We're going to be okay. You, me, the girls, and our little boy."

"I know. Just something I've been feeling."

The sound of cameras clicking and flashes going off when I take my spot behind the podium threaten to blind me, but I focus on a dark spot in the back of the room and address the room. "Thank you all for coming. I know everything was up in the air after our last game." The guys cheer and hold up the Stanley Cup. Yeah, we won the final and most important game of our careers. If any athlete decides when the right time is to make that life-altering move, it's after a championship win. "It's hard to know when to make the right decision to walk away or keep going. And there is no better or easier way to say this, but I'm officially announcing my retirement. I've given over twenty years to this game and ten years playing for my hometown. Who can say that they've committed to something for longer than an hour?" The crowd laughs and I use that as another second to gather my thoughts.

"This game was something I started with my dad, so walking away from something that he was an important part of, I'll never be able to thank him. But I know he's watching with a smile on his face. Thank you, to Coach Anderson for taking a chance on a rookie, on me. I've gained an incredible mentor and even more, a friend. Thank you, to the teammates who became like brothers. And as an only child that was all I ever wanted and you all made these last eleven years more memorable than I could have ever hoped for. Thank you, to Momma and Pops for shuffling me to my practices and cheering me on at my games. I don't know where I would be or who I would be if it weren't for you two. I want to give a special thank you to my wife. For the last ten years you have been by my side, cheering me on and helping me ice my aching body. You saw through the mask that I presented to everyone. You became my favorite cheerleader and just having you by my side through this insane sport I did, I'll never be able to tell you how grateful I am that you were there every step of the way. To my kids, who made the homecoming that much more special, thank you. And I want to give a final thank you to the fans. For standing by us through the good and bad. You all made stepping out onto the ice every game day one I'll never forget. While I'm hanging up my skates for the final time, hockey will never leave me. Thank you."

I turn to my wife and kids. Sarah with her teary expression and our kids with faces of joy. Then I turn to my team, who've been there with me through it all. And as I walk off the stage with my family by my side, I realize I'm still gaining more than anyone could hope for.

Later that night as Sarah and I crawl into bed, we just stare at each other. A million words pass between us but nothing comes out. Nothing needs to be said.

"I love you. And I'm so proud of you," she says and slides over into my arms.

I kiss her on the forehead and tuck her closer to my body. We still hate when any inch of space is between us, which makes our kids scrunch their faces up in disgust, which in turn makes us want to show more affection towards each other. "Thank you for making this last decade one I will never forget. I'm so glad you let it be me to love you."

RECIPES

Riley's Pasta

I love pasta and could eat it every single day. It's easy and a great way to get your veggies and protein in which is why I have Riley make it a couple of times in the book. And it's one that I've personally made when I had no clue what to make for dinner.

Recipe:
Ground Italian Sausage (cooked through)
Penne pasta (you can use whatever and cook to your desire)
Chopped or sliced bell peppers (let them sweat a little, you don't want them too crunchy)
Mushrooms (whole or sliced)
Alfredo sauce
Slap Ya Mama Cajun seasoning (use as much as you wish)

RECIPES

Chocolate Chess Pie

A typical dessert that's sure to hit all those cravings. My mom made has made this at Thanksgiving a few times and how can you say no to chocolate?

INGREDIENTS

-4 TBSP cocoa powder

   -1.5 cups of sugar

   -3 TBSP corn starch

   -2 large eggs, heated

   -4 TBSP unsalted butter, melted

   -1 (5 oz) can of evaporated milk

   -1 tsp vanilla extract

   -1 (9 in) unbaked pie crust (homemade or store bought is fine)

   -whipped cream (optional)

INSTRUCTIONS

-Preheat over to 350F

-In a large bowl, whisk together: cocoa powder, sugar, and corn starch. Add in the beaten eggs, melted butter, milk, and vanilla. Stir well to combine.

-Pour the mixture into the unbaked pie shell. DO NOT OVERFILL.

-Bake for 45 to 55 minutes or until a crust has formed completely across the top of the pie and is mostly set. There will still be some jiggle to the pie. Allow it to cool completely before slicing and serving as this will allow it to set even more.

-Serve with a dollop of whipped cream if desired

ACKNOWLEDGMENTS

This is my third time writing the acknowledgment for my books and every time I feel like I'm in front of a massive crowd at an awards show. The spotlight is on me.

Thank you to my cover designer, Kimberly, for making every cover design appointment so much fun.

Thank you to my alpha readers, Kalie and Sammie, for giving me the tough comments and reading through my gibberish typings.

Thank you to my beta readers, Cassandra and Caitlin.

Thank you to my ARC team, to Lemmy at Luna Literary Management for handling my ARCs, and to the ARC readers for giving this book a chance.

Thank you to you the reader for taking the chance on a indie author. I hope you loved Sarah and Riley's story as much as I loved writing it.

ABOUT THE AUTHOR

Elleese Black is a thirty-something millennial with a degree in Psychology from Virginia. She grew up reading romance books with swoon, tears, and all the HEAs.

When she's not writing or working, she's a cat mom to two wacky black cats, taking a CycleBar class, reading when she shouldn't, or doom scrolling until the wee hours of the night.

Newsletter

ALSO BY ELLEESE BLACK

The Night We Met

Make It Without You

Let It Be Me

Somewhere Only We Know - Late Summer 2025